D0370925

"Jack?"

Jack cracked one eye open and looked at the doctor, who was grinning broadly.

"You think you don't have the virus?" Eastman said. "The room you're in is dark. I can barely see your silhouette. And you're hearing me through soundproof glass. I'm not using a microphone."

"What?"

"Your brain," he said. "These readings—they're off the charts. It's incredible."

ALSO BY ROBISON WELLS

Variant
Feedback

Dead Zone
Going Dark: A Blackout Digital Novella

ROBISON WELLS

BLACK OUT

HARPER TEEN
An Imprint of HarperCollins Publishers

HarperTeen is an imprint of HarperCollins Publishers.

Blackout
Copyright © 2013 by Robison Wells
All rights reserved. Printed in the United States of America.
No part of this book may be used or reproduced in any manner whatsoever without
written permission except in the case of brief quotations embodied in critical articles
and reviews. For information address HarperCollins Children's Books, a division of
HarperCollins Publishers, 195 Broadway, New York, NY 10007.
www.epicreads.com

Library of Congress Cataloging-in-Publication Data
Wells, Robison E.
  Blackout / Robison Wells. — First edition.
    pages cm
  Summary: "A mysterious virus is spreading through America, infecting teenagers
with incredible powers—and a group of four teens are about to find their lives inter-
twined in a web of danger and catastrophic destruction"—Provided by publisher.
  ISBN 978-0-06-202613-2 (pbk.)
  [1. Supernatural—Fiction. 2. Ability—Fiction. 3. Virus diseases—Fiction. 4. Ter-
rorism—Fiction. 5. Science fiction.] I. Title.
  PZ7.W468413Bl 2013   2012045523
  [Fic]—dc23   CIP
                                                                              AC

Typography by Erin Fitzsimmons
14 15 16 17 18   LP/RRDH   10 9 8 7 6 5 4 3 2 1
❖

First paperback edition, 2014

To Mom, for everything

This book belongs to

_____

Chosen by the Langley Literacy
Association with donations from
TD Canda Trust

User: SusieMusie

Mood: Pissed Off

My stupid friends are nothing but power struggles
and politics. Sara invited Erica to see a movie Friday
night, but she invited Tyler to go to a party the same
precise time. She thinks it's funny, but I know she's
just going to stand one of them up. I don't even care
anymore. Let them fight.

ONE

"READY?" ALEC ASKED, LOOKING IN the rearview mirror at Dan, whose eyes were closed in a kind of nervous meditation.

"I'm good," Laura answered.

Alec ignored her. He wasn't concerned about Laura. She had the easy job.

"Dan? Ready?" he asked again. "It's time."

Dan didn't meet Alec's eyes, but opened the car door and stepped into the visitor parking lot of the Glen Canyon Dam. Their beat-up Chevy Bronco was one of only three vehicles there—the other two were desert-camouflaged Humvees.

Alec smiled. Soon there would be at least fifty thousand dead. Probably more. Lake Powell, the enormous reservoir just upriver from the Grand Canyon, got three million visitors per year, and even though it was September now—not peak season—there had to still be at least fifty thousand people on the lake.

Add to that anyone in the bottom of the Grand Canyon. All of the water from Lake Powell would scour the Grand Canyon and then pour into Lake Mead, overtopping the Hoover Dam and taking it out, too, in a violent flood. Alec wished he had better numbers to estimate the deaths. He wished he'd be there to watch it all happen.

Oh well. It would be in the news soon enough. And it would take hours for the water to get to Lake Mead, so there would be reporters waiting. He could watch the Hoover Dam topple from safety, five hundred miles away.

Besides, deaths weren't the numbers he was supposed to be most concerned about. Glen Canyon Dam produced 4.5 billion kilowatt hours of electricity per year, and Hoover generated another four. In one day he'd knock out enough power to light up Las Vegas for half a year.

He stepped to the back of the Bronco and clapped Dan on the shoulder. "For your mother and mine."

Dan nodded without making eye contact.

"Yeah."

They walked toward the visitor center in silence, Alec feeling a serene calm. This would be the biggest attack yet. Not just the biggest of theirs, but the biggest all across America. And rightly so—he was supposed to be setting the example.

A speedboat shot across the lake in the distance, leaving a

trail of white foam in its wake.

"Their country is falling apart and they go on vacation," Laura said, sounding amused.

"They have to relieve stress," Alec answered sarcastically. "They probably think being in the wilderness is safe."

If anything, the lake had more people on it than usual for this time of year, a fact he'd discovered yesterday when he'd tried to rent a small craft to scope out the dam. All he'd been able to get was an old houseboat, and he'd had to navigate through a bustling marina to where he could get a good view. From there, Alec made all his notes—security patrols, escape routes—and developed a quick plan. Laura had lain out in a bikini and taken in as much sun as she could before the cool September breezes forced her to pull her T-shirt back on. And Dan had just sat for hours, eyes transfixed on the mass of concrete.

They reached the visitor center. The glass doors were locked, but that had been expected.

Laura knocked, hard enough that Alec worried the doors might shatter. She was showing off. *Idiot.*

He took a breath and tried to clear his mind. It was time for his part of the plan. He'd rehearsed the conversation a hundred times in his head—trying to think of every possible variation, every surprise. He was ready.

A moment later a soldier appeared, dressed in the full combat fatigues of the National Guard, a rifle slung across his chest. Without opening the door, he gestured for them to go away.

Alec shook his head and held up a clipboard. "We have an appointment."

The soldier watched them for a few seconds, and then waved them off again.

"We have an appointment," Alec shouted again, through the glass. "We're from the University of Utah."

The guard sized them up. If he was worried, he didn't show it; he just seemed annoyed. All three were shorter than him. Alec was the oldest at nineteen, and skinny. Laura looked more like a ditzy cheerleader than a terrorist. Only Dan had any muscle, but he was short—maybe five foot six.

Alec was already working on the man's mind. Implanting memories was an imprecise science, but Alec was confident: the glass was thick, but not dense or leaded or bulletproof; the man was only about four feet away; Alec was fully prepared.

It would take a few moments.

The soldier opened the door about three inches. The handles inside were actually chained, and it was all Alec could do not to laugh. The whole front of the visitor center was glass, and they expected a chain to stop a break-in?

The guard spoke through the gap. "Can't you read the sign? Dam's closed until further notice."

Laura spoke. "We have an appointment."

"An appointment? For a bunch of kids?"

"Grad students," Alec said. "U of U. We're here to get the weekly samples." He held up a length of cotton rope and a handful of plastic tubes.

"There's no one here to have an appointment with," the soldier said, flustered. Alec could see the false memories beginning to take hold. "We're . . . the dam . . . it's on lockdown."

Alec held up the clipboard again. "I showed you our security clearance. We were here last week, remember?"

The soldier's brow furrowed. "Well . . ."

"We know it's a hassle," Alec said, "but if I don't get this data my thesis is gonna be shot."

The guard readjusted his rifle on his shoulder, uncomfortable and confused.

Alec tapped the clipboard a final time. "It's signed by your commanding officer," he said, prodding the memory that was slowly infecting the soldier's mind.

The soldier, looking completely flustered, nodded, and undid the padlock on the chain. "Just . . . just be quick, okay?" He turned his back to the group and led them into the visitor center, illuminated only by the large windows. The place had probably been closed to tourists since the United States went on high alert, three weeks before, and the building had a feeling of abandonment to it, as if the workers had left in the middle of what they were doing. A half-eaten sandwich sat on the information desk, the lettuce now brown and limp, the bread shriveled and stale. A scattering of papers lay on the floor in front of the cash register.

The guard led them to an elevator. He was walking more quickly now, with gained confidence as the memories solidified and began to fit more naturally into his mind.

He opened the door for them, smiling cheerfully at Laura and nodding to Alec and Dan. In a moment they were several stories down and walking out onto the top of the dam. A breeze blew Laura's hair across her face as she turned and said, "Five minutes. Promise."

Alec stayed beside the soldier, gently feeding a second set of memories into the man.

"Aren't you going with them?"

Alec shook his head. "I don't like heights."

Fifty yards away, Laura leaned over the edge of the dam and looked down at the lake thirty feet below. On tiptoe, she began to unwind the rope and lower it. There wasn't any point to this, other than to make it look like they were doing something somewhat scientific. She was the distraction and the getaway plan. Dan would do the real work.

The soldier's radio crackled to life. The voice on the other end sounded alarmed.

"Gulf Charlie Five, this is Gulf Charlie Four. Private Diamond, what are those kids doing on the dam? Over."

He pulled the radio from his belt. "They're from the U. They have papers signed by Lieutenant Kilpack. Over."

While Laura stretched out over the railing—she was wearing short shorts and a tank top for the explicit purpose of drawing the attention of whatever soldiers were watching—Dan had gotten down on one knee, his right hand flat on the cement.

The staticky voice spoke again. "No one's supposed to be out there, Diamond. Over."

Diamond glanced at Alec and spoke into the radio. "I don't know what to tell you. I have the written orders right here. Over."

Alec looked around for the other soldier, but there was no one in sight. There were the two empty military vehicles parked in the lot—there were military vehicles *everywhere* nowadays—but most of the manpower was focused on the bridge over the canyon. That was the more likely target. As far as the army knew, it was next to impossible to damage a dam this size from up on top. All three of them could have been strapped with C-4 and not made a significant dent in it. The military still hadn't figured out anything important; Dan was more powerful than any explosive.

"I'm going to make a call," the voice on the radio said. "Stand by. Over."

"It's fine," Diamond replied, a little nervousness in his voice. "I've got an officer with the sheriff's office right here next to me. Over."

Alec released a little tension in his jaw. That had been

tougher. It was easy to convince the man that the three of them were students, but much harder to immediately create a new, less-plausible story. Alec looked nothing like a police officer.

But, that's why he was in charge.

"Sorry, officer," Diamond said. "We'll get it sorted out."

A sudden shudder rolled through the concrete like a wave. Diamond and Alec both automatically reached for the wall for support.

The radio snapped to life. "Gulf Charlie Five, this is Gulf Charlie Four. Private Diamond, get those kids the hell off the dam."

Diamond began walking toward them. "Hey!"

Alec followed, right by his side.

There was another rumble, louder this time.

Come on, Dan, Alec thought. *Get it done.*

Twenty yards from the teens, the guardsman raised his rifle. "Hey, get over here."

Hurry up. Alec could fill the soldier's head with false memories, but he couldn't quickly override the soldier's deeply ingrained training to follow orders.

Laura dropped the rope and held up her hands, but Dan didn't move.

An alarm was sounding now, and Private Diamond stopped, training his rifle on the two teens.

"Turn around," he barked.

Dan ignored him.

There was a sharp crack, and for an instant Alec thought Diamond had pulled the trigger. But the sound was much louder than a gunshot, reverberating off the canyon walls and shaking the ground under their feet. The face of the cement was splintered with a thousand tiny cracks and a thin cloud of dust burst skyward.

"You have three seconds," Diamond shouted.

The radio was screaming at him to fire.

That was all Alec needed. If no one else was firing at Dan, then there weren't snipers. The voice on the other end of the radio was probably inside the dam itself, watching the four of them on security cameras. They'd be feeling the real impact of what Dan was doing.

Alec pulled the private's sidearm from the holster. There wasn't even time for Diamond to respond before Alec fired three shots into the soldier's neck and head.

The dam rumbled, deep and grinding, knocking Alec to his knees.

Ahead of him he saw Dan try to stand, wobbling on weak legs.

It was finally Laura's turn. She grabbed Dan and slung him over her shoulder as easily as if he'd been a stuffed toy. She ran toward Alec and the visitor center.

Alec took the soldier's rifle and radio, and then handed the pistol to Laura as she met them. He held the door open for her, and then chased after her up the emergency stair-well—she took them three at a time.

There was a ding of an elevator in the visitor center, and Alec spun and fired a short burst from the rifle in the direction of the sound.

"Door's locked," Laura shouted, and then Alec heard her smashing through the glass.

He fired another burst toward the elevators and then turned and ran, jumping through the broken glass door and sprinting to the Bronco.

"You do it?" Alec asked, barely containing his laughter. "You have time?"

Dan nodded weakly. "I did it. Damn thing's full of rebar, but I did it."

TWO

IT WASN'T HARD TO DISAPPEAR anymore. Six months ago Aubrey had hardly been able to control it, either to make it happen or stop it from happening. But now it was as natural as walking.

Nicole called it "twinkling," as in, "disappearing in the twinkling of an eye," but Aubrey hated that.

She hated a lot of things that Nicole did but put up with them anyway. Nicole had become her best friend. Her only real friend—the only one who knew Aubrey's secret. And so Aubrey left the dance floor of the Gunderson Barn, the location of the North Sanpete High homecoming dance, and headed outside. Her floor-length blue satin dress fluttered around her feet, and as she pushed through the crowds of dancing high school students, she vanished. No one noticed.

It wasn't fair, she thought, stepping into the cool September air. This was the first high school dance she'd ever attended. The first expensive evening gown she'd ever worn. The first time when a boy she didn't even know had asked her to dance—and Nate Butler, her date, had actually gotten angry about it. Boys were fighting over her. This wasn't the old life of Aubrey Parsons; it was much better.

But now she had to cut her night short, so that she could spy for Nicole.

Aubrey walked down the front steps, carefully moving around the couples who had gone outside seeking fresh air and privacy. Kelly—one of Nicole's entourage and therefore one of Aubrey's new friends—was in the shadows behind a tree, giggling with some guy. Aubrey ignored her.

The barn was just on the edge of Mount Pleasant, sprawled out on a wide field by the San Pitch River. Aubrey walked the uneven stone path toward the lawn in the back. Heels were new to her, too, and she was relieved that no one could see her take the shoes off and carry them.

It wasn't hard to find the boys. Aubrey had done a lot of spying for Nicole, and most of it had been much trickier than listening in on four stupid football players getting drunk in the dark. They sat in a row on a short brick wall, passing a bottle back and forth.

Nate was with them. He was the star linebacker, and he'd been following Aubrey around ever since she'd been under

Nicole's wing. She hadn't noticed him leave the dance floor to come outside—Aubrey had been spending more time with Nicole and the girls than with the boys.

Not that she minded that he'd left. She liked the idea of a boy doting on her—and he was supposedly a great catch—but she could barely carry on a conversation with him unless the topic was football, hunting, or video games.

The other three guys weren't as popular—not in Nicole's inner circle. Lewis was funny but had never done much around school other than crack jokes. Scott was rich—well, rich for their small farming town in central Utah. His family owned the slaughterhouse. And Thomas had recently moved to Mount Pleasant, and had done very little to distinguish himself other than walking on the football team and catching Nicole's eye. That's why Aubrey was spying—to see if Nicole should care about Thomas.

It wasn't fair. The entire reason that Aubrey spied for Nicole was so that Aubrey could be at things like the homecoming dance. That was their deal. Now she was missing that because of one of Nicole's whims.

And disappearing made Aubrey tired—she could only do it for so long—and she didn't want to spend the rest of the night dizzy and nauseated.

"This sucks," Scott said, wiping his mouth and handing the bottle to Thomas. "I knew it would be like this. Dances are always lame."

"You got here half an hour ago and only spent ten minutes inside," Lewis said.

"Is it going to get any better?" Scott asked.

"No." Lewis laughed and hopped up on the wall.

Thomas took a drink. "What's the deal with Kelly? She's hot."

"That's pretty much the deal with Kelly," Lewis answered.

"That's all I need." Thomas took another drink. "Who's she with?"

Lewis spread his arms out, walking unsteadily along the wall. "Everyone, at some point. She'll eventually get around to you."

The others laughed. Lewis stumbled and then jumped down to the ground.

Aubrey hated this. She wondered how long she'd have to stay and listen to get what Nicole wanted. Her spying didn't necessarily reveal everyone to be a jerk, but it wasn't uncommon. Everyone talked about other people behind their backs. Everyone gossiped. Everyone sucked.

Nate motioned for the bottle. "I probably need to get back in there."

"What's the deal with your girl?" Thomas said. Aubrey perked up. She had never been as interested in Nate as he was in her, but she couldn't help wondering what he would say.

"What about her?" Nate said.

"She's hot."

Aubrey felt herself blush.

Nate nodded.

"Here's what I want to know," Lewis said. "We've all been in school together since kindergarten." He was looking at Thomas but gesturing to the other two boys. "And so has little Aubrey Parsons. And until this year no one would give her a second glance."

Aubrey's chest tightened. Nothing they said would be good. But she couldn't get herself to leave—she needed to hear what Nate would say.

But he didn't say a word. He just shrugged.

"Why not?" Thomas was asking Lewis, but it was Scott who answered.

"Because she's trailer trash. Until she started hanging out with Nicole, I think she had like three old shirts that she wore over and over."

"And her dad's a drunk," Lewis added. "Like, slobbering, fall-down, filthy drunk."

"Just like you," Aubrey yelled, knowing they couldn't hear her. She felt tears welling up in her eyes but fought them off.

"So what?" Thomas said. "Like I said, she's hot. Didn't you see her tonight?"

Scott shook his head. "Nicole must have bought the dress. I think she buys all of Aubrey's clothes now."

That wasn't true, but Aubrey hated the real answer even more. She didn't want to think about it.

Nate smiled wryly. "Aubrey may be poor, but she makes up for it in other ways."

The group burst into laughter, and Aubrey ran forward, right in front of Nate. "I do not!" she screamed. "That's a lie, you pig!"

Maybe it was stupid and risky, but at that moment she didn't care: she jumped at Nate, both hands slamming into his chest. Partly from being unprepared and partly because of the alcohol, he tumbled off the low wall and into a patch of flowers. The open bottle lay on his shirt, spilling its contents onto his chest.

The other boys howled in delight as he struggled to get up, and Aubrey took a pleased step back.

Aubrey's invisibility wasn't like the movies. She still didn't understand how any of it worked—or how she'd ended up being able to do it—but from practicing over and over with Nicole, she knew it wasn't as plain as just disappearing. Instead, people simply didn't notice her. She could yell, or slap, or punch, and no one would detect it. They'd feel the punch—like Nate had—but they wouldn't recognize it for what it was. They'd think they'd slipped, or that they'd gotten a sudden muscle spasm, or that a wind (or drunkenness) had knocked them over. But they'd never see her, or hear her. It was like their minds just blocked her out completely.

Nate was looking stupid, awkwardly trying to climb back up off the lawn.

Aubrey checked her dress to make sure she hadn't been

splashed with any of the alcohol. The boys had stopped talking about girls and had switched to football. The North Sanpete Hawks had pummeled the Manti Templars in the homecoming game.

She was tired of spying. Who cared what these boys were saying? She was going back into the dance to tell Nicole that Nate could go to hell.

THREE

JACK COOPER SAT A QUARTER mile from the Gunderson Barn, up a hill in his dad's pickup. His mom had packed him a bologna sandwich for a midnight snack, but he was eating it now, mostly out of boredom.

Below him he could see the kids at the dance and could hear the blare of the music. It was too far to make out any faces, but Jack was fine with that. If he couldn't see them, then they couldn't see him. As if it wasn't bad enough that he was a janitor at his own high school, the school had asked him to clean up after the homecoming dance, too. It was time-and-a-half pay, and he couldn't say no to that, but he didn't want to even go down the hill until everyone was gone. He needed the money, but he didn't need to be seen.

He could easily spot the cops surrounding the barn. The

town only had four officers, but in light of recent events they'd asked for volunteers to come and guard the dance. Jack sighed. In light of recent events, no one should be leaving their house.

He'd only been a little kid when 9/11 happened—too young to even know about it, really—but there was a 9/11 every day now. Three straight weeks of terrorist attacks. No rhyme or reason. No arrests had been made, no suspects were being interrogated. Subways, government buildings, national landmarks, power plants, restaurants. Jack wondered how people had the courage to go outside anymore.

They didn't, he reminded himself. Except for little towns like Mount Pleasant that no terrorist would care about.

He clicked on the radio.

"*. . . take twenty to twenty-four hours for the water to travel the three hundred miles to Lake Mead. An unnamed representative of the Bureau of Reclamation said that if Hoover Dam overflows for a sustained period then that dam will likely fail. Hoover Dam officials have fully opened the spillways in an effort to dump as much water as possible before the bulk of Lake Powell arrives.*"

Jack sat up a little straighter. Had Lake Powell been attacked? The reporter started talking about evacuations on Lake Mead, and Jack changed to another station.

"*—we're told that the Glen Canyon Bridge is in danger of collapse due to rising water levels below what used to be the dam.*"

What *used to be* the dam?

This was the closest terrorist attack to Mount Pleasant yet—maybe only five hours away. He'd gone to Powell with a scout troop a couple of years ago and had caught the biggest fish of his life—a twelve-pound striped bass.

Could the lake really be gone? A wave of nausea washed over Jack, and he stepped outside the truck, leaning on the open door and sucking in a breath of fresh air. He could see through the massive barn doors below him, could see the kids dancing carefree while the world was falling apart. Shadows ran playfully on the lawn and in and out of the trees. His friends were down there.

His former friends.

It used to be the three of them—Jack Cooper, Aubrey Parsons, and Matt Ganza. Jack was always with one of them, for as long as he could remember. Aubrey was the smart one, tutoring Jack in almost every subject—except history, the one class he loved. Matt had never seemed to have a care in the world, except for sports, but he'd always been terrible at them. Now, suddenly he was the star of everything. Went from benchwarmer to starting quarterback. The basketball coach had already promised him a starting spot on the varsity team. He—regular old Ganza—was at the dance tonight with Nicole Samuelson, the homecoming queen.

And Aubrey. She was too good for anyone now. Last year, Jack had actually gotten the courage to ask her to junior prom, but she'd said no. She'd cried, told him she would if she could just afford a dress. And then she'd been too embarrassed to ever talk about it again—or to let him bring it up.

So now there was only Jack. Jack the friggin' janitor, waiting to clean up once everyone else had their fun.

He wondered if any of the kids he could see were Ganza or Aubrey. One of the guys sitting on the wall, one of the couples holding hands, the girl in the electric-blue dress.

None of them knew about Lake Powell. He wondered if he should go down and tell them.

In the distance, a long line of headlights approached the barn.

Wait a minute . . .

He pushed the door closed quickly, dousing the light in the cab. He climbed up into the bed of the truck and peered through the darkness ahead, trying to get a better look.

FOUR

AUBREY HAD ONLY MADE IT a few yards when something stopped her. There were two people in the shadows, watching the boys. Had they heard what Nate had said—what he had insinuated about her?

It was too dark to make out more than their vague shapes, but they were big. Obviously boys. Would Nate's comments spread even faster? Nicole could stop the gossip. Aubrey had to talk to her.

But if Nicole was going to stop the rumors, she'd have to know who had heard them. Aubrey walked toward the side of the barn, where giant timbers jutted out from the wall, creating a wide dark alcove. She felt light-headed and unsteady. She'd been invisible for too long. As she went on there were more—dark shapes hidden in the shadows all around her, all around the barn.

Aubrey took a step back, and barely caught herself from falling.

It wasn't just boys in the shadows. They were three soldiers—two crouched and one standing, all of them fully dressed in combat gear. They wore helmets and large goggles, and a black cloth covered their noses and mouths like a ski mask. The two men crouching held rifles at the ready, while the one standing had his slung over one shoulder.

Was this some kind of prank? The uniforms looked too real, and no high school student would be stupid enough to use guns as a joke—not with what was going on all over the country. Aubrey backed away, and then turned and ran toward where she'd seen the first dark shapes.

They were soldiers, too.

Her head was spinning. She needed to get back inside.

What if they weren't soldiers? What if they were terrorists in disguise?

She lifted her dress up almost to her knees and jogged toward the front doors. A caravan of school buses was pulling into the parking lot, led by a pair of army jeeps.

The place was being surrounded, and she didn't know why. She needed to tell someone. Nicole would know what to do.

Cautiously, she stepped through the open doors of the barn, but saw nothing out of the ordinary. The music was still playing and everyone was dancing and laughing.

She pushed through the crowd, bumping into more people than she normally would have, but she couldn't slow to be more careful. Besides, no one would notice her anyway. She hadn't reappeared. They might feel a movement, but to them it would seem like nothing more than a muscle twitch.

Near the speakers at the far side of the room, she spotted Nicole surrounded by a circle of girls. As Aubrey reached the group she started fading back in, and wormed her way into the center, becoming fully visible as she did.

"Aubrey," Nicole said, shouting over the blaring speakers. "You look terrible."

"I know. Can we go talk?"

"Later."

"No," Aubrey said, taking Nicole's arm. "Now."

Suddenly, the music stopped, and the dimmed lights were brought up to full strength. There were groans from the students and a few shouted at the DJ to turn things back on.

Wishing she were taller, Aubrey jumped up to look over the others' heads toward the door. She couldn't see any of the soldiers yet.

"What's going on?" Nicole asked.

Aubrey turned to her. "I don't know. I think we might be evacuated. The army's outside."

"The army?"

"I hope it's the army," Aubrey said under her breath.

A man appeared from the back of the barn—a soldier in camouflage, but not wearing all the gear or a helmet. He walked to the DJ table and took the microphone.

"I apologize for the inconvenience," the man said. "But we have to cut the evening short." He was smiling, but his eyes were grim and cold.

"They're all over outside," Aubrey whispered to Nicole. Aubrey's arms and legs felt weak, and her head was still fuzzy.

"First, I want to assure you that there is no reason for alarm," the man said. "When I give the order, we'll simply have you exit the building in a quiet and orderly fashion. The school district has sent buses which will take you back into town."

There was an outcry from the crowd, and the soldier motioned for everyone to be quiet. "In the interest of public safety, I'm going to need you to follow my instructions."

Aubrey craned her neck to look back toward the wide barn door, and saw at least a dozen soldiers. A few more had appeared from a side hallway. They were spreading out in the room, surrounding the students.

"Please," the soldier said, though his voice made the word sound like an order rather than a request, "walk in a single file line and keep your hands at your sides."

From over by the main door, Aubrey could hear a soldier bark a command at the students. The room was humming with whispers.

Nicole touched Aubrey's hand, her eyes frightened. "You don't think they're here for . . . you, right?"

Aubrey paused. She hadn't even thought about that. "What? Of course not. It's about the terrorists."

Nicole looked nervous—a look Aubrey had never seen on Nicole before. "Isn't that how it happens to people like you in movies, though?" she asked. "Testing?"

"This isn't a movie," Aubrey said, suddenly panicked. "It has to be something else. How would anyone have found out?"

Nicole shook her head.

"I'm going to go," Aubrey whispered.

Nicole grabbed her hand, but Aubrey was already vanishing. Aubrey, now invisible, brushed Nicole's hand away, and watched the puzzled look on her face as she reached and grasped for Aubrey's unseen body.

Aubrey didn't care right then how it worked. Panic was gripping her as Nicole's words sunk in.

Were they here for her?

Aubrey gave Nicole a final look, wondering when they'd talk again, and then forced her way out of the crowd into the night air.

The parking lot was brightly lit with floodlights mounted on the tops of four army jeeps. At the far end were the newly arrived school buses. A line of kids waited in the center of the lot, surrounded by more armed soldiers. She realized they were the people she'd seen outside, including the boys—the soldiers must have rounded them up before entering the barn.

She headed toward them—exhausted from being invisible for so long—hoping that something would let her know if the army was looking for her.

Two soldiers stood at the front of the line, one carrying a clipboard and the other holding a handful of what looked like plastic hospital bracelets.

Aubrey was out in the middle of the lights now. Her thin dress was doing nothing to stop the cold, and in her weakened condition she started shivering.

Kelly was almost at the front of the line, and the look on her face seemed more inconvenienced than worried. As the boy in front of her was directed to the buses, she stepped up to the soldiers.

"Name?" the man with the clipboard said.

"Kelly Wagner."

He looked through the papers on the clipboard until he found a black-and-white photocopied yearbook picture, and compared it to Kelly's face.

"How long is this going to take?" she said.

He ignored her, and peeled a sticker off his paperwork.

"Hold out your left wrist," the second man said, taking the sticker and pressing it onto one of the thick plastic bracelets.

Kelly obeyed, and the soldier strapped the bracelet on her arm. He tugged on it until Kelly squealed. He then motioned for her to hurry along, and a third soldier escorted her to a bus.

Aubrey moved to get a better view of the clipboard, but by now she could hardly stand. She waited through two more people, hoping to catch a glimpse of her own name on the list—to see if it was marked in some way.

Something rumbled, like the low growl of an animal.

The soldiers noticed it too, and they retreated away from the line of teens. The man with the bracelets dropped them and lifted his rifle, leveling it at the crowd. The other soldier twisted his headset microphone to his mouth.

"Possible Lambda," he said. "At the loading area. Over."

The soldiers' fear was contagious and Aubrey stumbled slowly back from the teens—from kids she'd known for as long as she could remember.

A loudspeaker squawked. "Attention, students. Please get down on the ground, and keep your hands in front of you."

The crowd was hesitant to move, and a few of the girls called out, saying that the asphalt would ruin their dresses.

Aubrey heard the rumble again. It wasn't an animal—it sounded like rock grinding against rock.

"Everyone get down," the voice commanded sharply. All the soldiers' guns were raised now, and the students slowly began to comply.

Aubrey reached the edge of the lit area. She couldn't stand any longer and rested on the bumper of a truck. She searched the faces for Nicole, but didn't see her—the line still wound all the way back into the barn.

Someone near the front of the line moved. It was Nate, only . . . it wasn't Nate. He was wearing the same boutonniere she'd pinned on his jacket earlier that night, the same garish tie, but his face was wrong. Aubrey rubbed her eyes to see if fatigue was blurring her vision, but he still looked off. His face and hands were black and rough, almost like the asphalt he was standing on. He stood fully erect, against the soldiers' orders.

The soldiers barked at him to get back down, then ordered him to come forward, but he didn't do either. His eyes— small and black—scanned across the crowd of students as though he was waiting for something.

The soldiers were screaming at Nate now, commanding him to listen and obey. He spoke words that Aubrey couldn't hear, and she almost thought she saw his grotesque face smile.

Then he lunged forward, running toward the nearest soldier. His footsteps were heavy and Aubrey thought she felt the ground shake. Rifles flashed all around the parking lot as the army opened fire on him, but Nate didn't stop. He collided with the soldier, tackling him to the ground with a horrible crunch. As the bullets hailed into Nate, he stood again, leaving the soldier crumpled in a motionless heap.

Aubrey dashed across the lawn, her bare feet stumbling. The soldiers weren't looking for her—they were looking for Nate, and he was some kind of monster. Or were they looking for both of them? At the edge of the lawn she plunged into the bushes, fighting her way through the tangled branches and sticks. Bullets continued to roar behind her, echoed by the screams of the terrified students.

Finally, she took a step and there was nothing beneath her. She flailed for something to grab, but fell.

FIVE

JACK WATCHED AS THE SOLDIERS fired at the—what was it? A gorilla?—but their guns seemed to have no effect.

The gorilla—no, it was human; it was wearing clothes—attacked another soldier, charging into the direct path of the bullets and leaping forward. The soldier was smashed to the pavement and didn't get up.

Several of the students began to creep away, crawling for safety or to escape. Jack saw two girls sprint from the school bus toward the denser brush.

And then the thing tried to run, thundering out of the parking lot and onto the empty road. Jack saw a soldier fire something else from his rifle—slower than a bullet and arcing like a thrown baseball. It hit the ground behind the creature and exploded in yellow fire and smoke. All the way up on the hill, Jack felt the shock wave thud into his chest and pass through his body.

How could this be happening? And what was that thing? Was it a terrorist? That seemed like the only explanation, though it didn't make any sense. Everyone assumed the terrorists were Islamic fundamentalists, or political extremists, or environmental activists. No one thought they were . . . monsters?

As the smoke cleared, the thing was struggling to stand.

Another grenade was launched—that's what it had to be—and this one was a direct hit.

Jack realized his hands were clutched on the sides of the truck's cab, his knuckles white and the sharp edges of rusty metal digging into his skin.

As the cloud of smoke and debris drifted away, the creature wasn't moving.

He didn't look menacing anymore. Just a man—just a kid, like Jack—lying motionless on the road, next to two craters in the asphalt.

Four soldiers moved out to check on him, and suddenly the rest of the army was back at work—corralling the kids who were trying to crawl away, and herding them all into some semblance of a line.

Jack realized suddenly that he was hearing screams. They'd been there all the time, he was sure, but he'd just noticed them now that the guns had stopped. They weren't frightened screams, or calls for help—they were wails, like uncontrollable sadness.

Few of the students would stand. Jack wondered how many had peed themselves, and then realized how stupid that was—someone had just died. Some teenager had just turned into some kind of monster and had then been gunned down, blown up, by the United States Army.

Jack watched as, one by one, the students were pulled from the ground, checked against paperwork, put in some kind of handcuffs, and led onto buses. There were medics there now, removing the bodies of three dead or, hopefully, unconscious soldiers. A truck beyond the floodlights took the motionless monster—now a regular boy—away.

The soldiers made a final sweep of the area—in and out of the barn, up into the brush, down through the river—and returned with a few more terrified kids.

And then they left, the buses in a tight convoy surrounded by Humvees.

And Jack was all by himself.

He stumbled to his knees and puked over the edge of the truck's bed, his whole body shaking.

What had he just seen? That was the homecoming dance—that was everybody he knew, all gone. When did teenagers at a dance become criminals?

No, not criminals. Police handle criminals. The army fights enemies.

A bunch of boys in hand-me-down suits and girls in skimpy dresses were enemies of America?

What was that thing, that monster? That must have been why the army was there. But then why did they take all the others away? Was the army protecting them or arresting them?

Jack didn't dare drive his truck to the barn—he didn't want any lights to make him a target—but he made the decision to hike down the grassy hill.

He moved slowly, instinctively using the slow, toe-to-heel footsteps he'd been taught over a lifetime of hunting deer and elk. The dark felt claustrophobic and heavy, like the night air was wrapping around him, crushing his chest. His breathing was rapid, even though he was hardly moving a mile per hour, and his heart raced.

When he got to the end of the brush, he stopped. The barn was wide open, the lights still on and crepe paper and balloons still adorning the doors.

A paper sign with the painted words "Hawks Forever" hung just inside the barn.

There were bullet holes in the sign.

Now that he was looking for them, he could see the holes everywhere, tiny dots of light punched through the wooden walls of the barn.

No one was here. The teachers were gone, and the DJ, and the local cops. Everyone had been taken.

It was a good thing he didn't have a date, Jack thought, and then began laughing until his laughs turned to sobs and he fell to his knees. What had happened here? What was happening to the world?

What would happen tomorrow?

He wiped his face, ashamed of himself even though there was no one to see him cry, and stood. Quietly, he crossed the lawn and entered the parking lot.

The asphalt was littered with shell casings. Dozens. Hundreds.

He kept moving out to the street, to the two craters blown into the roadbed. They looked like large potholes, only more violent, with grapefruit-sized hunks of asphalt scattered in all directions.

There was blood. In the darkness he might have mistaken it for spilled motor oil, but he'd seen where the gorilla kid had lain—where he'd died.

Jack turned away, feeling the nausea welling up inside of him again.

And then he saw her. A flash of blue and brown—a dress—entering the building.

He paused, frozen for a moment, frozen because everything felt dangerous. But it was just a girl. Someone the army had missed.

Jack hurried to the barn, his eyes darting back and forth between the door and the ground—he didn't want to step on any shells and scare her. He wanted answers, and maybe this girl would have some.

He stopped at the entrance, his stomach in his throat.

He peeked inside.

The girl sat at one of the round tables near the door, facing away from him. Her dress, blue and long, was covered in a layer of dark brown mud, and scratches up the back had torn and frayed the material. Her hair and neck were just as filthy. A long red scrape ran up her shoulder and under her dripping brunette hair.

She wasn't wearing any shoes.

She looked exhausted, her forearms resting on the table and her head hanging down. Jack guessed she must be in shock—one of the few who'd seen what happened but managed to stay hidden.

He wondered if he should say something, but was afraid she'd panic. Instead, he stepped inside the barn and began walking in a wide circle around her, staying far enough away to be non-threatening until he was in her view.

Her eyes were closed.

Aubrey.

He wondered how he hadn't recognized her before, but he wasn't used to seeing her in anything approaching a dress like this. The only times she ever wore a dress were to church, and for years those had just been the same floral prints she'd bought at his parents' thrift shop.

"Hey," Jack said, trying to sound as calm as possible.

Her head popped up, eyes open and terrified. They settled on Jack. She stared for just a few seconds and then bent over again.

Even now, after all that had happened, she didn't want to see him. What had he ever done to her?

"You okay?" he asked, a slight harshness to his voice.

Aubrey lifted her head, but didn't really make eye contact. Instead she gestured around the room at the destroyed decorations and spilled food. She pulled out the chair beside her, and Jack thought she was offering it to him until he saw the two bullet holes punched through the back.

"Do I look okay?" she said. "Is any of this okay?"

Jack came over anyway, staring at the sharp, torn metal edges of the folding chair.

"How did you get away?"

She pointed to her dress and then shook her head, plainly upset with herself. "I ran and fell in the river, like an idiot."

"Better than being out here," he said, sticking a finger through one of the jagged bullet holes.

He tried to imagine what she would have looked like if she hadn't been filthy with mud, if her makeup and hair weren't soaked.

She probably would have looked like one of Nicole's Barbie-doll clones, he thought. This wasn't the same Aubrey Parsons he used to know and—well, it wasn't the same Aubrey Parsons he used to know.

Jack sat down across from her. "Do you know what happened?"

She shook her head. "I know what I saw, but I have no idea what it was."

"What did you see?"

"I saw Nate Butler turn into some kind of monster—like he was made out of rock, like in a movie."

"That was Nate?"

"You saw it?" She looked surprised.

"Yeah," Jack said. He held up keys to the barn—keys he didn't need, since it was left wide open. "I was waiting for the dance to be over so I could clean the place up."

"Then you know what happened."

"I guess."

She looked so different. Even filthy, she was a different person than the one he'd known. Aubrey Parsons should have been wearing a T-shirt and jeans, not a strapless dress.

He stood, then walked to a small alcove by the front entrance. Rows of hangers held jackets and shawls—no one had been able to gather their belongings before being forced outside. He pulled out one of the boys' coats—thick, sheepskin, exactly like one Jack had always wanted. He then rooted around in the bags left on the floor below, digging through leftover decorations and extra boxes of cookies before he found a pair of girls' sneakers. Finally, he grabbed one of the shawls.

Jack took the clothes to Aubrey. "Here."

She picked up the shawl and wrapped it around her shoulders.

"No," he said. "Use that as a towel. Wear the coat."

Aubrey paused, then did as he'd instructed, whispering, "Thank you."

SIX

AUBREY WAS FREEZING. THE SHAWL wasn't much of a towel—it hardly absorbed anything—but she was glad to wipe the mud from her face. As embarrassing as it was to be seen like this, she was glad it was only Jack, not one of her new friends. Jack had grown up with her in the hills around Mount Pleasant— he'd seen her much messier.

"So what do we do now?" she asked.

"Your guess is as good as mine."

Jack was trying to put on a good game face, but she could tell he was scared. Why he was being kind to her was something she couldn't begin to understand.

"Do you think we can go back into town?"

"Did they say why they were here?" he asked. "I mean, I assume it was partly about Nate. . . ."

"Maybe it was all about him?" she said hopefully.

Jack just shrugged. "If they only wanted Nate, why take everyone else away even after they—after . . ."

"You can say it," Aubrey said, her voice emotionless. "After they killed him." She wondered if she was in shock. Nate brought her to the dance, after all. She'd seen him moments before he'd . . . whatever he'd done.

But this had to be related to her as well, to what she could do. When she'd first begun disappearing, it had freaked her out. Why did she, of all the people on the entire earth, have some bizarre evolutionary quirk? Now she knew she wasn't alone. Nate was something strange, too. He wasn't at all like Aubrey, but definitely something . . . inhuman.

And the military was here to find them.

Aubrey would have thought the army had better things to do than look for a seventeen-year-old invisible shoplifter and a boy who could . . . turn into rock? Was that what he had done?

She picked up the coat, shawl, and shoes. "I'm going to clean up."

"'Kay," Jack said. "But hurry. If they were rounding people up, you and I are going to be missing. They're going to look for us."

"Where should we go?"

"My house, I guess," he said. "Maybe we can figure out what's going on."

Aubrey nodded and turned toward the restroom, its door decorated with crepe paper and a poster-board sign that read "Hotties." Her hand lingered on it as she pushed the door open.

This was her first dance.

Ten minutes later they were in the field beside the road, trudging through two-foot-tall alfalfa. The rough stalks scratched Aubrey's ankles and snagged the frills of her dress, but it was ruined anyway.

Aubrey explained everything she'd seen and heard, lying where it was necessary so Jack wouldn't learn of her invisibility. She said she'd overheard the soldiers checking the students' identities, seen the soldiers tightening plastic bracelets onto the students' arms. Jack asked a lot of questions that she had no answers to.

They didn't dare drive, even though Jack had his truck and Aubrey knew where she could find the keys to Nicole's convertible Mustang. The plan was to stay off the road, get to Jack's house, and figure out what was going on. The soldiers had said the students would all be released the next day, and if that was true, Jack said, he'd just turn himself in. Aubrey said she would, too, but it was a lie. She'd disappear. Run. Get as far away as possible.

Where would she go?

"This won't get out of hand," Jack said, confidence in his

voice. "Name me a house in this town that doesn't have at least two guns, probably more. Parents aren't going to let the government lock up their kids."

Aubrey nodded. She knew it was true of most parents. Her dad . . . well, she'd be lucky if he was sober enough to say good-bye as she was taken away.

"Lake Powell was attacked," Jack said, and Aubrey stopped. "When?"

"I don't know. Today some time. That's the closest."

She shook her head. "No. There was that sabotage at Kennecott." People thought she was dumb—not caring about current events was almost a point of pride among Nicole's friends—but she was still Aubrey. She still read, even if it was alone, in her room. She still cared.

No, that wasn't true.

She hated what she knew she'd become. High school would be over soon, and then where would she be? Nicole wouldn't be around to make her popular anymore, and even though Aubrey could disappear and steal a homecoming dress, that didn't mean she could shoplift her way into college.

Aubrey had been a straight-A student until she'd become friends with Nicole. Nicole could afford to skip classes and get bad grades—her dad was the richest man in Sanpete County and owned at least half the turkey farms. Nicole would go to college, tuition paid in full, with letters of recommendation coming from the best names in central Utah—mayors, judges, state senators. But Aubrey needed a scholarship, and she was losing it every day, all in exchange for popularity.

"What happened to the lake?" she asked, turning and continuing to walk.

"It sounds like the dam broke," Jack answered. "I didn't hear a lot of details."

She nodded, and they walked in silence for a long time. If only she could talk to Nicole—the one person who knew her secret. At times, their relationship had felt more like a business partnership than a friendship, but they shared the deepest, darkest secret Aubrey could imagine—that she was *wrong*. Defective. So different that she wondered if she was human at all.

At first Nicole had joked that it was a miracle, that Aubrey was some angel sent to earth to do good works and fight crime. But it hadn't turned out that way. Not only was she a criminal, but her anomalies didn't end with invisibility. Her eyesight was getting bad—and not just something glasses would fix. Sometimes she couldn't see at all.

And the headaches were almost constant.

There wasn't a day that went by that she didn't wonder if she wasn't dying of a brain tumor.

But the one time she'd gone to the clinic her dad had been there within hours to yank her away, and yell at the receptionists and doctors—and Aubrey—for unnecessary medical care. She knew he wasn't paying any of the bills they'd sent.

He'd never even opened them; they just piled up by the door next to the rest of the mail that she wished he'd look at.

A brilliant white light burst on, less than a hundred yards away. Jack and Aubrey both dropped to their knees, and she went even farther, flattening herself in between a row of the crops. She instinctively started to disappear before she stopped herself.

"It's not a military truck," Jack said quietly.

Aubrey lifted her head enough to see the light. When it was pointed away from them, she could see someone standing in the back of a pickup.

"Maybe they're trying to find us?" she said hopefully. Jack was right—most of this town wouldn't stand for the kidnapping of their kids.

"No," Jack said. "Look how it's parked."

She strained to see, but to her it just looked like the outline of a pickup.

The beam flashed toward them again and she ducked.

"It's sideways," Jack said. "Like a roadblock."

He was right. Whoever was in the pickup was scanning a handheld halogen lamp back and forth across the field, blocking the one and only road to the barn.

The light hit the cab of the truck briefly, illuminating the man for an instant.

"He's got a rifle," Aubrey said, suddenly chilled despite the heavy sheepskin coat.

"It's Lance Halladay." Aubrey could hear the disgust in Jack's voice. "I bet Ian Morris is with him."

Lance and Ian were two people who made Mount Pleasant a little less pleasant. They were only a couple of years older than Aubrey and Jack, and probably would have been in jail if it wasn't a small town with a lenient police force. No big crimes, just a lot of public drunkenness and loitering. A ton of ogling and harassment, if that was illegal. Aubrey didn't know, and the police didn't seem to care.

"I don't think we should go this way," Aubrey said. The boys weren't out there to help straggling kids. They were there for . . . she didn't know. The one thing Aubrey knew was that she was somehow like Nate Butler, and he'd been killed.

"I think you're right."

They backed out of the field, crawling on their hands and knees through the harvest-ready crops until they felt they were far enough away. Aubrey stood, feeling weaker than ever. Normally she would only stay invisible for a few minutes—fifteen at the most. Tonight, she'd spied for at least twenty-five, and then she'd hidden from the soldiers on and off for another hour as they swept the area for runaways.

But there was nothing she could do about it now. Her only other option was to sit down on a rock and wait for someone to find her.

"What if we just turn ourselves in?" Jack asked. "You told

me the soldiers said this was for our own safety."

"No," she answered firmly.

He nodded, and Aubrey wondered what he was thinking. They used to be so close. She used to be able to read him like a book. That was less than a year ago, but it felt like a decade.

They crossed two more long fields, her dress snagging on barbed wire when she climbed both fences. Each time it made her want to cry—the dress had been gorgeous, the prettiest thing she'd ever owned. Stolen.

"Do you hear that?" Jack asked, stopping and grabbing her arm.

Aubrey listened, straining to hear anything besides the cold canyon wind. "What?"

"Voices," he said, and then carefully climbed up the short embankment to the road. He ducked, and pointed.

Aubrey was right behind him, and saw the shapes in the distance—three cars across this road. None had their lights on; instead, half a dozen flashlights moved violently around the makeshift roadblock.

"They're arguing," Jack said, but Aubrey still couldn't hear it.

Was she losing her hearing along with her sight?

"About what?"

He shrugged, and then motioned for her to cross the road to the next field. "Can't tell."

"Why would they do this?" she asked.

"You think they're looking for us?"

"Who else?"

"Terrorists," he said, like the answer was obvious. "Whoever hit Lake Powell." He scrambled down the other side of road. This wasn't a cultivated field—just rocky undeveloped land. She expected him to offer her a hand, but he didn't.

"But what about Nate?" Aubrey asked as she carefully followed after him.

"You know more about Nate than I do," Jack said.

"Hardly anything, really."

"I'm just saying—"

She stopped, suddenly letting out her fear, disguised as anger. "I don't understand anything about what he did."

"I don't care," Jack answered. "All I'm saying is you knew him better than me."

"Well, I didn't know . . . whatever he was. Whatever he did back there."

"I don't care," Jack said again. He started walking, forcing her to follow if she wanted to talk. "I have no idea what happened with him. I'm just saying that the military has their hands full right now. They'd only stop the dance if people were in danger."

"What danger?" She wasn't trying to be belligerent, but part of her wanted—needed—to justify Nate's actions. If she was anything like him, then he couldn't be dangerous, could he? Could *she*?

"Terrorists hit Lake Powell. Maybe they're coming here next." He turned and kept walking away from the road.

"To do what?" Aubrey asked, exasperated. "Blow up a turkey farm?"

"They could target Wasatch Academy," he answered. "The dorms. Or Walmart."

"Walmart?"

"They hit malls last week."

Aubrey pulled the oversized coat closer around her. She'd gotten the dress just before the mall disasters on the West Coast. She wasn't sure of the final count, but the attacks were staggered—three one day, five the next, six more the day after. Nothing in Utah, of course. It was too small to care about. Well, that was what she'd thought until tonight.

But what about Nate? Did that have anything to do with the attacks?

"Where are we headed?" she asked Jack. She'd just realized the roadblocks were forcing them away from Jack's house.

He shrugged without turning back. "Into town. To the school. It seems like the most logical meeting place."

"So we just turn ourselves in?"

He glanced over his shoulder. "You and I know Mount Pleasant inside and out. We can sneak up close, see what's going on."

She thought about that for a minute. They might know

every alley and broken fence, but they weren't the US Army. They didn't have night vision binoculars and who knew what else. And she couldn't turn invisible with Jack.

"No," she said, and stopped.

He turned around, annoyed. "What?"

"Let's go to my house. Check the news. Find out what's happened."

"Why?"

Aubrey started to cry. It was fake at first—something Nicole had taught her to help her get her way—but once the tears came they didn't stop. "My date just turned into a monster, and then they killed him. It's the middle of the night and you want us to spy on the people who did it. I want to go home."

Jack hesitated.

"Come on, Jack," she sobbed. "Let's go home."

SEVEN

"SLOW DOWN," ALEC SAID, SITTING up straighter in the passenger seat. His head was throbbing, and he'd been trying to sleep, but Laura drove too fast. They were asking to get pulled over.

The escape had gone perfectly to plan—better than he could have hoped. Only a few vehicles had tailed them as they flew out of the Glen Canyon Dam parking lot—Dan had shaken the canyon walls and must have damaged the bridge over the Colorado River—and the Bronco had quickly lost their pursuers in the maze of dirt roads to the west. They exchanged the stolen Bronco for a pickup, and then headed north through the Grand Staircase–Escalante National Monument, one of the most godforsaken stretches of wilderness in the country.

Laura drove—she'd had plenty of time that day to rest while the other two prepared for the attack, and both Alec and Dan were worn out and hurting. Dan could usually just sleep off his problems, but Alec's always resulted in a migraine. Laura, so far as they'd seen, didn't have any significant side effects. But her mutations were simple—strength, toughness, endurance. She was their tank, their human escape plan.

Human. Alec smiled tiredly. He was better than human now.

He turned on the radio again, the noise sending electric bolts of pain through his forehead.

". . . *expected to be a complete loss, though the damage could have been far worse. The brunt of the explosion took place fairly high up on the dam; had it been lower, the hole would be growing significantly faster and the evacuation process would be that much more difficult.*"

"Dammit." He sat quietly, watching the darkness out the windows. *The evacuation process.* He had thought that breaking the dam would be like popping an inflatable pool, sending all the water—and boaters—flushing down the Grand Canyon. But for hours they'd heard news anchors talk about the slow descent of the water, like bathwater slowly draining out of a tub.

He punched the dashboard. "Dammit. Dammit. Dammit!"

"It was a stretch," Dan said quietly and defensively. "You knew that. I was working with concrete, not natural rock; it was over a hundred feet thick."

Alec didn't say anything, though of course it was all true. He'd known it going in.

"We killed the dam," Laura said, her hands tight on the steering wheel. "I don't see what the big deal is."

She never saw what the big deal was, Alec thought, but he kept his mouth shut. Not because he couldn't have out-argued her, but because he had a headache and it wasn't worth his time. Something caught his attention and he turned up the radio again.

"*. . . want to emphasize that the suspects in this bombing are three young people, between seventeen and twenty-five years of age. They were last seen heading west on Highway 89 in a late model Bronco.*"

The newsman gave their basic descriptions, which were vague enough to give Alec a little peace.

"So you want solid rock, huh?" he asked.

Dan, lying down in the backseat, grunted a yes. Dan always did better with natural stone than with synthetics.

Alec pulled out his smartphone and began scrolling through lists he'd made over the last several months.

"*. . . We have breaking news from Michigan—the power grid in Detroit has been on and off all night, and there have been reports of damage to electrical substations throughout the city. We also have had unconfirmed reports of blackouts in the northeast, including many portions . . .*"

"Attacking substations?" Alec said back to the radio. "Weak, guys. Weak."

Laura laughed. "That's why we're the best."

That's why I'm *the best*, he thought.

He continued flipping through the list on his smartphone. He had potential targets researched all over the area—good targets, too. Railroads, mines, even a handful of power plants. And being in the middle of nowhere in Utah hopefully meant there wouldn't be too many guards.

"Hey," Laura said, and pointed ahead into the darkness.

Alec peered forward. Bright floodlights illuminated the highway and made his headache even worse. Two vehicles were stopped across the road.

"You ready?" Laura asked.

He didn't answer. Of course he was ready.

She slowed as they approached. The lead car was marked as the Wayne County Sheriff's Department. A portly man with a thick mustache walked around the front of the cruiser.

"You know what to do," Alec whispered, suddenly nervous. Local authorities were always a wild card—he wasn't sure how paranoid they would be, or how strictly they'd follow guidelines of police protocol. The only thing Alec needed was time, but he wouldn't get that if the officer had a "shoot first, ask questions later" approach.

Laura stopped the car and shifted into park. She unrolled her window.

The officer clicked on his flashlight and began walking toward them, his hand resting on his holstered gun.

Alec wondered how alert Dan was in the back. That's where the stolen rifle was, under a blanket, and Dan was probably still too weak to use it. Alec had the pistol under his own seat.

He tried to push all of those thoughts out of his mind. He focused on the officer.

"Where ya headin'?" the officer asked, peering in the windows. He shone his light in Laura's face, then Alec's, then at Dan.

"Home," Laura said, her voice scared. "We were camping down in Kodachrome Basin, but we heard about the dam on the radio. We figured it was time to go."

"License?"

Laura fumbled for it, digging in her jeans pockets first, and then leaning over to the glove compartment. She wasn't really looking for it, Alec knew. She was wasting time.

The memory he was trying to place was a simple one—that the officer had heard the suspects had been spotted at roadblock in St. George—four hours to the west. It was the easiest kind of memory to plant. Just a simple fact. The officer could build the rest of the story in his own mind.

Laura turned to the window and handed the truck's fake insurance card. "Here's this. Still looking for the license. Sorry—we left in a rush and I'm not sure where I put everything."

"Take your time," the officer said.

Dammit. A second man was walking over from the cars. Alec could only work on one mind at once.

Laura's eyes met Alec's as she turned back to dig through the glove compartment again.

"Where's home?" the officer asked.

"Denver," she answered.

"That's a long way to drive."

"We were just trying to get away from everything," she said, finally grabbing the license and handing it to the officer. "We left right after the stadium came down last week. Figured we'd go somewhere safe."

Alec switched his focus to the second man, but he had to be more careful now. The memory had to be perfect—it had to match the first officer's exactly.

It was quiet for several seconds as the men looked at the driver's license of Laura Hansen, the all-American blonde from Lakewood, Colorado. It wasn't even a forgery—she'd lived there for ten years with her sleeper-agent parents, groomed and prepared for this as all of them were. All Colorado natives, all graduates of Colorado public high schools.

Keep talking, Laura.

But she was quiet, the officers several feet away, back from the window so they could watch everyone.

Dan sat up in the backseat and stretched. Probably trying to show he wasn't a threat, that he wasn't attempting to hide anything.

Alec was pouring the information into the second man's mind. Three suspects, all matching the description of the terrorists, were spotted at a roadblock just outside of St. George. Three suspects. The call came in on the radio. The sighting only happened half an hour ago.

What were the men doing back there? It wasn't the first time that Alec wished he could read thoughts as well as influence them.

Were their minds resisting the new memories? The whole reason for the roadblock was probably to watch for suspects, so the notion that the suspects had been seen half an hour ago would be hard to reconcile in their minds. Why were they still stopping cars? Who were they still looking for?

The officer reappeared at the car window, his flashlight blocking Alec's view of him.

He handed Laura's license and insurance back to her. "The bad news is that you're going to run into a lot of traffic a couple miles up the road. Everyone's doing the same thing you are, coming up outta Bullfrog. How far are you fixin' to drive tonight?"

"Until we get tired," Laura said.

The officer stepped back and patted the hood of the truck. "Well, be safe. Stay awake."

Laura stuffed the license and insurance back into the glove compartment, thanked the officer, and then steered the car through the roadblock.

"That was a close one," Dan said.

"Easy," Alec answered. "Have I ever failed you?"

"I could have taken them both," Laura said.

Alec ignored that. It was her answer for everything, and it would leave a huge trail for police to follow.

He pulled out his smartphone again. "Dan, you want natural stone?"

Dan yawned. "You find something?"

Alec opened a picture and handed the phone back to Dan. "How's that?"

"Where is it?"

"Maybe an hour and a half away. Depends on the traffic."

Laura turned to look at him, the grin on her face illuminated by the glow of the phone. "Two in one day?"

Alec looked in the rearview mirror. "Better get some sleep, Dan."

EIGHT

"IF ANYONE WAS THERE, WE'D have seen them by now," Jack whispered.

Aubrey knew he was probably right, but he didn't have as much to lose as she did. Jack wasn't a freak. The army hadn't shown up at the dance to take him.

As Aubrey and Jack waited in the tall, dry grass behind her trailer park, the disaster at the Gunderson Barn kept replaying in her mind. One thing was nagging at her.

A soldier had referred to Nate as a "possible Lambda." What was a Lambda? She knew lambda was a letter in the Greek alphabet, she'd heard about it in physics—a lambda particle—and she'd seen lambda used in math before. But it wasn't really what it meant that was nagging her; it was that it meant *something*. Whatever Nate was, he was a possible

Lambda. The army knew about Lambdas. They knew about freaks.

Am I a Lambda?

The thought both scared and exhilarated her. Whatever made Aubrey invisible had a name. Someone was researching it. Maybe someone was looking for a cure.

Maybe. Or maybe they were looking for Lambdas to exterminate them.

"It's been fifteen minutes," Jack said, looking at his watch.

There were lights on in a few of the mobile homes, including hers, but nothing had moved. A car drove down the highway every minute or two, never slowing to glance at the run-down trailer park.

Cautiously, Aubrey stood and then squeezed through a break in the fence as she'd done a thousand times before. Jack hurried behind her and they slipped quietly down the dirt road to the second home on the right. It was filthy, more so than it used to be, now that Aubrey had a life other than helping her dad. She felt a twinge of embarrassment.

No, it's just Jack. He's been here almost every day since we were little.

The door was unlocked, as usual, and Aubrey stepped inside. Jack followed her.

"What the hell are you doing here?" Her father's voice was slurred and loud, breaking through the small amount of calm they'd felt out in the darkness. He stood in the kitchen, fiddling with a can of something.

Aubrey stepped to her father and gave him a hug. "Just here to change clothes, Daddy."

"What happened to your dress?" he nearly shouted. He had about ten days' worth of unshaven beard, and his long gray hair was out of place as if he'd been sleeping.

"It's been a long night," she said.

Jack spoke up. "Do you mind if I turn on the news?"

"Go ahead," her father replied, his hands and voice shaking. "It's all crap."

Jack sat on the well-worn couch and found the remote for the old TV.

Aubrey helped her dad as he fumbled with the can opener, cutting the top off a small can of generic chili.

"... *those reports from a few minutes ago that the Glen Canyon Dam terrorists had been apprehended are now being called false. Officials are urging everyone—including those on blogs and social media—to not spread unconfirmed rumors.*"

Aubrey paused in front of the TV. She saw for the first time the footage of the collapsed dam—the crumbled cement clinging to the canyon walls as a torrent of water spewed into the Grand Canyon. There were still boats on the lake, kicking up a stream of churning white foam as they fought the current to reach the marina. It had still been light when these videos were taken; she wondered how much worse it was now.

"I'm going to change," she mumbled, and headed to her room.

She closed the door behind her and leaned against the wall, taking in a deep breath.

Her room was small—a tiny space with thin walls and a linoleum floor—but she felt safe for the first time that night. It was the one place in the entire town where she didn't have to put on a show, where she didn't have to be someone else.

Sometimes, in her room, she didn't even feel like her dad's caretaker. In her room—she was free.

She took off the heavy sheepskin coat and inspected her dress in front of the mirror on her closet door. It was a complete loss. Aside from the mud stains, which were everywhere, the satin was snagged and scratched from every time she'd pushed through bushes or waded through alfalfa. Even if she could get it cleaned, it would look terrible. She slipped it off and tossed it in a pile in the corner.

First dance, over.

She wondered where she was going, what clothes she should wear. Her wardrobe was extensive now—all stolen from the mall in the city—but most of what Nicole had talked Aubrey into getting was too delicate for the uncertainty that lay ahead. The expensive jeans, the loose, thin tops, the cute sandals. Aubrey didn't know where she was going, but she knew she'd be on her own, and that the few times she'd be around people she'd be invisible.

She picked a pair of jeans that, while still expensive, seemed durable, like they could handle the outdoors. She layered her tops—a T-shirt, a long-sleeve button-up plaid, and a sweater. She didn't have nice hiking boots, so she pulled on a recently acquired pair of cross trainers.

She looked at herself in the mirror. She wasn't the old worn-out Aubrey she used to be, but she wasn't the stylish popular girl Nicole had helped her become, either. She was half and half. She wasn't anyone.

Aubrey plopped down on the bed and put her head in her hands. What was she going to do? She could take her .22 with her, but she couldn't live off the land, not forever. And going into the city wouldn't help: sure, she'd have access to food and clothes that she could steal on a whim, but she'd be homeless. She couldn't stay invisible forever.

She wanted to cry, but stopped herself. It wouldn't help anything, and she had cried enough that night.

Jack was on the edge of his seat, staring at the TV when Aubrey came back out of her room. He didn't look up.

"What's the news?" she asked, sitting on the arm of the couch.

"Roundups," he said. "It's not just here."

Aubrey's stomach turned, and she slid down onto the seat next to him.

"Apparently it started a couple days ago," he said, giving

her a quick glance. "They've been keeping it quiet. It's mostly rumors at this point, but it's happening all over the place. The official word is that it's for protection, but others say it's for some kind of testing. The National Guard has been going door to door."

"Testing," she repeated. Her chest felt hollow, as if she were collapsing in on herself.

"Maybe the terrorists spread poison or something," Jack said.

Aubrey nodded, though she knew he was wrong. She didn't know what her invisibility had to do with terrorists, but she knew—she just knew—they were after her.

Jack met her gaze. "We should turn ourselves in."

She was suddenly panicked. "What? No."

"What if we've been poisoned? If they're testing for something, what if we have it?"

"We don't," she said, standing up. She nervously ran a hand through her hair. Everything was falling apart.

"Here, look." Jack pointed to the TV. "This is up by Salt Lake."

It was a helicopter view of a dark road. Below them was a long convoy of vehicles. The news anchors were speculating about the destination of the convoy, listing half a dozen military installations in Utah and Idaho. They weren't explaining anything about who was in the buses or why.

"Why would they be testing people somewhere else?"

Aubrey asked, trying to breathe calmly. "Why not just do it here, in the high school gym or something?"

"Maybe we're contagious?"

"No," she said.

"I really think we need to turn ourselves in," he said. "What if we're making your dad sick?"

"No," Aubrey repeated, and suddenly realized that her dad was gone. "Where did he go?"

Jack's eyes didn't leave the screen. "He said he was going outside for a smoke."

"Great." Her voice was quiet and angry.

"Listen," Jack said, muting the TV and turning to face her. His voice was even, but nervous. "I know that tonight was crazy. I know you and Nate were close."

"We weren't close," she snapped, pacing into the kitchen.

"Okay," he said. "Whatever. This sucks, but the important thing is that we don't get into more trouble."

"You don't understand," she said, moving her hands like she couldn't figure out where to put them—from her hips to her face to her hair.

"What is going on?"

She was on the other side of the kitchen counter from him, and grabbed onto the edge for support. She didn't want to tell him. She couldn't.

She had to.

"Turn off the TV for a second," she said.

Jack fumbled with the remote and then clicked it off. "What's going on?" he repeated.

She was hyperventilating. She and Nicole had sworn that neither of them would tell another soul. But now Nicole was on a bus heading who-knows-where.

Aubrey stepped out from behind the counter, her knees feeling weak.

"Look at me."

"What?"

"Just watch." And then she disappeared. She saw the look on his face that she'd seen on so many others as she'd practiced. In their minds, she hadn't just blinked out of sight, but she wasn't there anymore. Confusion spread across his face.

"Where did you go?" he asked.

She reappeared, and his eyes slowly focused back on her.

She spoke before he could. "Tell me what you saw."

He was plainly puzzled. "I'm not sure. Did you go back behind the counter?"

"Nope," she said. "Right here the whole time."

"But . . ." he started.

"Jack," she said, taking an anxious step toward him. "This is why I can't turn myself in. I'm like Nate."

He just stared, more confused than scared, which Aubrey considered a small victory. "You're not like Nate," he finally said.

"I don't know what Nate was," she said. "But he was different. And I'm different, too. I think they're testing to find us."

Now Jack stood up. "What are you?"

Her eyes narrowed. "I'm Aubrey, same as I've always been."

Jack shook his head. "The Aubrey I knew couldn't do . . . what did you do again?"

"I can disappear," she said, her voice shaking. "I can't explain it, so don't ask me to."

"It wasn't like you disappeared," he said.

"I know. Here, watch again."

A second time she vanished, and once again Jack stared, flustered. He reached an arm out, swiping through the air. She grabbed his hand and reappeared.

He flinched as she came back, and pulled his hand away. "What are you doing?"

She didn't want him to be like this. She wanted him to be impressed, amazed. That's how Nicole had been. She'd immediately seen how valuable Aubrey could be.

"How do you do . . . that?" he asked.

"I just do," she said. "Now do you see why I can't turn myself in? This has to be what they're testing for."

Jack nodded blankly.

She couldn't stand the strange way he was watching her. He was her oldest friend and he was looking at her like she was someone—something—foreign and strange. Like she was a freak.

He was right.

Her fingers clutched the edge of the counter.

After a long pause, Jack spoke. "The Pattens' cabin."

"What?"

"Eric Patten's cabin. His family left town to go be with his grandma in Montana. We could go to their cabin—no one will be there."

She tilted her head slightly toward him. "What do you mean 'we'? You should turn yourself in."

"Yeah, right."

Aubrey turned around again. He looked tired, but he was standing firm, rubbing the back of his neck while he thought.

"If they're testing for . . . whatever it is you can do, then that means they aren't searching for me. If I get caught then I'll just say I was afraid and running."

"Why?"

"Because I'm not going to leave you."

Suddenly she was less scared of him than for him. Nate had been killed. What would happen if they found out Jack was helping her? "I can take care of myself. You're not the only one who knows how to fish and hunt."

His head was down, staring at the cluttered mess as he rubbed his neck.

"I've been to the Pattens' cabin," Aubrey continued. "I can find it. They have food storage there." She didn't add that she could steal anything else she needed from the grocery store.

Jack still gazed at the floor, not responding.

"I'm going to pack," she said, and took a step toward her bedroom.

"I thought your dad stopped smoking."

"Huh? Well, he did for a while." She hadn't seen him smoke in a long time. The little spare money he had usually went for cheap beer.

Jack bent over and picked up a paper from the floor. It was wrinkled, with torn corners where it had been taped to something. He handed it to her.

The font was bold and simple, with an official seal top and center.

WE NEED YOUR HELP

The Centers for Disease Control and Prevention has identified a highly contagious virus in your area. By order of the President of the United States and the Federal Emergency Management Agency, all persons between the ages of 13 and 20 are to be tested and quarantined for the protection of both themselves and others.

We appreciate your cooperation with this action. Because of the major threat this poses to public health and national security, it is of utmost importance that all citizens comply. Financial compensation will be granted for any help rendered in fulfillment of this request.

Aubrey's hands began to shake before she got to the bottom of the letter. Finally, she looked up at Jack. "Financial compensation?"

"There's a bounty on you—on us both. That's why we kept seeing those roadblocks. Lance and Ian—they were trying to get reward money."

She ran to the front door. For the first time in her life she hoped her dad was sitting on the front porch smoking. She twisted the knob, then peered outside.

Darkness. No one was there.

Not even her dad.

A blazing light filled her eyes. For an instant she felt Jack's hand on her arm, pulling her back, but she disappeared, slipping out of his grip. She stumbled through the trailer, blindly forcing herself to the back door. Before she got there a foot kicked it in.

"Aubrey!"

It was Jack's voice but she couldn't see anything. Her vision was blurry, trails of the brilliant-white floodlights seared into her eyes.

Something flew through the window in a spray of glass.

She screamed. Jack was yelling. He couldn't hear her while she was invisible.

The room began to fill with a glowing white light.

Jack bumped into her and knocked her down without knowing he'd done it.

She couldn't breathe.

Her eyes stung and she wiped at them wildly as tears flowed down her face.

Was the trailer on fire? She couldn't get any air.

Jack wasn't yelling for her anymore. She couldn't see him.

This was her fault. He had wanted to turn himself in.

She reappeared, sucked in a draft of burning air. "Jack!" she called out.

In a moment he was there, grabbing her hand, pulling her from the trailer, away from the bright, stinging smoke.

He twisted her arm behind her back, and the two of them stumbled down the stairs to where she landed, face down in the dirt.

He grabbed her other hand.

She could barely open her swollen eyes.

"Aubrey," a choking voice said.

She cracked one bleary eye. Jack was beside her, pinned to the ground, his arms bound behind his back.

She felt the tug of cuffs being tightened on her wrists.

"Stay here," Jack said.

Every impulse in her urged Aubrey to disappear, to slip away from the soldiers and run. But it was too much. She was handcuffed. Her dad had turned her in—sold his own daughter out for beer money.

And as tough as she was—or pretended to be—there was something in Jack's insistence that he stay with her that she'd liked. They would have been on the run together. A friend who wasn't using her.

She'd stay.

NINE

DAN WAS STILL CRAWLING OUT of the car as Laura hurried to the edge of the cliff, excited about Alec's unexpected new goal. She peered over the rim of the canyon, into what looked like a black river of darkness. "It says here," Alec said, shining a flashlight on a plaque next to the rest stop parking lot, "that they named it Eagle Canyon because pioneers thought it was so deep not even an eagle could fly out of it."

Laura looked down again, at the pitch-black bottom, and at the enormous steel beams that held up the short bridge.

It wasn't a big target. No one was guarding it, which made it even more perfect. She guessed that most of the people who drove over this bridge never realized they were crossing such a deep gorge. It was maybe eighty yards wide, in a stretch of canyon country called the San Rafael Swell. Interstate 70 swerved and climbed through the rugged terrain, and even Laura hadn't noticed the bridge when she passed over it. Alec had to point out the turnoff.

"There are two bridges," Alec said to Dan, who still looked exhausted. "The eastbound and westbound are separate, maybe forty feet between them. The plaque says the rocks are limestone and sandstone."

Dan stood up and stretched. "Now you're talking."

Laura climbed over the edge of the cliff, testing the strength of the notoriously grainy and brittle rock. She slipped her hand into a fissure and clenched a fist, creating an ironlike anchor point.

This was what she loved: using her strength for something real. She'd spent the last month doing nothing but hauling an exhausted Dan over her shoulder like a rag doll. Her parts of the plans were never any fun.

Alec didn't help. He thought she was stupid, just because she was the lowest-ranking member of the group. She wasn't even the youngest—she was nineteen, only three months younger than Alec—but he treated her like she was a little kid, like she didn't know how to do anything.

She leapt sideways, hundreds of feet above the canyon floor, and caught another outcrop of stone. She wished she wasn't wearing shoes—they only slowed her down. Her feet and toes were just as tough and unbreakable as the rest of her.

"Can you climb from here?" Alec asked impatiently.

"Sure," she said, leaping again to the side and catching herself deftly. She couldn't even see her landing spot clearly—it was just a craggy outline in the darkness—but she knew she could grab hold of it. It was like a playground, like a circus high-wire act.

"You look like an orangutan," Dan said, a smile in his voice.

Laura laughed, and swung with one arm, leaping up to where the boys stood.

"You done?" Alec said, the snide frown on his face illuminated only by moonlight.

"We can climb down here easy," she said. "Lots of hand holds. Dan, are you strong enough to hang on?"

He held up his wrists. There was a rope tied between them. "Alec already helped out with that."

Laura smiled. Alec probably thought it was ingenious. He thought everything he did was brilliant.

"Try to just crack the supports," Alec said. "Leave it on a hair trigger for the next eighteen-wheeler that drives over it."

Dan nodded. "I'll see what I can do."

He put his arms, tied together at the wrists, over Laura's head. He'd ride on her back all the way down the cliff.

"Dan," Alec said, his tone more serious. "For your mother and mine."

"Yeah," Dan answered quietly.

With that, Laura hunched over, lifting Dan off the ground

so she could move freely. He smelled of sweat, but she probably did too. They'd been on the run for hours, and sitting in an old car.

She stepped down to a ledge.

"Try not to choke me," she said, and leapt toward another rock.

TEN

JACK SAT BESIDE AUBREY, BUT neither of them talked. Two
soldiers were behind them in the bus, and Jack was sure he
didn't have to warn Aubrey to be quiet about her—was it
invisibility? She was an expert at keeping secrets. At lying.

The two of them had cooperated at her dad's trailer.
They'd given their names and ages, and her dad had con-
firmed them—with a constant request for extra financial
compensation. The man had tried everything: claimed that
Aubrey's job was his only source of income; claimed that she
helped him with his handyman jobs around the trailer park;
claimed that he was disabled and needed her to help him
around the house.

The army had given Jack and Aubrey bracelets, just like
the ones they'd used at the Gunderson Barn. They also got

plastic handcuffs because they had tried to run. They were considered dangerous.

Jack still didn't know what to think about Aubrey. It was true—she was exactly what the army was looking for. If it was anyone else, he thought he'd just urge them to tell the truth, to turn themselves in. But this was Aubrey.

She'd lied to him. She'd ditched him. She'd given up a lifelong friendship in favor of parties, malls, convertibles, and dresses. And it wasn't like he'd forgiven her for any of that. The truth was, when the black ops guys burst into the trailer with tear gas and machine guns, she'd disappeared. She'd tried to escape on her own, to leave Jack by himself yet again. Even in the chaos and the smoke, he'd known.

But he wouldn't turn her in. He couldn't. He'd seen the look on her face when she'd confessed what she could do, that she had some kind of superpower. It wasn't a look of guilt, like she'd been caught, and it wasn't a look of shame, like she was admitting how poorly she'd treated him. It was a look of fear. Fear of what she could do. Fear of who she was.

He didn't trust her. He didn't know if he ever could. But he wasn't going to turn her in.

She was Aubrey Parsons.

The bus pulled into the parking lot of North Sanpete High School, entering a hive of military activity. There were at least eight Humvees and two other buses. Tables were set up on the asphalt and soldiers sat at laptops. Others patrolled the perimeter with M-16s and night-vision goggles.

When their bus parked, an officer told Jack and Aubrey to stay where they were, and then he and all but one of the soldiers left the bus. The last man stood at the door, his focus more on what was going on in the parking lot than on the two teenagers he was guarding.

Aubrey was fidgeting in her seat. "These cuffs are digging in to me."

"I know," Jack answered with a nod.

"Where is everyone?" she asked, her voice a whisper so the guard at the front of the bus couldn't hear.

"Maybe in the school?" Jack said.

"Maybe. But where are the other buses?"

He shrugged, and felt the awkward pain of his twisted arms. "Moved on to the next town? Ephraim or Manti? Mount Pleasant was probably an easy target because we were all at the dance. It'll be harder to round up the other kids."

All the more reason for offering a reward, Jack thought, though he wondered where that money was going to come from. There were a lot of kids, and he still doubted that most parents would give their kids up without a fight.

An idea struck him, and made him sick to his stomach. "What if they're testing for something different? Something else besides what you've got—what you can do."

"What do you mean?"

He made certain he was talking too quietly for the guard to hear. "There're terrorists all over the country. And as of today they're in Utah. What if something was put into our water supply, or our food? What if this has nothing to do with Nate or you? What if it's a real virus?"

Aubrey let out a long slow breath and then smiled for the first time in hours. "I don't know whether to be happy about that or horrified."

Jack chuckled softly.

The guard stepped farther down the steps so he was looking outside.

"So how does it work?" Jack asked. "It's not invisibility like in the comic books."

She paused for several seconds and then spoke. "Here's my best guess. I don't think I'm actually changing—I don't think my skin goes transparent or anything like that. I mean, my clothes disappear too, and people can't hear me when I'm gone. I think, instead—and I know this is going to sound crazy—but I think that my brain talks to your brain and tells you I'm not there. So your brain just ignores any sign of me. Does that sound nuts?"

Jack thought it over for a moment. "Yes. But not any crazier than just turning invisible."

She smiled again, and then leaned forward to try to take pressure off her bound hands.

"How long have you been able to do it?" he asked.

Aubrey was silent for several seconds, like she was try-ing to decide what to say. "About six months," she finally answered. "It was in March. I'd been at a church activity and all of a sudden I couldn't see."

"Really?"

"Yeah. So, my leader drove me to the clinic and they were going to do tests, but my eyesight came back. I was sitting in an exam room and someone walked in, and I freaked out—I was just wearing one of those flimsy hospital gowns—and I realized they couldn't see me. Something about wanting to be hidden made me just disappear."

"That's so weird."

"Tell me about it."

"How could you tell they couldn't see you?"

"Because they just stood there and stared, and then started looking all around—in the bathroom, in the hallway—and they couldn't hear me or see me. They were sure I'd just been there—they just couldn't figure out where I'd gone. I finally reappeared, by accident. It took a long time to control it."

"So the hospital knows?"

Aubrey looked instantly uncomfortable, turning to gaze out the window into the darkness. Jack wished he was back with the old Aubrey. They never used to have secrets.

He prodded. "Did they do tests?"

She slumped back in her seat, her weight on her bound hands again. "It wasn't a doctor."

"Your dad?" he asked.

"No." She let out a long breath, and then laughed. "I was about to swear you to secrecy, but who are you going to tell? The army?"

Jack grinned. "If I could reach, I'd cross my heart."

"Nicole," Aubrey said. "Probably the best-kept secret in Mount Pleasant is that Nicole Samuelson, the queen bee of North Sanpete, has kidney failure. She's on dialysis. She walked in thinking it was her room."

"Seriously?"

She was getting fidgety again, like she'd just realized she'd told some enormous confidential secret.

"You can't tell anyone," Aubrey said, making eye contact for the first time since they'd sat down. "She'd kill me."

Jack opened his mouth, but stopped himself. He carefully considered his words. He didn't know how much of the old Aubrey was still there, but maybe it didn't matter. They were tied up, on a bus to who-knows-where, captured by the military for some mysterious testing.

And besides, he'd wanted answers to this for a long time.

"That's when you became Nicole's friend," he said.

"Yeah, you can call it that," she said. She laughed again, but it was colder, more bitter. "We were never friends. Nicole asked the nurse if she could get her dialysis in that room, and of course they let her because she's a Samuelson. So we shared it, and she talked to me. And she told me what she'd seen. I was freaking out, and I didn't know what to say."

Jack could imagine it all. That was the old Aubrey—the Aubrey Parsons who was too shy to talk during class at all, even though she knew every answer. She was probably as terrified of Nicole as she was of what was happening to her body.

"I didn't become her friend," Aubrey said. "I became her spy. In exchange, I got to hang out with her. She invited me to things. She—well, you know the rest."

The idea made him mad, and he didn't try to hide it. Aubrey never needed Nicole to make Jack like her. Honestly, Aubrey was prettier than Nicole. She wasn't the Scandinavian bubbleheaded blonde that Nicole was—the bland generic beauty that the movies tried to convince him was gorgeous. Aubrey was tall, with long, straight brown hair and eyes that were a stark gray, eyes that reminded him of fresh snow on the mountains.

And honestly, he liked her better in jeans and a T-shirt than a fancy ball gown.

There was a noise at the front of the bus, and the soldier snapped to attention. On command, he hopped to the top step and took a clipboard from another man.

A voice shouted at a line of teens outside the bus. Jack strained to hear.

". . . to take you to the testing and quarantine facilities. The rest of your classmates have already been moved there.

You are the last batch from this county."

"This county," Jack repeated, but Aubrey hushed him.

"This will not take long, but it will require your participation. Congress has declared martial law. You kids know what that means? It means that we're the police now. It means that if you have any problems, you will talk to us, and if you cause any problems, you'll answer to us."

There was a long pause. Someone was asking something. Aubrey whispered under her breath, but Jack didn't catch it.

"Listen," the soldier continued. "We're on your side. You're American citizens and we'll treat you with as much respect as our orders allow. We have kids of our own."

Jack heard the response to that. "Then why are we in handcuffs?"

"All will be explained when we reach the quarantine area. I'm authorized to tell you two things. First, the virus that we're testing for—it's being spread by the terrorists. And second, all known terrorist subjects have been teenagers."

Six more teens were on the bus now, though Jack didn't know any of them. Four were from Manti, the town twenty miles to the south, and two others had managed to escape the shooting at the dance. Jack perked up when the seventh was called.

"Name and town?" the officer on the top step barked.

Matt looked terrified. He was the youngest of the group

so far, small, thin, and drowned in his dirtied suit and tie. "Matt Ganza," he said. "I'm from Mount Pleasant."

"What school?"

"North Sanpete High. I'm sorry, I shouldn't have left the dance. I'm really sorry."

The officer ignored him, and flipped through a thick notebook. Finally, he held it up, comparing a picture to Matt's face.

"Okay," the officer said, and another soldier immediately grabbed Matt's wrist and slipped a plastic bracelet onto it. He cinched it tight and Matt grimaced.

The officer ordered Matt to find a seat. His eyes met Jack's, but he turned quickly and sat toward the front.

They moved to the next person in line—Nicole. The soldier helped her up much more gently than he'd done with Matt.

Aubrey stared for a moment and then looked down at her lap.

"Name?" the officer asked.

"Nicole Samuelson," she said. She was still wearing her dress—a skimpy, shimmering thing that looked like it was made out of giant sequins. She was six feet tall normally, and in her heels she towered over the soldier.

How had she managed to escape the dance without a torn dress or broken stilettos?

The officer flipped through the notebook. "Also from North Sanpete?"

"Yes," she said, smiling happily as though she was excited they were there. "Go Hawks!"

The man smirked. Jack couldn't believe it. Nicole was flirting with the soldiers.

The other soldier attached her bracelet, so gently it almost looked loose on her wrist.

When she turned to walk down the aisle of the bus and saw Aubrey, Nicole's face broke into a smile and she gave her a wink. She sat down next to Matt.

Four more students got on, all younger than Jack. They looked scared. Two were in their pajamas; they hadn't been at the dance—someone had turned them in.

They were all prisoners now.

ELEVEN

LAURA SAT ON A WIDE flat stone, eating from a can of peaches while Dan washed in a cold creek.

The Eagle Canyon bridge had gone better than they could have hoped for. Dan was able to fracture the sandstone easily, and Laura even got a piece of the action, pulling shattered boulders away from the support struts. She knew Dan could move all the rock himself, but she liked being down there, rolling up her sleeves and doing something—anything—with her powers.

They'd loosened the rock around both bridges, enough that one of them began to creak and sway slightly before they'd made a run for it. Laura followed Alec's orders and ran north out of the canyon rather than trying to climb the cliff face. She probably carried Dan five miles before rendezvousing with Alec and the truck. And, just before the truck doors closed, a loud rumbling roar echoed up the canyon. The bridge had fallen.

Then it was time for a real escape. They drove through the little town of Ferron, avoided another roadblock, and headed for the Manti-La Sal mountains. They needed somewhere to lie low, and they needed to get off the streets.

There was a reservoir directly above the town, and Alec spent half an hour talking about taking out that dam, too. But it could wait. They were leaving a big enough trail as it was.

After an hour on a narrow dirt road, they pulled off into the brush and set up camp in the dark. They each had a pup tent and sleeping bag in the back of the truck, and Laura was curled up in her bag, drifting off to sleep before the others had even staked their tents.

There was a bright light and the sound of an engine. It was loud and rattling, like an old utility truck.

Laura rolled over. She unzipped the tent about an inch so she could look out. A set of headlights shone through the trees.

As quietly as she could, Laura climbed out of the sleeping bag. This was her moment—it was her job to ensure the security of the whole team.

"Hey!"

The voice was young, female. Laura felt her heart sink a little—she wouldn't even have to try.

A shape passed in front of the lights, and then another. There were two of them. They were just silhouettes, but one was taller than the other, with broader shoulders. Both had the wide-brimmed hats of forest rangers.

"Hello!" Alec called back with a wave.

As they moved out of the path of the beams Laura could see them better—a man and woman, both wearing green jackets and khaki pants. Neither looked much older than Laura or Alec. Probably fresh out of college. They had radios on their belts and other basic gear, but no weapons that she could distinguish.

Laura pulled on a sweatshirt, and wished she could change from her boxers to jeans without shaking the tent.

"How's it going?" the woman asked.

"Great," Alec answered, a smile in his voice. "Gorgeous night, isn't it?"

Dan had opened his small daypack and was sitting on a rock, chomping on a granola bar, presumably so that he'd look too preoccupied to get into conversation.

"It is," the woman answered, and moved her arm—she was checking her watch. "I saw your lights heading up the canyon. A little late to go camping?"

Alec reached into his back pocket and pulled out a folded map. "We heard about Lake Powell," he said, his voice grave.

"We just wanted to get away from everything." He pointed to something on the map. The woman listened intently as he talked, commenting on a few of the landmarks and laughing at his jokes.

Laura knew enough about law enforcement, however, to know that something was wrong. The man wasn't paying attention to Alec; he was staring at Dan, and Laura's tent. His hand rested uneasily on his radio.

How long had they been watching? Had they seen the guns? Alec had the rifle, and Dan had the pistol. Either one might have been left out, unhidden when the forest rangers showed up.

The tent's zipper was going to be too noisy. Laura pivoted to the back side of the tent. Gently, she plunged her utility knife into the nylon wall of the tent and slid it upward. In ten silent seconds, Laura's tent was open.

There was no reason for Laura to hold back. The worst-case scenario was she'd charge one and the other would go for their radio. But people didn't act like that. They wouldn't go for their radio and stand there waiting to be attacked. They'd run. And Laura could outrun either one.

"Just so you guys know," the woman said, "it's a red burn season, so no campfires."

Yeah right, Laura thought. The rangers wouldn't follow them here at four in the morning to give them a friendly reminder about fires.

Dan pointed toward Laura's pack and talked with a mouth

full of granola. "We've been using one of the small back-packing stoves. The salesman in town said it was legal."

"It is," the man said, obviously still nervous. "One more thing—have you been watching the news?"

"Listening to the radio," Alec said. "But the reception's not very good up here. Why?"

"Well—" The man stopped himself, as though he didn't know what to say. "I was just . . . curious."

"Don't worry," Alec said, laughing. "We're not supposed to be in school or anything. Laura and I are nineteen." He pointed toward her tent. "Dan's eighteen—just graduated in June."

"I'm sure everything is fine," the woman said with a phony laugh. The man, more stilted, put the radio to his lips. "CC Eight, this is CC Station. CC Eight, this—"

Laura couldn't wait any longer. She leapt from her hiding place, bounding across rocks with superhuman strength. It only took her two strides to reach the man and she brought her fist down hard on his hand, knocking the radio to the ground. She heard his bones break under her powerful blow. He stumbled and tripped on a root, falling on his back.

"Don't move!" the woman shouted, her voice panicked. She'd yanked a canister of Mace from her belt, and she pointed it toward the group. With her other hand, she struggled to free the radio from its clip.

Dan was standing, his pistol leveled at the ranger.

"No, stop," the woman said, pleading. "I don't care who

you are. I don't think they should be locking people up, either."

Laura still focused on the man, but her ears perked up.

"Drop the radio," Alec said calmly.

She looked terrified. "Let him go!"

"Drop the radio," Alec repeated, his voice quiet and cold. "I know you're only a ranger, but allow me to explain something. The mace you're holding is not going to stop a bullet."

She was sweating despite the cool air, and her teeth were clenched as she looked back and forth between Dan and Alec.

"Drop—"

"Let him go," she begged. "I won't tell anyone you were here! Listen, I think what they're doing is terrible. They took my little sister yesterday—I would love it if she could have escaped into the mountains like you."

Alec paused for a moment. "Laura," he finally said. Laura glanced at him and he pointed to the man on the ground in front of her. She smiled.

"Wait!" the woman shouted, but it was too late. In hardly a heartbeat, Laura yanked the man up by his crippled arm, then grabbed his collar and threw him backward through the night air. There was the sound of splintering trees and bones, and Alec refocused his attention on the woman.

She was crying now, and the mace fell from her fingers to the ground. Somewhere out of sight, the man was gasping his last breaths. Both walkie-talkies were squawking "CC Eight this is CC Station, come in. CC Three this is CC Station . . ."

Alec looked at Laura. "Get the radios."

She took a deep breath and trekked barefoot over the rocky terrain to find the man and his radio. He was maybe twenty-five feet away, shattered and broken at the base of an uprooted tree.

She bent down to retrieve the gear, and then trudged back over to the woman, who merely stared at Laura, defeated, as she approached. The ranger was no match for any of them—smaller and lighter, without any combat training and now without even her mace. She didn't even know who they were. Laura wondered if the woman had made the connection between them and the destroyed dam.

Laura stood in front of her, looked into the woman's eyes, and unclipped her radio. "Don't fight," Laura said.

For some reason, Laura hoped this one lived. She looked . . . nice. Besides, forest rangers weren't really law enforcement, were they? They weren't the enemy.

"Please . . ." the woman started, but her voice trailed away into nothing.

"Now," Alec said, leaning down to look at the ranger. He touched her name tag. "Ms. Brown. I have some questions for you."

TWELVE

NO ONE WAS TALKING AS the bus pulled onto the highway.

Jack was laying his head back on the seat, but his eyes were open a thin slit. He didn't look like he'd last long. Aubrey wished she could sleep. Normally after staying invisible as long as she had that night she'd nap all afternoon or go to bed early. She definitely wouldn't stay up all night. But her heart wasn't letting her relax—it was pounding in her chest, adrenaline pulsing through her arms and legs. It was claustrophobic and dark—she didn't realize how much she relied on her ability to disappear until she felt completely trapped and knew that she couldn't escape.

They stopped three times over the next few hours. Each one looked like a roadblock. Soldiers were on the road, fully armed and looking cautious and jumpy. Empty cars were pulled over on the side of the road into a jumble of makeshift parking lots. Beside the third roadblock several of the cars were blackened and burned, and at least one soldier appeared to be injured.

Their caravan was headed north, Aubrey was sure. She knew the road well enough—another fifty miles and they'd be in Salt Lake. But she didn't know what that meant.

The eastern sky was turning a faint gray when they turned off the interstate and headed west. They passed the suburbs of Provo and were once again on narrow country roads that wound over low hills. Little rural towns that she'd never heard of before—Faust and Clover—whizzed past as the sun crested the mountains to the east.

Finally they arrived at a gate. As she stared into the distance on the other side of the fence, she could see they were being watched. She spotted at least three Humvees, and two things that looked kind of like tanks. A helicopter sounded low in the sky, though she couldn't tell where it was.

She elbowed Jack, who startled awake.

"Hey," she whispered.

"Where are we?"

She pointed to a sign. "Dugway Proving Grounds."

He rubbed his face. "Dugway?"

"You know it?" she asked.

"Some kind of military test facility. The place is enormous—it's like a bomb range for the air force." He glanced around him, trying to get his bearings. "Did I really sleep that long?"

"Look," she said, pointing to a wide sign hung on the chain-link fence.

WARNING: RESTRICTED AREA.
USE OF DEADLY FORCE AUTHORIZED.

She balled her hands into fists, and bent her head down to take a few deep, long breaths. She was expecting a hospital. Not a bomb range.

There were more murmurs around the bus and a soldier at the front stood and faced them. "Almost there, folks. Maybe half an hour now."

I should have run, Aubrey thought. *What am I doing here?*

The landscape was barren desert. There wasn't a plant more than two feet tall, and the bus windows were pelted by grains of salty sand. It seemed to get more bleak and desolate with every mile.

Jack nudged her. "It'll be okay."

She nodded, but didn't answer. It would be okay for him. He wasn't a freak.

The bus crested a hill and the uninhabited desert suddenly transformed into a small valley of bustling activity. There were a handful of permanent structures—some metal ware-houses, others squat and cinder block—but the majority of the valley and hills were covered in olive-green tents. Tall chain-link fences with razor wire ran in every direction, separating one building from another and creating restricted pathways.

Each corner was guarded by a wooden tower.

Everything looked new and hastily built, but there was already tumbleweed blown up along the base of the fences.

Jack thought it would be okay. He didn't know what he was talking about.

The convoy drove through one chain-link fence, then maneuvered around a short maze of cement barriers before entering one of the large warehouses.

A few minutes later there was the sound of engines—other vehicles moving away from them—and then a metallic thud as the warehouse doors closed. The interior was lit with dim floodlights.

The bus door opened and a soldier who looked older than the others entered. "Welcome to Temporary Quarantine Camp 14. Please exit the bus in an orderly fashion. This can be as simple or as hard as you'd like."

Jack gave Aubrey a nervous smile and they slowly made their way to the front of the bus. The soldier there unlatched their handcuffs, though he didn't remove their ID bracelets.

Aubrey followed Jack down the stairs and onto the dirt floor of the warehouse.

A banner hung on the far wall reading "Intake Station 2."

There was a catwalk around the perimeter of the warehouse, almost at the ceiling, and at least twenty armed soldiers stood there, cautiously watching the teens as though they were prison inmates.

She walked around the bus to where the others were gathering, and noticed that two more buses were behind them, and dozens of other students were there, people she'd never seen before.

Jack pulled her away from the crowd. There was fear in his eyes. "I shouldn't have told you to stay."

"Where else would I have gone?" she whispered.

"Look at this," Jack said, keeping his voice low. "You'd rather be here?"

She glanced up at the soldiers—one appeared to be aiming a machine gun right at her. "What else was I supposed to do? Hide in the mountains for a few more weeks, starving and freezing? They'd have found me eventually."

"They're going to find out—" Jack paused.

Aubrey took a step closer to him. "What about you? You think I should have just left you alone here?"

He didn't answer, his frustration plain on his face. She knew that her words didn't carry much weight. She'd abandoned him plenty of times in the last six months. And besides—what help could she be?

Jack looked into her eyes, his lips tightly sealed. A loudspeaker squawked as someone prepared to talk.

Jack leaned close to her, his voice barely audible. "If you want to help me, promise that you will stay safe. Don't let them find out what you can do. Promise me."

Aubrey smiled, and touched his arm. "Okay."

"Promise?"

"I promise."

"Good."

Nicole was moving from Matt over to Aubrey, but before she got a chance to say anything, the loudspeaker blared to life. The voice was older and rough.

"This is Intake Station Two at the Dugway Assessment Facility. You have been brought here in accordance with Executive Order 16309 and the Emergency Protection Act. This is for your welfare, and is in the best interests of both public health and national security."

Nicole exchanged a glance with Aubrey. Aubrey would have expected Nicole to be angry, but instead she looked scared.

"At the east end of the building you will see a metal door," the speaker continued. "Please proceed to that door in an orderly fashion for identification and your initial assessment. And please note that your cooperation is appreciated and will be rewarded. Thank you."

Nicole turned to Aubrey. "What are you going to do?"

"What do you mean?"

"Can you escape?"

Aubrey glanced at Jack. His face was tense and anxious. "Not now," she said.

Nicole looked confused. "Why not? They're going to test us. This has to be about whatever you and Nate are."

Aubrey shook her head. She looked at the door; a few students were slowly moving toward it. "Where could I go? The doors are locked."

Nicole scowled, and she turned so her back was to Jack. "You could have warned me last night," she whispered, her voice harsh and low. "After everything I did for you."

"I—I'm sorry. I tried."

"You were too stupid to even save yourself," Nicole snapped. "And too selfish to save anyone else."

"Selfish?" Aubrey said. "I've been your slave for six months."

"How is it slavery," Nicole said, "if you're getting something out of it? This was a partnership."

Jack leaned in close. "Can both of you keep it down?" he said. "Who knows who's listening?"

Nicole's eyes were cold and bitter. Aubrey wanted to say something—wanted to scream at her—but Nicole finally turned and began marching quickly toward the door. Matt, who'd been waiting for her, didn't meet Aubrey's eyes, but followed in Nicole's wake.

Aubrey seethed. Nicole had no right calling anyone selfish.

"Come on," Jack said, taking Aubrey by the elbow. She reluctantly followed.

There were at least thirty teens in front of them in line and another ten or twelve behind.

"Whatever is happening," Jack breathed, "you can't let them know." His hand found her hand, and she took it out of sheer terror.

"I won't," she said. "Quiet."

The line was slow, but steady. Aubrey felt like they were being led to their doom—that something sinister was waiting behind that door. But, when they finally got inside, it was just a generic, boring office. Two soldiers sat behind a desk at the front, and the line wound past them and toward a long table where medics were doing something Aubrey couldn't see. Ten armed men were watching the line.

Aubrey reached the first intake worker.

"Left hand on the desk," the young soldier said, and pointed to a rectangle that had been drawn on the desk with marker. Aubrey let go of Jack and then laid her palm on the table.

"State your name," the soldier said, peering at the bracelet on her wrist.

"Aubrey Parsons," she said.

The soldier turned to the man next to him. "Aubrey Parsons. One-one-seven-W-S-L."

There was a brief pause while the man typed on a laptop.

"Aubrey Parsons, one-one-seven-W-S-L. Confirmed."

The soldier, for the first time, looked her in the eyes. He seemed uncomfortable. "Please proceed to the medics for a cheek swab."

"Why?"

"Testing," he said. "Please move along."

Testing. It could be for anything, she told herself. Any disease. The terrorists could have put anything in the air or the water or the mail or the food. But she'd had half a dozen blood tests in the hospital when she'd gone blind, and no one had found any irregularities.

Still, visions of vicious experiments filled her brain: Aubrey, lying on an operating table, tubes and needles every-where. Or running through some scientist's obstacle course: How long could she stay invisible? How far could she push it?

Aubrey turned and looked at Jack, who had just been con-firmed at the desk. She smiled at him halfheartedly, and then faded out.

He looked confused, but then Aubrey saw him suppress a worried smile. She turned, watching the faces of the guards, but none of them seemed to notice anything out of the ordi-nary. Even if there had only been a few teenagers, the guards would have questioned whether she'd even been there in the first place. In the long line of faces passing in front of them, they didn't seem to notice her disappearance at all.

Being more careful than usual, Aubrey gently slid out of

line, stepping around the other teenagers and heading toward the medics' table. There were probably fifteen students between Jack and the medics.

The procedure seemed simple enough: Aubrey watched a boy arrive, and the medics checked his bracelet. A medic then opened a fresh swab kit—it looked like a thick envelope—and wrote the boy's name and number on it. The medic removed a long cotton-tipped stick from the kit and swabbed the inside of the boy's cheek, rubbing hard for a few seconds, and then placed the swab back into the kit and set it in a box behind the table.

She could switch her swab with someone else's. It wouldn't be hard—just go through the line as normal and then disappear when she was done, transferring her swab into a different kit.

But that was a problem. She didn't want to get tested—but she didn't want to just trade swabs. She didn't want to make someone else end up with her test results. She was tired of making other people pay so she could do whatever she wanted. Sure, she was still being dishonest, but there had to be a way that wouldn't get someone else hurt.

She looked back down the line. Another problem with this plan was that she was just guessing about who to switch with. She needed someone healthy—someone who the medics would never question. It couldn't be Jack; Aubrey didn't know if the tests could tell if someone was a boy or girl, but it was better to be safe than sorry. It couldn't be Nicole, either; she had that kidney problem that kept putting her in the hospital.

Aubrey scanned the waiting people. Four down was a girl who seemed to be perfect. Tall, slender. She was wearing shorts and her legs looked like those of a runner. Aubrey stepped closer to the girl. Her teeth were straight, she wasn't wearing contact lenses, and her skin was smooth. It wasn't much to go on, but it was the best that Aubrey could do.

The girl got to the table.

"Hand on the table," the medic said. "What's your name?"

"Kristy Smith."

Another medic confirmed it in his laptop—checking her bracelet number against the master list—and then the first set to work swabbing her cheek. He rubbed the cotton inside her mouth for a moment, and then set the swab back into the kit. Aubrey moved quickly, snatching it away immediately and tucking it into her jacket pocket. Then, she gently bumped the kit off the edge of the table.

The medic swore and bent over to get the kit. He was down under the table for a few minutes searching, and Aubrey snuck back into line. Jack had left a space between him and the boy in front, and Aubrey was able to slip in and reappear.

"Oh," he whispered, smiling. "Hi."

She turned and motioned for him to be quiet. Ahead of

them, the medic was swabbing Kristy Smith's mouth a second time.

Minutes later Aubrey and Jack reached the medic's table,
and she went through all of the motions as usual, a surge of
adrenaline going through her body as she realized that it all
might work.

The medic finished rubbing her cheek and then placed her
swab in the kit, closed it, and set it in the box behind him.

As soon as she was away from the table she vanished again,
running behind the table and switching out Kristy Smith's
stolen swab with her own. Aubrey was able to make it back
to Jack just as he was leaving the testing room.

"How are you?" he said, reaching forward to touch her
arm.

"Good," she said. "I hope."

User: SusieMusie

Mood: Tired

I feel like I have a train running through my head. I should never drink. But isn't Saturday for drinking? Erica says so but I'm the one stuck in the passenger seat while she goes from party to party, getting plastered. Sara isn't any better. I need new friends.

THIRTEEN

LAURA CLIMBED OUT OF THE torn hole in her tent and peered into the morning light. It was an hour or two past sunrise, but despite all the events of yesterday—and despite having marched five miles into the forest with Ranger Brown over her shoulder—Laura hadn't been able to sleep.

The sky was cloudy. Rain would be coming soon, probably before noon, which would help in their coming hike. Assuming that the country could spare any manpower, low clouds and heavy rain would hamper any kind of helicopter search.

So much for lying low. Now they'd need to get back off this mountain somehow. There were targets to the east— Alec had been excited about the power plants that dotted this part of the state—but escape might be their first priority.

Standing now, Laura stretched and took a deep breath of the crisp mountain air. Dan was the only member of the group who didn't have to wear a thick coat in these Wyoming mountains. Something about his abilities gave him a constant feeling of being overheated. Maybe he should have been wearing a coat anyway—maybe it was all in his head— but you couldn't convince him of that. He said the cold air actually felt good to him. Laura was already shivering as she bent down and got her coat—a puffy purple one she'd stolen from the backseat of a car last week.

Ranger Brown was still where Laura had dropped her, in an uncomfortable slump beside a large granite boulder. She was bound with duct tape at her ankles and knees, and her hands were taped behind her back. As Laura approached, she could see a glimmer of light reflecting off Brown's eyes. She was awake.

"Don't worry," Laura said, watching the woman. "I'm not going to hurt you."

The ranger's gaze was fixed on Laura, but she didn't try to move or struggle. Alec had removed Brown's shoes, throwing them into a nearby creek. He'd said it would be harder for Brown to run that way, though the amount of tape binding her ankles made the bare feet unnecessary. Now, the poor woman just looked cold.

Laura knelt down beside her, the ranger's terrified eyes watching Laura's every movement. With her left hand she reached out and grasped one of Brown's feet. Brown twitched at the touch, pulling back instinctively, but Laura held tight and the resistance faded. Brown's skin was icy and rough. Laura reached one hand into the pocket of her coat and retrieved a pair of her own wool socks, and then proceeded to pull them onto Brown's feet.

The ranger looked confused and opened her mouth to speak, but Laura motioned for Brown to stay quiet.

A voice broke the silence. "They've instituted martial law."

Laura, startled and embarrassed, saw Alec sitting motionless on a rock about twenty feet away. His pale skin and sunken features made him appear ghostly in the dim light.

Laura let go of Brown's foot and stood. "You heard something?" Alec had kept both of the rangers' radios, and had listened for hours while they hiked.

Alec shook his head. "They've ceased all radio traffic."

"They know we're listening?"

"Probably."

"Then what?"

"I got some information from her," Alec said, nodding slightly toward Brown. "The military seems to have figured out two things: they know our network is made up of teenagers."

Laura sat on a log near Alec, leaning forward. "Have they caught anyone?"

He nodded. "She doesn't know anything about it, but they must have. Because the other thing they've figured out is that our abilities are caused by a virus."

"What? But they're not."

"Remember that crap she was spewing last night about the police taking teens?"

Laura nodded.

He took a swig from his canteen and then continued. "They're doing it because teens—American teenagers—are getting abilities. And, since the government can test for it, that means they must have captured someone; they must have some strain of the virus to compare it to."

"But it's not a virus," Laura said again. She didn't catch it. She was injected with it as a baby. Her parents told her.

Alec rolled his eyes. "It must have mutated. How long since your abilities manifested?"

Laura was flustered now. This wasn't how it was supposed to work. She was supposed to be superior to everyone. "Uh, I don't know. Two years?"

"See, you should have had them before that—they were supposed to come around age twelve or thirteen. Mine came late, too."

Laura was trying to think clearly, but this was the first significant problem in their plan she'd encountered. Every chase, every attack—those were things she could handle. But this was different. The entire system was flawed. And everything hinged on this.

Alec was still talking to Laura, but stared at the ranger. "I think it was broken from the beginning. We didn't get our powers when we were supposed to. We got physical side effects, which we weren't supposed to. And now it's spreading like a virus."

"So what do we do?"

"We do a better job of hiding. We go for targets that will slow their study—hospitals, labs, the damned CDC if we can get it."

"Should we speed up our attacks on the scheduled targets?"

"I'll think about it," he said. "I wish I knew how the testing works. How do they know if someone has been tested? Complete quarantine? Some kind of identifying mark? If it's something simple like a tattoo, then we need to get ourselves tattoos. If we can look like we've been tested, then we can walk around without suspicion."

Laura pointed at the ranger. "What do we do with her? She's seen everything. She heard us talking. She saw what I did to the other one."

"It will be useful to have a hostage," Alec answered. "They're probably trying to find us right now."

"We won't be dealing with police," Laura said, almost surprised that she was arguing with Alec. "It will be the US Army, maybe special forces. They won't be negotiating for hostages."

"Then we'll kill her," Alec said.

Laura stood. "We could have just left her there, by the cars. What good did bringing her do? She slowed us down—and I won't be able to carry both her and Dan if we need his powers."

"You're right," Alec said. He slowly stood from his rock, twisting his neck and back to stretch the muscles. "But I want more information from her."

"What more does she know?"

Alec took a step toward Laura. Alec was the highest rank of the three of them and Laura knew she was pushing it.

Alec smiled. "I don't know. Let's ask."

He brushed past Laura and knelt beside Brown.

"Leave me alone," she whispered. "I don't know anything."

Alec, his back to Laura now, didn't respond. He simply sat there and stared at the girl. Laura didn't want to watch, but couldn't look away. She knew what Alec was doing—playing with Brown's mind. After a tense moment, Brown looked puzzled and smiled nervously.

"What's going on, Alec?" she said.

His voice was soft and soothing. "What's your name?"

Brown paused for a moment, her gaze darting up to Laura. "You know my name," Brown said. "Take this tape off."

"Humor me," Alec said. "What's your name?"

"This isn't funny," she said, and her face contorted in another wave of confusion. She shrieked, flailing uselessly against the restraints.

"Here are the rules," Alec said, his voice suddenly filled with hatred. "I'm going to ask you some questions. If I like your answer, you'll be fine. If I don't, you'll get more of the same."

She froze, her eyes wide and terrified. Laura shuddered to think what memories Alec was stuffing into the girl's brain.

"Good," Alec said. "Now, what is your name?"

"Gina," she whispered. "Gina Lynn Brown."

Laura watched for a moment, and then turned back to her tent.

FOURTEEN

"AT LEAST IT'S NOT BREAD and water," Aubrey said, looking down at the pouch in her hands. It was military rations—vacuum-sealed tuna casserole.

Jack smiled. "I don't know if this is much better."

"It's warmed up. That's something."

They were in another warehouse, this one smaller and without guards. The floor was cement, and along three of the walls were long rows of cots. There had to be at least two hundred, but only about half were occupied—maybe fifty by the kids who had gone through the testing with Aubrey, and about that same number who had already been in the warehouse when the others had arrived. The fourth wall was lined with portable restrooms.

The center of the warehouse was a hodgepodge of tables and chairs, not in any order. A few minutes before, six soldiers had entered the warehouse with two metal carts, each stacked with military MREs—Meals, Ready-to-Eat—and dense cookies, like power bars.

A steel catwalk ran along the walls, high up, like in the other warehouse, but no guards were on it. There were only four doors. Two were up at the level of the catwalk, a third was connected to the testing offices, and on the far side of the warehouse was a twenty-foot-tall opening with a retractable metal covering. It was open, but no one was going out there—it seemed to be a long path, like a chain-link tunnel, with walls and roof.

Matt approached Aubrey and Jack's table. "Can I sit here?"

Aubrey nodded. "Sure."

Matt inspected his packet—bold black letters declared it to be spaghetti—and then he tore the top open.

"Have you heard what they said about this place?" he said, looking unenthusiastically inside the pouch.

"What do you mean?" Jack asked.

"All the kids in Utah are here," Matt said. "Everyone."

"That's impossible," Aubrey said. There were way too many teenagers in the state to fit into one . . . what was it? A prison? A camp?

Matt shrugged. "That's what they said. And some kids from Nevada and Idaho, too."

"That's what who said?" Jack asked, after swallowing a bite of food.

"The others," Matt said. "The guys in line." He was

ignoring his food now, staring outside. "There's a kid named Sibley. He's been here for three days."

Jack tore open his cookie. It was thick like a brownie, and a shower of crumbs fell on the table as he cracked it in half. "Three days makes him an expert?"

Matt didn't answer.

Aubrey looked down at her food and poked at it with her plastic fork. She wondered what her dad would eat without her around to cook for him. That world—her life—seemed far away.

"I'm one of them," Matt said, still staring.

Aubrey speared a noodle and pulled it out of the pouch. "One of what?"

"Like Nate," he said. "And Sibley."

Jack's head sprang up. Aubrey felt her heart beat faster but tried not to show it.

Matt's eyes met Aubrey's and then Jack's. "We don't have to pretend like that stuff with Nate didn't happen. We can talk about it. We *should* talk about it."

Aubrey took a deep breath and choked on a noodle. She coughed until the scratch went away. There was a third besides her and Nate? A third and a fourth?

"You know how I'm on the varsity basketball team?" Matt continued. "Even though I've never been any good?"

Aubrey nodded, holding her breath. Basketball season was months away, but the paper had already written about Matt being a potential all-American in both football and basket-ball. And not just the *Sanpete Messenger*, but the state papers. There was even talk about Matt getting featured on ESPN.

"I can't miss a shot," Matt said, finally turning his head to look at them.

Jack snorted, obviously annoyed. Aubrey knew they used to play together. "That's good basketball. It's not . . . what-ever Nate was."

Matt's face reddened. He spoke slower and more clearly. "No. I mean I can't miss a shot. I can't blow a pass, even if the receiver stinks. I sometimes miss on purpose during games so that people don't find out about me."

"Right," Jack said sarcastically. "I miss shots on purpose, too. That's why I didn't make the team."

"I'm serious," Matt said, getting frustrated. He looked around, searching for something, and finally grabbed his heavy cookie. "Point to something."

Jack laughed, and pointed at a garbage can halfway across the warehouse.

Matt rolled his eyes. "Too easy."

"Really?" Jack scoffed. "Then try the can by the wall—the red plastic one."

Matt turned to Aubrey. "I'm serious. I can't miss a shot."

She smiled uncertainly, and then gestured to a far cot. "Do you see the boy with the shaved head? See his baseball cap next to him?"

Matt grinned, and then turned and, without any preparation, threw the cookie. It spun through the air, crossing over a dozen tables, and landed squarely in the sleeping boy's hat.

Matt turned back to Aubrey. "Can I have yours?" Amazed, she handed him her cookie.

Without looking, he threw it behind him, over his shoulder, and then turned to watch as it wobbled through the air. It looked like it was going to fall short and to the left, but to Aubrey's amazement the cookie plunked down into the same baseball cap.

A few people, who hadn't been paying attention fully, clapped when they saw what he'd done.

"I can't miss a shot," Matt said again.

Jack lowered his voice, suddenly serious. "Why are you doing this in here? They'll find you."

Matt picked up his pouch again and looked inside. "They already swabbed my mouth. It's too late."

Aubrey glanced at Jack. Their eyes met for a moment and then she turned to Matt. "How do you know that's what the test was about?"

"The guys who've been here longer," Matt said. "They told me that's what happens." He set his pouch down on the table and stood. "Come on. I'll take you to meet Sibley and the others."

FIFTEEN

LAURA KNELT IN THE DRY mountain grass. She carefully rolled her tent into a neat package, and then slipped it into its green nylon bag.

She hadn't slept much. She was amazed that Dan had been able to sleep through the forest ranger's cries, but he'd always had the worst reactions to using his powers. He'd probably be tired for days.

Gina Brown had known more than she'd let on, just as Alec had expected. Yes, she was just a forest ranger in an obscure part of central Utah, but she'd been monitoring her radio, and even the forest service was being conscripted into service.

"You need to hurry," Alec called out to Dan, who was still moving sluggishly around the campsite. "They could be here any minute."

One of the most important bits of information Brown had was that this roundup of all the teenagers was somewhat localized—a huge number of soldiers had moved into the West earlier in the week. With Brown's disappearance, and the collapsed Eagle Canyon bridge only forty miles away, it was almost certain that troops would be on the mountain soon, if they weren't there already.

Worse, Brown told of an enormous army base that had sprung up in the desert west of Salt Lake City. Laura had assumed the three of them were in the middle of nowhere— a thousand miles from any of the real action—but now it sounded like they were only a few hundred miles from one of the largest military centers in the United States.

She glanced over at Brown, who lay awkwardly on her back, staring at the sky. She was quiet now, her mind having been ravaged. Alec hadn't held back, fully aware of the consequences. So many memories had been inserted during the night, most of them conflicting. Some were horrifically violent and others were reassuring her with warmth and trust. Laura didn't know if Alec had ever done this before, but the results were appalling. Gina's cries—cries of intense pain but also of joyful rescue—had gone on for hours until her mind just couldn't take any more.

"Come on," Alec demanded. He shoved the last of his gear into his bag and threw it to Laura.

She wanted to ask what Alec was going to do with Brown, but knew that asking wouldn't help anything. If the ranger was lucky, he'd shoot her. If she was unlucky, he'd leave her there to die—her mind too scrambled to know how to survive on her own.

Laura looked at the ranger again, and their eyes met. There was no emotion or movement. If Brown hadn't blinked, Laura would have assumed she was dead.

"Dan," Alec called. "Laura. Come check this out." He had unfolded the map.

Laura was strapping on the heavy frame pack, adjusting the straps around her chest and hips as she and Dan met Alec.

"Keep your eyes on the map," Alec said quietly. "Don't look up. They're here."

"Where?" Dan asked. He finally seemed alert.

"I saw movement in the trees to the west, near the two dead pines."

Laura forced herself to keep her head down. "You're sure it's the army?"

Alec nodded. "Uniforms."

"Why haven't they shot us already?" Laura said.

"They're not in position yet," Alec said. "At least, I don't think they are. And maybe they're trying to figure out what we can do—what our powers are. Maybe they want to capture us alive."

"How many?"

"Doesn't matter," Alec said with a smile. He jabbed the map. "We're only four miles from the road if we go cross-country. Laura can do that in—how long?"

She pursed her lips and looked down the rough slope at the forested terrain. "If the ground is like that, thirty minutes. Maybe forty."

"How fast can you do it carrying someone?"

Laura thought about Brown lying on the grass. When she'd heard that the soldiers had arrived, she'd been relieved, thinking that the girl might live. "She doesn't know anything else," Laura said. "She'll slow us down."

Alec almost couldn't contain his glee. "You won't be carrying her, Laura. You'll be carrying me."

"What?"

"It's simple," Alec said, grinning. "You can carry me faster than I could run myself. And we'll be in a big hurry."

"Why?" Dan said, annoyance in his voice. "Where will you be going without me?"

"We'll be running from you," Alec said. "And you'll be chasing after us. I need you to start an avalanche."

Dan looked at the long dry grass under their feet, confused.

"They can't chase us if the mountain is falling down around them."

Dan stammered for a moment. "I'd have to touch it. I couldn't run."

Alec was so pleased with himself he looked like his smile

would rip into his cheeks. "You don't need to run. Just tear this mountain to hell and protect yourself. When the soldiers are taken care of, follow us."

Laura had pulled a bag of toiletries out of the frame pack, and had the contents splayed on a rock as though she was looking for something. Alec paced impatiently, barking the occasional order for her to hurry.

"I'm going to go pee," Dan called.

"Fine," Alec yelled, mock exasperation in his voice. "Take your time. We'll be waiting here another hour for Laura."

This still didn't feel safe, Laura thought. At any moment, one of them was going to get a sniper's bullet in the back of the head.

She looked over her shoulder. She couldn't see Brown. If the military didn't immediately move in for her, she'd die in the avalanche.

"I've counted four," Alec said quietly as he walked past Laura.

"Five," she said. She couldn't be sure they were all different people, though. "Light infantry. M4 carbines."

Alec stepped next to her, digging in the frame pack. She peered inside and saw his hand wrapped around the pistol.

"When it happens," he said, "we'll both run—give them two targets instead of one. When I tire out, you carry me."

Laura nodded. She took a pair of gloves from the

pack—Alec wouldn't stop her now—and walked to the bush where Brown lay. She knelt down at the ranger's side.

"I'm sorry, Gina," Laura said. "This will be better than being crushed."

With a single quick snap, Laura broke Gina Brown's neck.

She had just stood when a plume of dust exploded in front of her. Alec was already running, and gunfire erupted. Laura jumped forward, doing a tuck-and-roll down the rocky hill, and then darted for the trees.

Laura could hear bullets hitting the ground around her, but only for an instant before the sound was drowned out by the deep, shuddering groans of erupting earth.

A boulder, twice as big as her head, flew over her shoulder, and Laura sped up, hurtling wildly through the path of an earthquake.

SIXTEEN

"THEY'RE CALLING IT THE FREAK WAR," Sibley said. Aubrey, Jack, and a few others were sitting on nearby cots, listening as he spoke. "This thing that we've got, this disease, it didn't start in America. They think it started in Russia, maybe, or China. No one's sure. Before we even knew that we were getting sick, they had already diagnosed it and were training the freaks to fight."

"They?" Jack said.

"Whoever it is," Sibley answered. "Nobody knows." He seemed to enjoy being the center of attention, the only one who knew what was going on. And he probably didn't know very much—just more than the other teens in the warehouse. Or he could have been making it all up.

"So there's a whole army of . . . ?" Aubrey started but

didn't know what word described people like her and Matt and Nate.

Sibley shook his head. "No, not an army. There's not enough of us for that. They're terrorists."

Aubrey leaned forward. "What do you mean 'not enough of *us*'?"

He smirked. "I'm not dangerous, so don't worry. Sitting right here, I can do exactly nothing."

"What can you do somewhere else?" Aubrey asked, her eyes wide in the dim light of the warehouse.

"I can kill plants," he said, looking almost embarrassed. "It's not even a dramatic death. I touch them, and they'll die over the next couple days. If it's something big, like a tree, it'll die in a couple weeks."

"Wait," Jack said, looking at Aubrey, concern spreading across his face. "This is a disease?"

Sibley laughed. "Well, it sure as hell isn't the X-Men. I don't know how it works, but everyone who has some kind of power—even stupid ones like mine—have a lot of side effects. Ever since I started, I've been getting ulcers. And if I get cut, I'll bleed for weeks."

Aubrey's eyes met Jack's, and she nodded. The fatigue of disappearing was one thing, but the blindness—it scared her to death.

"So, if it's a disease," Aubrey said, "then why is every-one different? If we all got a cold then we'd have the same symptoms. Why can you kill plants and someone else can turn into a monster?"

"I'm not a doctor," Sibley said. "I don't know. But what about something like schizophrenia? Two people may be schizophrenic, but they don't have the same hallucinations. They don't act the same. They just act different from normal people."

"So what are we doing here?" Jack asked.

Sibley shrugged. "Your guess is as good as mine." He gestured around the room. "Aaron over there is sure that we're being protected from the war, because he's an idiot who believes everything he's told. That girl there with the red hair thinks that the government is going to run tests on us like lab rats. Those two guys with the blond hair think that the Freaks are going to be trained as supersoldiers, but I think they watch too many movies. Maybe we're going to be locked up—prisoners. Or, maybe they'll just lobotomize us all."

Jack took Aubrey's hand in his. His palm felt rough and dry, but she squeezed it tight and flashed him a weak smile. Somehow, holding his hand made it easier to breathe.

"Are there more?" Jack said. "More like you?"

"You mean here?" Sibley asked. "The test results come in every day. I don't know why mine haven't shown up yet. They don't seem to come in order." He stood up and walked to the enormous open door. Jack and Aubrey followed him, along with a few others. The chain-link walkway stretched fifty yards to a gate. Four guard towers, two on each side of the path, watched the open space.

"You see that?" Sibley said, pointing. "Your name gets called on a speaker, and you walk down to that door. It unlocks, you go through, and it locks behind you. Then they give you the news, Positive or Negative for the virus."

"How many Positives?" Aubrey asked, staring at the door.

"Enough," he said, and for the first time his voice broke. He *was* scared. "I don't know. Maybe one out of twenty? Maybe less. I've been here three days, and I've seen eight or ten. Most of them freak out—they don't think they're sick, or they try to use their abilities to get out."

"Where do they go?" Jack asked. "The Positives?"

"Over to the right," Sibley said, gesturing to a squat cement structure. He coughed, regaining his composure. "They try to fight, but it's no use."

"Why?"

"Ever seen those sound guns the army has? They call it 'nonlethal force'—a huge directed blast of sound that knocks you down."

Jack nodded and squeezed Aubrey's hand. "Well, we won't have to worry about that."

For now, they were safe. Aubrey had dodged the blood test, but she could still be found out. She scanned the room, a thought nagging her. Nicole was at a table near the center of the room, now surrounded by six of the best-looking guys there. She was laughing.

Nicole knew Aubrey's secret. What would she say if Aubrey was declared Negative? Would Nicole turn her in?

Suddenly Aubrey noticed that the catwalk had guards on it—fifteen already, but more were entering through the small doors high up, close to the ceiling. She pointed it out to Jack.

"More kids are coming," Sibley said with a sigh. "You'd better find a cot while you can. Last night people were sleeping on the floor."

SEVENTEEN

IT WAS A DISASTER. Whatever hopes Laura had of finding Alec were dashed within seconds of the avalanche. The air was suddenly so thick with dust that she could barely see two feet in front of her, and she was buffeted by rocks the whole way down.

She had to just ride it out, skittering and jumping in the loosening debris field as the whole face of the mountain collapsed. It was destruction like she'd never seen—it was Dan finally letting loose. Pure, unchecked devastation.

Laura could run ahead of it, her unnaturally strong legs able to balance on the tumbling mass of dirt, boulders, and trees. And when she got to the bottom, she dashed up the mountain on the other side. The avalanche crashed just below her, waves pounding into a rocky cliff. As she ran, splintered wood and shattered rock flew all around her.

She didn't stop until she reached the next crest, and the rumbling, grinding earthquake behind her had come to a halt.

The view was choked with dust, and she couldn't make out more than the dark scar that once had been covered with trees and vegetation. She didn't know how to judge the size of the crater—five football fields? Ten? Fifty? It had to be more than that. It was one whole side of the mountain torn loose.

The plan had been to carry Alec when he couldn't outrun it any longer, but they'd been separated almost immediately. And if Laura could barely stay ahead of the avalanche, did Alec have any chance?

Laura waited. She waited for the dust to clear, for someone to move, for a voice—anything.

But there was nothing. The mountain seemed dead.

The army had to have backup somewhere. The few soldiers they'd seen in the woods couldn't have been everyone. And just because she couldn't see through the dust didn't mean they couldn't. They might be in helicopters, with thermal imaging. They might have snipers posted on this very mountain.

She scanned the scar one more time, looking for something, anything.

She checked her jeans pocket for her smartphone. She'd never needed it with Alec around, but he was gone now.

Laura was on her own.

EIGHTEEN

AUBREY WOKE WITH A START, frightened from her already uneasy sleep by the sound of a loudspeaker. The morning sky outside was dark blue, the sun not yet over the horizon.

This was the third time she'd heard the loudspeaker. It came on twice during the night, once taking three girls to be judged and later taking two boys. All five were declared Negative and were released, gleeful, from the chain-link cage and put in a waiting jeep.

The voice on the loudspeaker was metallic and cold. Aubrey would have thought it was a computer, except she could hear the voice take a breath just before it read the names.

"John Sibley, please proceed to the exit gate."

Nearly everyone in the warehouse rose to their feet as

Sibley stood from his cot, but no one said a word. He nervously attempted to straighten his rumpled shirt, and then crossed to the large overhead door that led toward judgment. He'd be a Positive—a Lambda?—that was certain. Unlike some of the other judgments, there wasn't a question this time—no one doubted where Sibley would end up.

He was trying to put on a brave face, trying to keep up his air of confidence, but fear was peeking through. It was like watching a prisoner walk to the death chamber. No one knew what would happen to the Positives, but images of giant needles and dissection and experimentation loomed in everyone's mind.

Aubrey felt nauseated as she watched the boy step out into the cool morning air of the chain-link tunnel. What made her any different from him? She was infected just like he was. Neither one of them deserved whatever fate awaited the Positives, but was it fair that she'd be safe?

"Go get 'em, Sibley!" a boy in the warehouse yelled, though if Sibley heard it he didn't respond.

As he got farther down the guarded walkway, a mass of kids gathered at the door. A few even stepped outside, but kept an eye on the watchtowers—no one was sure how far they were allowed to go. Each tower housed at least three armed guards, and each was mounted with a strange, round black disk.

Even back where they were, Aubrey heard the electric

buzz as the gate unlocked. Sibley hesitated only a moment before opening it, and then stepped through. The gate led to a small room made of more chain-link, with doors to the left and to the right. On the left, standing back from the little room, were another three armed soldiers in combat fatigues, and an armored truck.

On the right was a chain-link tunnel leading to another building—a squat, cement structure with no windows.

"John Sibley," the voice announced. "Positive."

A boy in the crowd swore.

There was another buzz and the door on the right swung open. Sibley turned back to look at the kids in the warehouse, and offered a small wave.

One of the soldiers on the left leveled his rifle at Sibley, and the metallic voice said, "John Sibley, please continue to your right."

Sibley paused, glancing at the soldiers, and then up at the nearest watchtowers.

"John Sibley, please continue to your right," the voice repeated. Sibley flipped the bird at the towers, then turned and walked quietly down the tunnel and out of sight.

Aubrey felt Jack's shoulder touch hers. "He'll be all right," Jack said quietly.

"You don't know that."

"This is America," he answered. "They can't do anything too terrible."

Aubrey didn't answer. If someone had told her last week that American soldiers were going to round up—or shoot—innocent teenagers just because they had an infection, she wouldn't have believed that either.

But was Nate innocent? Did he really attack the soldiers, or was he just trying to defend himself? It all seemed like such a blur now.

"Kara Meyers," the voice called.

A blonde girl about Aubrey's age let out a quiet gasp, and another girl assured her everything would be fine.

"Kara Meyers," the voice repeated. "Please proceed to the exit gate."

Aubrey watched as the girl hugged her friend, tears streaming down her face. Aubrey moved to take Jack's hand, but stopped herself.

"Kara Meyers—"

"I'm coming," she shouted angrily, and quickly stepped out of the group into the empty walkway.

"We'll be fine," Jack whispered to Aubrey. "They never swabbed your cheek."

"What if they saw something?" she asked.

Kara was walking slowly past the watchtowers. Aubrey glanced at Nicole, who was hanging back from the crowd, standing alone. Their eyes met for a moment, and Aubrey could see terror in Nicole's face.

The sound of the clanking gate drew Aubrey's gaze back

to Kara, who now stood, small and fragile, in the chain-link room.

"Kara Meyers," the voice announced. "Negative."

There was a sigh of relief in the warehouse. Kara's friend let out a cheer of support, and a small applause erupted as the door on the left swung open and Kara stepped out to the waiting soldiers. They smiled at her, and one put his hand on her shoulder as he led her to the waiting armored vehicle.

The speaker squawked again. "Aubrey Parsons."

Panic swept through her body, and she turned to Jack, throwing her arms around him.

"It's okay," he said, his voice weak. "You'll be okay." He hugged her tightly, one arm around her waist and the other cradling her neck. "Whatever happens, you'll be okay. I'll make sure."

"How?" she whispered, tears flowing freely down her face.

"I don't know. But I'll get you out."

"Aubrey Parsons. Please proceed to the exit gate."

She pulled back from him, her hands still gripping his shoulders. "Promise me. If I go Positive that you won't try anything stupid. Don't get killed."

"I'll get you out," he said, his eyes hard and dark.

"Promise me," she demanded. "Now."

"I won't do anything stupid."

He pulled her closer. She couldn't be a Positive.

"Aubrey Parsons, proceed now to the exit gate or you will be extracted."

Jack ended the embrace and took a step back.

"Go," he said urgently, taking her elbow and pointing her to the walkway. "I'll meet you down there."

"Okay," she whispered.

She squeezed his hand briefly and then stepped out onto the dirt path.

The gate that had seemed so far away suddenly felt too close, and the high chain-link walls made her claustrophobic, even though she could see through them.

The soldiers at the side were watching her approach. They looked nervous, as though she might attack at any moment. Had that happened before? Like Nate?

She wondered what she'd do, if she could actually do something powerful. If she had powers like Sibley had talked about, if she could fight. Would she break out? Would she attack the soldiers to rescue Jack?

Would Jack attack the soldiers to rescue her?

He'd never forgotten her, even when she'd betrayed him and left him alone. It seemed so obvious to her now, and she wondered what had made her forget about him all of this time. She wanted to make it right. If that was even possible.

And then she was at the gate, too soon.

There was a loud buzz, and the gate unlatched. She grabbed the heavy metal handle and pulled it open, and went inside. Up close, she could see that the room wasn't chain-link like everything else was—the walls and roof were made up of tightly spaced steel rods. It wasn't a room; it was a reinforced cage.

She turned to look back at the warehouse, but had a hard time picking Jack out of the crowd. Her eyes just weren't good enough anymore. She wished she could see his face.

The door fell closed and locked.

Aubrey held her breath. When they declared her a Positive, she would also be a criminal. They'd know she tried to hide it and falsified records. Would they care? Would she go to jail? Would it be a war crime?

"Aubrey Parsons," the voice said. "Negative."

An uncontrollable smile broke across her face, and she waved back at the group as they cheered.

The door on the left clicked open. She rushed out to the soldiers, feeling elated and free. The towers weren't watching her now, and the fences weren't trying to hold her in.

A soldier approached her, smiling. "Sorry to make you go through that. Hop in the vehicle and we'll get you out of here."

Grinning, Aubrey jogged to the large armored truck and climbed into the backseat next to Kara. She'd done it.

"Jack Cooper."

She left the door open to watch Jack as he came down the path. He walked faster than the others had, almost running by the time he got to the gate. Aubrey shouted to him and cheered as the door opened and he stepped into the cage. They'd be back home soon, and things would be different.

"Jack Cooper," the voice said. "Positive."

"What?" The smile faded from her face.

Jack stood in the center of the cage, not moving. Kara took Aubrey's hand, but Aubrey shook her away.

"No," Jack shouted. "I'm not sick. I'm not Positive."

"Jack Cooper," the voice said calmly, "please proceed to your right."

Aubrey leapt from the truck, running to the cage. She could hear a flurry of voices behind her, and the tinny squawk of the loudspeaker, but she ignored it. Jack met her at the wall of steel, yanking and tugging on the gate.

"Jack," she shrieked, reaching through the bars to touch him. She could only get her hand in up to her wrist.

The loudspeaker blared. "Step back!"

Jack grabbed her hand, a look of panic in his eyes.

"I'll disappear right now, right here," she whispered fiercely. "They'll have to take me with you."

"Don't you dare." He let go of her hand and tried to push her away. "You're free. I'll get out."

"But I can do it right now, and then I can go with you," Aubrey insisted, forcing her hands between the bars and grabbing his shirt.

"No! If you're free you can get me out. Who knows what

will happen if we're both Positives?" He took her hand in his own.

"I want to come with you!"

"No. You get me out."

"I will," she promised,

"Step back!" the voice repeated. "We will use force."

"Go," he said, pushing her hand through the fence. "Don't get killed like this."

Pain burst through Aubrey's head and rippled down her body. It was as though she were being beaten with a baseball bat, but couldn't tell where she was getting hit. She saw Jack stumble and collapse. Her legs felt like overcooked noodles, and she could barely muster the strength to bring her weak arms to her ears. Noise was coming from somewhere—piercing, thundering noise that seemed to sap all of her energy and cripple her brain.

And then, as suddenly as the noise came, it disappeared, leaving her crumpled in a heap, unable to move.

She felt a hand on her shoulder, and saw that she was being dragged away from the cage.

The world was silent. Whatever had happened had completely deafened her.

"Jack," she shouted, though she couldn't hear her own voice. "I'll get you out."

NINETEEN

ALEC SAT UP GINGERLY AND swung his legs over the side of the bed. He took a breath and wheezed at the pain. He tried to focus his bleary eyes. A bare, hardwood floor. A worn La-Z-Boy draped with an afghan. A stack of quilts. A plate of food—a sandwich and potato chips—that he hadn't touched.

"I'm sorry ma'am," a young man's voice said in the other room. "Nobody hates this more than me. They took my own nephew, little Levi. Yeah, you know him."

Alec couldn't hear the old woman's voice, but he could hear the old man snoring loudly in a neighboring room.

"Listen," the young man said. "I know you're just trying to do right by this boy. We heard about Parley's car accident, and we know you're just trying to protect him."

Alec stood and crept toward the door on bruised legs.

The woman's voice shook with Parkinson's. "I've seen the news. If we took the boy to the hospital then you would have taken him away."

She'd been easy to play. Her mind was so decrepit as it was that he hardly had to try to implant new memories—memories of her husband driving the old 1970s Chevy Impala into town and hitting Alec as he was crossing the street. Memories of Alec being a boy she knew—a grandson of a neighbor. That was all it took. People in this little town—even ancient people like Mr. and Mrs. Lyon—had no love for the government, and the thought that the army was stealing kids was abhorrent. And so the old couple had taken him in, treated his injuries as best they could, and let him sleep.

After a twenty-five-mile hike out of the mountains, with at least one arm broken from the avalanche and a hundred black bruises, all Alec wanted to do was sleep. He didn't know how long he had been out, or how his arm had ended up in a bandage.

That was probably what did him in, though. Mrs. Lyon would have been too trusting, too concerned. She would have sought help and that's how the police found out.

Alec looked at the window, with its heavy wooden frame and its thick leaded glass. There was no way he could open it with one hand.

Dan had been too reckless. Laura had abandoned him. Alec had saved their asses a hundred times and they just let him get caught in the avalanche. Left him to die, buried up to his waist, one arm broken and the other smashed.

"Please tell me where the boy is," the young man said.

Think of a story. Think of a story.

But his mind was too blurred. There wouldn't be any getting out of this. Alec cursed himself. He'd snuck into the bathroom less than an hour before and found an old bottle of narcotic painkillers. Two Lortab to take away the excruciating pain.

And now his mind was so muddled, so numb, that he couldn't concentrate. He couldn't implant a memory. He wondered if he could even speak coherently.

He sat back on the bed.

"Mrs. Lyon," the man said, his voice more firm. "Please tell me where the boy is. I have half the guys from Castle Dale surrounding the house. We have orders from the army."

Alec couldn't fight; he couldn't use his mental abilities. He could barely stand.

Laura and Dan were as good as dead. Traitors. If Alec ever made it out of this house alive, Laura and Dan would pay.

"He's badly injured," Mrs. Lyon said, her voice quivering. "My Parley—he just can't see as well as he used to, and he didn't mean to hit the boy."

"Is he back here?"

There were heavy footsteps on the wooden floor, and the door was pushed open fast and deliberately.

Whether there was a gun pointed at him, Alec had no idea—all he could see was the blinding bulb of a flashlight as it passed back and forth across the room.

Alec couldn't even raise an arm to block the beam.

"What's your name, son?"

"Alec Moore."

"I heard you had a nasty accident."

Alec just nodded his head.

"What were you doing out on the road?"

"Hitchhiking," Alec said, repeating the same story he'd told Mrs. Lyon. "Trying to get up north."

"Well," the man said, turning off his flashlight and revealing himself to be a stocky man with a goatee and a deputy uniform. "We've got orders to take you up to Price—there's a quarantine on. But I think we'll make a pit stop at the clinic and see if we can't get you patched up."

Alec nodded again. He knew there were things he needed to do—stories he needed to create and memories to manipulate to get himself through the quarantine. But it would have to wait until the drugs had worn off.

"Can you walk?" the deputy asked.

"A little."

"I'll bring in some of my guys. Don't worry. We'll get you taken care of."

TWENTY

AUBREY'S EYES BURNED, AND SHE didn't bother to wipe away the tears that were dripping down her flushed cheeks as the armored transport sped away from Jack and the other Positives. Something had failed, something had gone wrong. She'd changed her own test results—had someone changed Jack's?

None of the other teens in the transport said anything. Kara, the girl who had been picked just before Aubrey, sat directly across from her, their knees almost touching. Kara's hands were clasped in her lap, and she looked relieved and happy. Aubrey wished that she could feel the same way. It's how she should have felt, how she'd expected to feel if she was declared Negative.

There were seven other teens, and they all shared Kara's look of joy.

But maybe they were too relieved. What if everything was backward? Maybe the army told the Positives that they were actually Negative, so that they wouldn't try to fight and escape? Right now Jack could be on his way back home, and Aubrey and Kara were headed to prison—or worse.

"Are you okay?" someone asked.

Aubrey looked to her left. A boy—probably three or four years younger than Aubrey—was watching her.

She shook her head.

"We're safe," he said. His face, still round and babyish, was shining with optimism. "My sister told me back there: if we're Negatives, we get to go home."

Kara jumped in, giving Aubrey a reassuring look. "Soon, I'm sure. Maybe not today."

"My sister told me that they couldn't keep us here long," the boy continued. "She said it's illegal."

Another girl, who Aubrey recognized from the warehouse, laughed. "It was illegal to kidnap us in the first place. Why would they start following the laws now?"

The truck came to a stop, and there was a long, uncomfortable pause before the back hatch opened and sunlight poured into the vehicle, followed by a gust of wind and sand.

A soldier stood in the hatchway, his hands on his hips. Aubrey knew almost nothing about the military, but could tell that this man wasn't a normal infantryman. He didn't wear a helmet—he had a camouflage cap—and his jacket had quite a few more patches and markings than most of the soldiers' she'd seen.

He took a step closer to the vehicle and rested his hand on the door. He spoke, but his words sounded memorized, and he looked bored—almost annoyed. "All of your test results have come back negative, and the United States Army, on behalf of your country, extends its gratitude that you've been willing to submit to these procedures. I'm sure you have questions, and I can promise you that they will all be answered. But first, we need to get you through decontamination."

The young boy spoke up, looking concerned. "What's that?"

"You've all been in close proximity to people who have a serious illness. You need to be disinfected before you go any farther."

The boy said something else, but the man talked over him. "Now, if you'll all exit the vehicle, we'll get this taken care of quickly and easily."

The nine teens carefully filed out of the armored transport, ducking their heads as the ceiling was too low for all but the boy to stand. Aubrey was the second-to-last out, followed by Kara.

They were standing in front of another long chain-link fence topped with razor wire. On the other side, stretching out for what seemed like miles, was an endless row of enormous canvas tents, desert camouflage and buffeted by the wind.

Just like at the warehouse, the fence was guarded with watchtowers.

Aubrey touched Kara's arm and whispered, "It doesn't seem like they're sending us home."

Kara frowned, and brushed her long blonde hair from her face. She looked sick. "I'm sure it's just temporary."

The soldier led the small group across the dusty road to a wide canvas tent that appeared to be the only entrance through the fence.

"This shouldn't take long," he shouted, to be heard over the wind, "provided you listen to instructions and do as you're told."

He stepped up onto a low wooden platform, and opened the door to the tent. "Males on the left, females on the right."

The first in line—an overweight boy—nervously peeked his head in the door.

"Come on," the officer snapped. "Hurry up."

Aubrey grabbed Kara's elbow again. "Hey."

"It'll be okay," Kara said, though her face was pale.

"You're not actually a Positive, are you?" Aubrey asked, trying to keep her voice low.

Kara looked surprised. "No! Are you kidding?"

Aubrey forced a smile. "I just wonder if they made a mistake. Maybe they think we're Positives."

Kara glanced up at the door ahead of them, and the officer standing grimly beside it. "I'm not a Positive."

They reached the door and entered a small, cramped room. The boys—there were six of them—were in a line heading left, and the three girls were waiting for a door on the right.

"Where are you from?" Kara asked. Aubrey guessed she was trying to make conversation to keep her mind off the situation.

"Mount Pleasant."

"I love that area," Kara said, putting on a big nervous grin. "I have an aunt in Manti."

"Did you know anyone else back there?" Aubrey asked, keeping her voice low. "Back at the warehouse?"

Kara looked embarrassed, and shook her head. "No. I'm from Park City. I don't know where they took my friends, but—" If the door hadn't opened, Aubrey guessed that Kara would have started to cry.

"Come in," a woman said, holding the door for them. "Quickly, please."

Aubrey glanced back at the boys, still waiting in their line and anxiously watching to see what happened to the girls. Her eyes met the young boy's, and she smiled.

"Hurry," the woman said.

Aubrey turned and entered the room.

The soldier couldn't have been very old, but her face was

grim and uncompassionate. She asked for the girls' names and personal information, and checked them against a paper on her clipboard, and again against the girls' bracelets. Kara was eighteen, which surprised Aubrey—Kara looked younger than that. The other girl—a fifteen-year-old from Roosevelt—was named Betsy Blackhair.

The soldier hung the clipboard on a hook. She then opened a cabinet and pulled from it three garbage bags, and three tiny bars of soap, each about an inch square.

"Strip down," she said, handing the girls the bags and soap. "Put everything you have in the bags, leave them with me, and then go in the next room for a shower."

"What will happen to our clothes?" Betsy asked.

"They will be disinfected," the soldier answered. "You can keep any metal jewelry, but you'll have to scrub it in the shower. There's a clock in there—you'll need to wash for fourteen minutes, and that means really washing, not just standing there. If you don't scrub yourselves, Corporal Smith will do it, and she uses a stiff brush." The soldier smiled at that, but the girls didn't laugh.

Aubrey removed her clothes and shoes and stuffed them haphazardly into the bag, not bothering to fold them the way Kara was doing. The situation was uncomfortable enough, and she wanted to go straight into the shower rather than stand and wait naked.

The soldier made Kara cut off a cloth bracelet that was

tied around her ankle. Not waiting, Aubrey cracked the door to the next room, peeking inside to make sure it was safe to go in.

The room had a single pipe in the center, with four shower heads branching off of it. A wide plastic sign hung on one side of the room, giving directions for how they should shower, with simple illustrations beside each instruction. Corporal Smith, a matronly woman wearing a green rain poncho over her combat fatigues, motioned her in.

The water was lukewarm, and the soap was gritty and harsh. Aubrey followed the sign step-by-step, watching the clock as the directions told her to scrub her hair for two minutes, then her face and neck for one minute, and so on. By the time she was finished she felt like her body had been rubbed with a cheese grater, and she smelled of ammonia.

Done before the other girls, she took a towel from Corporal Smith and then moved to the next room. The towel was small, not covering much as she tried to wrap it around herself, and it was as rough as sandpaper on her already stinging skin. Another female soldier—this one younger than the others, and with a kinder face—asked Aubrey's size and then handed her a bundle of clothes.

Aubrey looked at the pile, pleasantly surprised. The clothes appeared to be new—a button-up blouse, a pair of jeans, sandals, some plain underwear, and a bra. "I was expecting coveralls or something like that."

The soldier smiled. "You're lucky. You wouldn't have liked the jumpsuits—a whole lot of olive green. But the shipments never came in, so the CO sent a couple trucks into Salt Lake and cleaned out all the department stores."

Aubrey turned her back to the soldier and quickly tried to dry off with the nonabsorbent towel.

"Most of our supplies are like that," the soldier said. She sounded tired, like she was making small talk to stay awake. "None of the shipments are coming through anymore. Just more and more of you guys."

"You're expecting a lot of people here?" Aubrey asked.

"We already have a lot. You're the stragglers."

"Really?"

"Sure. You came from . . . Intake Two, I think." She checked a clipboard. "Yes. Two. And there are thirty-two intake stations."

Aubrey turned to look over her shoulder. "That many?"

"Yes." The woman nodded, and Aubrey turned back to dressing.

"So how many of us are here?"

"I don't know. But there's been a steady stream for five days. Hundreds of girls have been through this room. Maybe thousands."

Aubrey slipped on her shirt and began buttoning it. "When do we get to leave?"

"I'm not at liberty to say. Even if I knew."

λ

Aubrey sat on a narrow wooden bench with the eight other teens who had just finished decontamination. The wind was still blowing and Aubrey knew that the dust from the dirt road had to be gluing itself to her long wet hair.

No one was talking. The astringent soap and indignity of the showers seemed to have sapped the elation that they'd felt earlier at being declared Negative. Now they simply sat, staring at the endless rows of tents, wondering how they'd ever get back home.

A soldier stood nearby, watching the road for the bus that he promised would come.

"Who was he?" Kara asked quietly. "The boy back there?"

"A friend," Aubrey said, not even knowing what to call him. "An old friend." She cared for him. It seemed that right now she missed him more than anyone else—more than her so-called best friend. More than her dad. Jack had rescued her. He'd fought for her and lied for her, tried his best to hide her. And now he was facing the punishment that should have been hers.

No, she thought. Even if she hadn't changed her own test result, that wouldn't have helped him. She was on the outside now, and she could get him out. Somehow.

"What was his name?"

"Jack Cooper," Aubrey said. "He'll be okay."

"Of course," Kara said.

A plume of dust appeared in the distance, and the soldier told them to stand for the bus.

"How about you?" Aubrey asked, watching the bus approach. It was a regular city bus, the side marked with the words "Utah Transit Authority." "You're from Park City?"

"Yeah," Kara said. Her voice was quiet, almost embarrassed. "My mom's a secretary in the sheriff's office. She heard what was happening and tried to hide me. We got caught in a roadblock on the Wyoming border."

Aubrey smiled. "We tried to run too. Didn't get very far."

"I think most of us are like that," Betsy said. "Fugitives, I mean. I went to my grandma's house out on the reservation. I didn't think anyone would look there. They came in the middle of the night."

Aubrey thought back to what the woman had told her after her shower. They were the stragglers. Maybe the rest of her school was already here, in one of the hundreds of olive-drab military tents.

The bus door opened and the soldier gestured for the group to climb aboard. Aubrey was the last on, and even though there were plenty of empty seats, she sat next to Kara.

The bus drove east, passing tent after tent. All of them looked the same, with nothing to distinguish them other than a large number stenciled on the canvas. After about half a mile, the bus turned north, tents now on both sides in a seemingly endless array.

"My cousins are here somewhere," Kara said. "My mom tried to get her sister to come with us, to run, but she wouldn't. I guess it doesn't matter now."

"Who was with you at the warehouse?" Aubrey asked. "You hugged someone."

Kara shook her head. "I don't know her, really. We both got caught at the same roadblock."

The road was bumpy and the bus was moving more slowly. They weren't passing the front of the tents now, just the wide windowless sides, and it was harder to pick out the faces of teens.

Other vehicles were moving among the tents, too. Trucks parked in front of several, some appearing to carry supplies and others picking up garbage.

"Can I ask you a question?" Kara said, still looking out the window.

"Sure."

"Did you know that Jack was . . . one of . . . ?"

Aubrey shook her head. "No. And he isn't. He can't be."

Kara nodded and thought for a moment. "I've heard that some people aren't even aware they have it."

"This isn't like that," Aubrey said. "He's not sick. There must have been a mistake."

"I mean," Kara said, talking slowly, "if he's sick, then maybe he gave it to you?"

"He's not sick," Aubrey insisted.

"Okay."

The bus turned one more time and then stopped in front of Tent 209. A Humvee was waiting for them, and six soldiers stood in front of the door. Slowly, Aubrey and the others filed off the bus, and one of the soldiers directed them into the large tent.

Aubrey paused just inside the door as her eyes adjusted to the darkness.

The layout wasn't unlike the warehouse they'd left earlier—bunk beds lined the walls, and two tables were in the center. In one corner was a row of shelves, stocked floor to ceiling with boxes. The floor was wood, and sand showed beneath the slats.

"Everyone please gather in the center of the room," one of the soldiers said. "Feel free to take a seat."

"I don't know if this is better or worse," Kara said.

Aubrey smiled and chose a seat. Kara and Betsy sat with her.

"When are we going home?" the young boy asked, but the soldier merely pointed him toward a chair.

A man walked in front of them. He was the first soldier Aubrey had seen who was not wearing fatigues. Instead, he wore a more formal uniform, with a green jacket and tie. Medals and insignias were pinned to his chest.

"My name is Major Bowman," he said, his voice soft but emotionless. "You are in Relocation Center Five, Tent 209.

I know that this must seem very foreign, perhaps even a little scary, but I assure you, everything that has been done is for your safety."

One of the boys, who had been wearing all black before decontamination and sported the beginnings of a thin beard, swore and laughed. "This is not for our safety."

Bowman scowled at him and continued talking. "You may have had friends who were detained for further questioning. Trust me—they will be fine. They have showed the early warning signs of a debilitating disease, and it is in the interest of national health to quarantine them temporarily."

The boy swore again.

Bowman took a step forward. "What is your name, son?"

"Simon Fisher," the boy said. "So what?"

"Simon Fisher," Bowman repeated, staring down at the boy. "You're a tough guy, huh? Weren't you found in the freezer of a burger shop? Hiding all alone behind a bag of frozen fries?"

"We shouldn't have to hide from the government," Simon answered. His voice was firm, but he looked unsure of himself.

"Let me tell you something," Bowman said, stepping forward and leaning down until his face was right in front of Simon's. Bowman's voice remained as calm as before, but it was hard and cold. "You fled the police and military, and you were lucky that you didn't get shot when we found you. You wouldn't have been the first. My division has lost more than two hundred men in the past five days, just trying to keep little brats like you alive."

Bowman took a step back and again addressed the group. "We have limited manpower here. You'll notice very few guards. But we're not going to have any trouble, are we?"

No one in the group spoke. Aubrey felt sick.

"Let me be clear," Bowman said. "We have a method for dealing with those who are causing trouble. Tent 209 can be retested for the disease. And, in my experience, there's a strange correlation between those who cause trouble and those who get sent to quarantine."

Simon opened his mouth to speak, but didn't say anything.

"I've also found," Bowman said, sitting on the edge of a table, "that if one person in a tent goes to quarantine, then others in the tent get sent to quarantine as well. So you'll be well served by keeping an eye on your friends."

Aubrey glanced at Kara and their gaze met for a moment. Kara looked terrified, and Aubrey felt the same. If this was what it was like for the Negatives, how were things for the Positives? For Jack?

Bowman stared at them for a moment, and then stood and turned. He pointed at the shelves in the corner, and a soldier standing next to them. "This is your primary point of contact for all needs. This man will provide you with all necessaries: food, clothes, blankets. If you have a problem, talk to him. He's assigned to Tents 201 to 220." He looked back at the group, his eyes meeting Aubrey's. "Other than that, your orders are to wait. Do not think that you have been forgotten and that you need to register a complaint. You will be returned to your homes as soon as the crisis has passed."

The young boy raised his hand. Aubrey cringed, hoping he wouldn't make Bowman angry.

"Excuse me," the boy said. "What is the crisis? No one really knows."

Bowman glared at the boy for a moment and then put his hands behind his back. "From our best estimates, 180,000 Americans have been killed in the last three weeks. The origin of the terrorists, if it is known at all, has not been divulged to me. But we do know that the attackers have the illness for which you were all screened, and we know that the illness makes people dangerous."

Aubrey's heart sank, nausea and fear swelling inside her.

"For now," Bowman said, his expression slightly softened, "proceed to the supply station. They have orientation packets for you. We'll get you home as soon as we can."

User: SusieMusie

Mood: Pissed off

Have you ever seen that movie Chicago? Erica =
Roxie, and Sara = Velma. Both should be locked up
ASAP. They're both crazy and they deserve each
other. They are a severe, SEVERE pain in my butt.

TWENTY-ONE

JACK'S CELL WAS BARE AND cramped, the floor too small for him to lie flat. Other than the miniature size, it seemed like the prisons he'd seen on TV: bare cement and cinder block, steel bars for a door, and fitted with its own steel toilet.

He'd been there for sixteen hours—the soldiers hadn't taken his watch or even frisked him. Although two had escorted him down the narrow corridor to his cell, the men seemed almost afraid to touch him, let alone talk to him. He wasn't a threat in any way—he felt weak and drained of energy, his head still ringing from the noise weapon outside, and his hearing was only now beginning to come back.

The others in the prison had been a blur as he was marched to his cell. They'd stood at the bars of their cells, calling to him, yelling at the soldiers, but he hadn't been able to hear a word of it.

One way the prison was different from the ones he'd seen on TV: it wasn't segregated. He'd seen both boys and girls in the cells he'd passed, and now he could hear their muffled voices: sometimes talking, often yelling, and occasionally crying. If there was any pattern it was that they were all teenagers. Jack was among the older ones, he guessed, but no one looked more than eighteen or nineteen. The most talk-ative, a guy named Eddie, claimed he was twenty-one, but Jack didn't believe him.

Most of the conversation was about escape, but none of it made much sense to him. The soldiers were keeping them all drugged—some yellow powder that they mixed into the water—so his head felt cloudy, but Jack tried to sort out the details in his mind. Eddie talked about riots in Salt Lake and news reports of a rebellion. Others spoke of a girl who could burn white-hot and still be fine, or a boy who could hold his breath for days.

But even those conversations were scarce. No one said much at all, other than to curse at the soldiers when they brought in a new prisoner, or to complain about the food.

Jack hadn't complained yet. He'd stayed completely quiet. From his cell, he could see only three others—the one directly across from him and the two on either side: num-bers thirty-two, thirty-three, and thirty-four. They were all empty. And Jack didn't feel like talking to anyone.

He wondered if he'd ever see Aubrey again. No one in

the prison knew what lay before them, but all of them agreed that it couldn't be good. They were being treated like hardened criminals, like violent killers. After treatment like this, no one was just going to let them go home.

Worse than the thought that he'd never see Aubrey again was knowing that she'd try to rescue him. Two days ago he would have considered Aubrey lost to him—a former friend who couldn't be counted on for anything. But now she was different. She'd try to get him out, or, worse yet, reveal herself and try to get into the prison with him. He prayed she wouldn't.

And Jack didn't belong here. He wasn't a Positive. He couldn't do anything unusual. Something had gone wrong. Maybe there was someone else, someone like Aubrey, who switched the test results. Someone else was marked as a Negative and Jack was a Positive.

A familiar clank echoed down the hall as the main door was unlocked and opened. It felt too soon for food, but Jack obediently pushed his flimsy plastic bowl under the door for his evening ration.

Eddie, as usual, was the first to start talking.

"I don't suppose you've got me a lawyer yet?" he said.

"Shut up, Eleven," the soldier snapped back. They referred to everyone by their numbers, but Jack didn't even know what his was. He figured that was a good thing. Stay out of the way and survive.

"Oh, good," Eddie continued, "you're bringing us more friends. What did this one do?"

Jack couldn't hear a response from the soldier. Instead, he heard the voice of Josi, another prisoner who seemed to have a little more sense.

"What's your name, kid?" she asked.

"His name is Thirty-One, I bet," Eddie answered, laughing.

"What is it?" Josi asked again.

"Cesar," another voice said. "Cesar Carbajal."

"What do you do?" another one shouted.

"And what did they do to you?" Eddie added.

Cesar didn't answer, but a moment later Jack could hear the screech of metal on concrete as a nearby door opened. He probably was thirty-one, like Eddie had said.

"Well, welcome to hell, Cesar Carbajal," another teen said. "Let me tell you how this place works: you stay here, freezing at night and burning up in the day, and no one tells you anything. And then, at some point, you get hauled away."

Eddie piped up. "Why don't you tell Cesar where he gets taken, Private?"

"That's Sergeant," the soldier's voice barked. "And shut up all of you or I'll turn on the water."

Jack looked up at the ceiling and the sprinkler head that was embedded in the cement. That was the punishment for talking back, and they gave it to everyone, no matter who had been harassing them.

"Bring it on," Eddie shouted. "I need a shower."

Several of the other prisoners yelled at Eddie to shut up.

The metal cell door closed with another squeal, and locked into place.

"We're getting two more today," the soldier bellowed. "If I hear so much as a word from any of you, I'm turning it on."

A moment later the main door closed.

"Don't do it to us again, Eddie," Josi said. "I can't take it anymore."

"If they weren't pumping me full of this yellow crap . . . ," he answered.

"Then what?" she said, with an unhappy laugh. "You'd punch through the ceiling and fly away?"

He didn't answer.

"What is it you do again?" she said, continuing to needle him. "You never say, but I bet it's absolutely amazing."

There was silence for a moment. *Two more*, Jack thought, looking at the empty cells across from him. *I'm going to get company.*

"What do you do, Carbajal?" another voice called out.

There was no answer.

"They drug you in here," the voice said again. "Valium or Klonopin, or something. It makes you tired, and screws up your head. If you can do something to get us out of here, do it now."

Josi jumped in before Carbajal had time to respond. "And if you can do it, it had better be awesome enough to get us *all* out of our cells, out of this building, and off of this military base. Because if it can't do that, don't even try it. You'll just get yourself shot, and maybe us, too."

"I—" Carbajal began. "It's stupid. It's a dumb trick. I can count things. That's it."

"You count things?" someone asked. "Big deal."

"I mean," Carbajal said, sounding frustrated, "I can see anything for a couple seconds and tell you how many things are there. Like a bunch of ants, or people in a stadium."

"Really?" Josi asked. "How fast? How big?"

"Pretty fast. And big, but not too big to look at. Like, I tried to count the stars but I couldn't because I kept having to turn my head to see them all, and that messes it up."

"That's a solid Lam 2," Eddie said.

Josi laughed. "You don't even know what that means."

"I told you," Eddie answered. "I heard it from the guards. Lambda 2 means no military use."

"And they explained this all to you?" Josi said.

"I'm not an idiot."

"That's debatable."

Another voice, one Jack didn't recognize, shouted, "Quiet! He's coming back."

The room fell silent. After several seconds, the main door opened again.

No one said anything this time, and Jack couldn't make

out much more than the sound of footsteps scraping on the cement. It surprised him that the new prisoner wasn't even making noise.

A soldier appeared in front of Jack's cell, and he could see that two other men were carrying the prisoner this time. The boy appeared to be unconscious.

They laid him in the cell, slumped in a heap. Jack only caught a glance at the boy's face, but thought he recognized him from the warehouse. Now all Jack could see were the boy's feet and lower legs, motionless.

The soldiers' boots clunked down the otherwise silent hall. A moment later, the door opened.

"So you beat him unconscious and now you're just going to leave him?" It wasn't Eddie—it was Josi.

The sergeant yelled back, "I told you to shut up."

"This is against the law," she shouted, and the prison erupted with angry bellows and threats.

Jack curled up against the wall, and wrapped his arms around his knees. An instant later there was a deep clank and the sound of rushing water. The sprinkler head burst open, pouring down a hard spray like a wide-mouthed fire hose.

The water stung his skin, and Jack had to put his face down to be able to breathe. The others' shouts were drowned out by the noise.

Oh, Aubrey, Jack thought. *Don't do anything stupid. Don't get put in here.*

λ

They turned off the sprinklers much sooner than usual, and Jack lifted his head to take a deep breath. The water ran out of his cell to a long drain that flowed down the center of the hallway. The drains never could keep up with the volume, however, and two inches of standing water were still in the hall when the main door opened again.

The long room was silent.

"Is this where I'll be staying?" a girl's voice asked. It was sweet and clear—it didn't seem to fit in the prison.

"Right down here," the soldier responded, with an uncomfortable cough.

"Okay."

Finally they came into view, the soldier and a very tall blonde girl—Nicole. Something about her seemed so out of place in the prison. Everyone else was ragged and filthy and soaked, and Nicole was her usual self: confident, happy, and beautiful.

The soldier, who appeared to be trying to avoid making eye contact with her, opened the cell door and motioned for her to enter.

"Thank you," she said, stepping inside and turning to face him. He paused for a moment and Jack expected him to say something, but then the soldier swung the door closed and locked it. He bent over and set a large bottle of water outside her cell, the yellow tint bright and obvious.

As the soldier disappeared from view, Nicole flashed a smile at Jack, and then turned to look at her tiny cell. Nicole was taller than Jack, and he guessed the low ceilings and close walls would probably bother her a lot more than they did him.

The door closed with a bang, and Jack waited for the others to start up their usual questions, but the corridor remained quiet.

Still standing, Nicole turned back to face Jack. The smile was gone from her face, but she still looked surprisingly pleasant. "What happens now?"

"Nothing," Jack said, his voice tired and scratchy. "We wait."

Something about seeing Nicole was refreshing, even though they had never been friends. But even in this damp prison, with Nicole wearing the baggy, oversized clothes the military had given her to wear instead of her homecoming dress, Jack had trouble taking his eyes off her.

"It looks like they're making some mistakes," he said, rubbing his hand through his hair to wring the water out of it.

"Apparently," she said softly.

Nicole wrapped her long, slender fingers around the bars and shook the door as though testing it.

Finally, Eddie spoke up.

"What's your name?"

"Nicole," she called back. "What's yours?"

"Eddie Shaw," he answered. His voice seemed to have lost all of its anger. He didn't sound like himself.

"How long have you been here, Eddie?"

"Four days."

"What happens?" Nicole reached up and touched the sprinkler on the ceiling, and then pointed at the water on the floor. Jack nodded.

"We wait," Eddie said. "They come and take us eventually."

"Take us where?"

"I don't know. Testing, I guess. Hey—what can you do?"

Nicole looked around for a place to sit, but didn't appear to like the idea of sitting on the wet, dirty concrete, or on the edge of the metal toilet at the back of her cell, so she leaned on the bars instead.

"Can everyone in here do things?" she asked.

"Everyone in here failed their test," Josi answered.

"What's your name?"

"Josi."

"What can you do, Josi?"

There was a pause, and then Josi's voice sounded embarrassed. "It's weird. Just a brain thing. I'm good at remembering stuff."

"How about you, Eddie?" Nicole asked.

"It's . . . nothing," he said.

Nicole pressed her face against the bars, trying to look down the corridor. "No, tell me. I'm sure it's great."

Jack watched Nicole with awe, wondering how someone could be so gentle and sincere. Had she always been like that?

"It's nothing amazing," he said. "I mean, it's amazing, but it's not amazing, not like some of the others."

"What is it?"

"I have hot breath."

Josi, who had been pestering Eddie the entire time Jack had been in the prison, laughed. "That's it? You have hot breath?"

"It's more than just a little hot," he said defensively. "It's really hot. Like, I can blow into a cup of water and it'll boil."

Josi laughed again, and Jack could hear the snorts and jeers of other prisoners. "You're a human microwave?"

"You don't get it," Eddie said.

Nicole's eyes met Jack's, and she smiled warmly. She pointed, and then mouthed the words, "What can you do?"

Jack shook his head. He wasn't supposed to be there. He should be with the Negatives, with Aubrey.

Or should he be here with Nicole? She seemed so fragile, so helpless. She needed his help here in prison more than Aubrey needed it with the Negatives, didn't she? He could protect her.

"How about you?" Eddie asked. "What do you do, Nicole?"

"I'm here by mistake," she said with confidence. "I think they have me mixed up with someone else."

"Well, good luck," Josi said. "Half the people in here claim they're Negatives, but the guards don't listen."

Nicole stepped back from the bars and finally sat down on floor. "Maybe they'll listen to me."

TWENTY-TWO

A BULLETIN BOARD HAD BEEN erected outside Tent 114, a place where some of the higher-ranking soldiers had offices, and Aubrey and Betsy stood in front, poring over the information for news about home. The first day it had been newspapers, the *Salt Lake Tribune* and the *New York Times*, the front pages stapled to the corkboard. But since then there had only been internet printouts, with short summaries of news.

Aubrey took it all to be a good sign—the army was trying to help. They weren't blocking the Negatives from information about the outside world. On Aubrey's second day in the tent they'd even been allowed to write letters home. Aubrey wrote one to her dad. She told him where she was, and what it was like, and how she'd never forgive him for trading her for beer. She'd signed her name, folded it neatly, and then crumpled it and threw it in the trash.

She wondered where she'd go if she ever got out of here.

"Hey Betsy," Aubrey said, tapping a loose white paper that was thumbtacked in the corner of the corkboard. "From your place. 'The Uintah and Ouray Indian Reservation reports that all previously missing children have been accounted for.'"

Betsy moved to the paper and read the short paragraph carefully.

"They're accounted for," she said with a frown. "That doesn't mean they're alive."

"It's something," Aubrey said. She stepped back from the board, getting a wide view. They'd come here three times a day for the last two days, and very little changed. There'd been no news out of Sanpete County other than a two-day-old mention of a skirmish at a roadblock near Manti. The article listed a few names, but they were no one Aubrey knew.

Betsy turned to face Aubrey. "Ready?"

Aubrey took a final glance at the board and then nodded.

"They're in a good position, I guess," Betsy said as they turned and started back toward Tent 209. "There's not much on the reservation that would be a target for terrorists."

"Any idea where everyone went?" Aubrey asked.

"I think we had more time than most," Betsy said, and then shared a wry smile. "This isn't the first time the Utes have fought the government. And we know the backcountry inside and out."

"If everyone's accounted for, they should be here. Right?" Aubrey had tried looking through the bunkers for people she knew, but it was hard. The army had strict rules about moving around the camp and you couldn't go into any tent other than your own.

"Maybe. A lot went down to the South Reservation. Maybe they had better luck. Or got sent to a different camp." Betsy nodded and put her hands in the pockets of her jeans. It was the beginning of October now, and the winds were getting colder.

"Did you grow up in Roosevelt?"

"No," Betsy said. "I'm from the middle of nowhere— Whiterocks. Ever heard of it?"

Aubrey shook her head.

"No one has," Betsy said with a laugh. "When I was six, my father moved me up to Roosevelt to live with my aunt. Better schools. I used to worry so much about grades. Last year, I actually freaked out because I got a B in Trig. I mean, I thought my life was over. Now I wonder if any of that will ever matter."

"It will," Aubrey said. "Wars end. Think of it: there's more than three hundred million people in the United States. Even if Major Bowman's estimate is accurate—180,000 people killed—then there's still three hundred million who have to go on with their lives."

Betsy nodded, exhaling a reluctant laugh. "That's kind of a callous way to look at it."

"It's not callous," Aubrey said. Somehow, talking about it—even if Aubrey wasn't sure if she believed it—made her feel more confident. "It's just true. You'll still go to college. Life will get back to normal."

"But—"

"Well," Aubrey corrected, "it won't go back to *normal*. But it will go back to better than this."

Betsy grinned. "It'd be hard to be any worse."

Aubrey laughed and looked out to the south. Several hundred yards away she could see the fence that surrounded the bunkers, and one of the many watchtowers. She'd been to the fence every day—fifteen-foot-tall chain-link, topped with razor wire. An identical second fence stood thirty feet past it. It wasn't clear if it was intended to keep people out or in. Aubrey had heard rumors about antiaircraft guns somewhere among the tents, but she hadn't seen them.

She touched Betsy's arm as they approached Tent 209. "I think I'm going to walk some more," Aubrey said. "I'm really getting sick of being in there."

Betsy smiled and nodded. "Want company?"

"Sure."

They turned away from their tent and headed south. Aubrey was sure that Betsy knew where they were going—Betsy had walked with her before.

"Hey guys!"

Aubrey turned to see Kara running from the tent. A guy was walking behind her.

"Where've you been?" Kara asked. "We got new people in the tent next door. A bus came with eight newbies." She lowered her voice to a whisper so only Betsy and Aubrey could hear. "And they're all *guys*—cute ones."

Aubrey looked up at the approaching boy. He was tall, with blond hair and a thin face. One arm was in a cast and sling, and he had two black eyes. As he reached the girls he stretched out his hand.

"Alec Moore," he said.

"Aubrey," she answered.

Betsy shook his hand. "I'm Betsy Blackhair. We were just going for a walk. Want to come?"

Alec looked surprised. "They let you do that? I thought we were kind of confined to the tent."

"No," Kara said, laughing more than the situation warranted. "As long as we're back by six o'clock. They shut the tents after dark, and they have a roll call to make sure we're there. I heard about a boy who was out past curfew and they sent him to some detention or something."

Alec looked at his watch. "Then I guess we have a little time. Where are we headed?"

Aubrey turned and began walking. She hadn't really

wanted so much company.

"The fence, I bet," Kara said. "It gives a gorgeous view, especially this time of night."

"Sounds good," Alec said.

They walked for several minutes, and Aubrey let Kara and Betsy do most of the talking. Alec was from a private school up in Salt Lake and was thinking of joining the Air Force Academy. He said that he'd been talking to the soldiers earlier—even the guards at the warehouse—about life in the military. Listening to him talk, you'd think that nothing had ever happened—that they hadn't been torn from their friends and families and imprisoned with no chance to appeal.

"How were you caught, Alec?" Aubrey asked, her curiosity about his injuries finally overcoming her.

"Caught?" Alec said. "I wasn't caught—I was rescued."

She looked back at him and saw that Kara's arm was slipped into his. She was positively beaming.

"Rescued?" Aubrey said, not trying very hard to mask her annoyance. "You just got here. Were you running from the police?"

"Oh no," Alec answered. "I was camping. We'd been up there for a week before an avalanche chased us off the mountain. We didn't even know about the evacuations until search and rescue found us."

"That sounds scary," Kara said.

"We all made it out okay," Alec said, winking his black

eye. "Kind of exciting, really."

Aubrey frowned. "How were you camping for a week? Weren't you in school?"

"Private school," he answered. "Year round. I was off track."

They cleared the last bunker and reached the fence. The ground sloped to the south, taking a sharp decline just after the second fence. In the distance, Aubrey could see where they came from—a large collection of buildings all connected by fences and watchtowers. From this distance she just couldn't tell which one had been hers. One of them, she had to hope, still held Jack.

Aubrey remembered her promise. She wouldn't do anything stupid. But she also remembered Jack's desperate plea—if she was going to get him out, she couldn't let anyone find out she was a Positive, a Lambda.

She looked at the fence in front of her. There was no way she could cut it—she hadn't seen anything like cable cutters in the tent, even in the supply station. And one glance at the razor wire was enough to tell her that she couldn't climb it. Even with being able to disappear, this fence was impossible to cross.

Maybe she could go back to the decontamination rooms, she thought. They'd be guarded, but guards were easier to avoid than razor wire.

Of course, the fences weren't her only problem. The

buildings were surrounded by armored vehicles, tanks, watchtowers, and there always seemed to be hundreds of infantrymen nearby—drilling or working or patrolling.

Aubrey tried to picture Jack, tried to guess where he was and what he was doing. He'd be safe, she thought. Eventually they'd realize that he wasn't a Positive. Maybe he was already released, back in one of the tents and trying to find her.

She lost her train of thought for a moment—as she stared at the buildings she couldn't remember what she was looking for. It had been too long since she'd had a normal life—too long since decent food and a good night's rest.

"Hey, wait a minute." Aubrey turned and looked up at Alec. "Aren't you . . ."

It was hard to picture. She could see his face. She knew that she'd seen him somewhere before. But where? On the bus? In the warehouse? Or was it longer ago than that?

Alec looked equally confused.

"Alec Moore, right?" she asked.

He nodded.

"Oh my gosh," she said with a laugh. "Did you go to Mount Pleasant Elementary? Third and fourth grade?"

Alec's face brightened. "You're from Mount Pleasant?"

Aubrey felt a sense of elation—in all of this camp she'd finally found someone that she knew. Granted it was years before, but she knew him. "Aubrey Parsons," she said happily. "I'm Aubrey Parsons!"

She jumped forward, throwing her arms around him. He hugged her back.

"Aubrey," he said. "Holy cow, you've grown up. Man, it's been a long time."

"Yeah," Aubrey said, stepping back to look at him. "You're so . . . tall."

Kara looked a little peeved that Aubrey had a connection with Alec, but Aubrey didn't care. She'd spent the last four days searching for some sign of home, and here was someone right in front of her. Aubrey couldn't remember much about Alec—it had been a long time—but they'd been friends. They'd been friends back when Aubrey had friends.

"Oh, wow," she said, feeling happier than she had in a long time. "This is great."

TWENTY-THREE

NICOLE DIDN'T LAST LONG IN the prison. Before the soldiers had even brought in anyone new, Jack watched as two guards and an officer came and took her away.

The cells seemed to be getting colder, though Jack wondered if that was just because he'd never been able to get fully dry. The other Positives couldn't seem to keep their mouths shut, and the sprinklers were turned on at least twice a day. Jack was able to keep time for the first two days, but eventually water got into his watch and it stopped. He wasn't sure how many more hours had passed—there were no windows, and the lights were always on—but Jack tried to keep track of how often the guards brought food; he guessed he'd been in his cell about three days.

By his count, three more people had been brought in to

the prison and four had been taken away. Eddie and Josi were gone now, but Matt Ganza was there. He hadn't said a word since he'd been brought in, and he was too far down the row to have a private conversation with Jack.

The boy who had been brought in unconscious never woke up and was carried off by medics.

The only thing that kept Jack's spirits up was the hope that Aubrey was working on getting him out—maybe trying to get him retested. Part of him doubted it. He didn't want to doubt. He wanted to sit confidently in his cell, certain that she was harassing the guards day and night.

But she'd abandoned him before.

A metallic clank sounded as the far door opened. The kids still argued, but without the same enthusiasm they'd had before. They'd been here too long, and knew it wasn't doing any good. The newer prisoners weren't talkers, and the old ones were tired of getting soaked all the time.

The guards appeared in front of Jack's cell, putting the new prisoner into Nicole's former cell. She thanked them, just as Nicole had done, and they left her with a bottle of drugged water.

"Hi," Jack said, as the girl inspected her tiny cell.

"Hi," she answered, turning to face him. She was short, probably just over five feet tall, with light blonde hair that fell just to her chin. Like most of the prisoners who'd been brought in, she looked tired.

"I'm Jack," he said.

"Laura," she answered.

Another girl from somewhere down the corridor shouted out the same question she did of all new prisoners. "Any news from outside?"

Laura sat down on the concrete cross-legged. She was probably short enough that she could lay flat on the floor, and Jack envied that. "I've been in the warehouse for two days," Laura answered. "No new people have been brought in since last night. The last one to come in said that the TVs aren't broadcasting anymore. He said that there's a draft now."

"Do they know who the terrorists are yet?" Jack asked.

"No," Laura said, picking up the water bottle and peering at the yellow specks floating in it.

Jack leaned against the cinder-block wall and stared at the ceiling. Could it be that he was actually safer in prison?

"What do you do?" Matt asked. He was in a cell to Jack's right—Jack couldn't see him.

Jack looked back at Laura, who seemed surprised by the question.

"Excuse me?"

"What's your power?" Matt said. "You're a Positive. That means you can do something."

"Oh," Laura said. She balled her small hand into a fist and punched the cement floor. With no more apparent effort than if she was squashing a bug, the cement splintered and cracked.

The corridor suddenly erupted with noise.

"What was that? What did she do?"

"She punched the freaking floor! Like a jackhammer or something."

"Don't drink the water! It'll mess with your head!"

"Get the bars! Get us out of here!"

Laura, with a contented smile on her face, didn't move. Her eyes met Jack's, and he moved forward to his door so he could talk over the noise.

"Why don't you escape?" he said. "Can you break the bars?"

"Probably," she said, gripping the steel in her hands. "I think so. But I'm not going anywhere."

"Why not?" someone else shouted. "You could fight your way out."

The other prisoners yelled in agreement, pleading for her to break them all free, but she shook her head. Jack wondered if Laura was like Aubrey—maybe using her ability too much made her tired. Maybe she knew she couldn't fight long enough to get free.

"No," Laura said, still smiling, though obviously over-whelmed by the shouts. "Haven't you guys been listening to what's happening out there? Think about it for a minute. What if the army isn't bad? What if they really are locking us up for our protection?"

A girl somewhere down the corridor screamed, "You

haven't been in here! They wouldn't treat us like this if they cared about us."

"But we get out, don't we?" Laura answered. "They don't just leave us in these cells, right?"

"I've been here for days," the girl answered. "A week, maybe."

"But they have to take us somewhere eventually. If I escape, they'll hunt me. They'll think I'm a terrorist."

Another voice called out, "They already think we're terrorists."

"So you want me to prove them right?" Laura said. "I break us all out and we run—how many of us will get shot? If I punch an infantryman I'll kill him, and then what does that make me?"

"What if they dissect us?" Matt asked. "What if they cut every one of us open and find out how we do what we do?"

"They already know how we do it," Laura insisted. "Do you think they developed that cheek swab test without knowing what they're testing for?"

Matt didn't respond, and the room was quiet for a moment. Jack watched Laura's face as she waited for someone else to say something. She didn't look angry—she looked confident.

"I'm sorry," Laura said. "I know you've probably been waiting for something like this, someone to get you out of here. But I'm not afraid of the army. In fact, if I don't cause any trouble—if you guys don't cause any trouble—then maybe they'll treat us like people instead of prisoners."

"They already treat us like prisoners," someone down the corridor muttered. "And none of us have done anything yet."

Jack thought about the night at the homecoming dance. If Nate had surrendered instead of attacking, would they have let him live? But what about kicking in Aubrey's door and tackling a teenage girl to the ground? That wasn't a military that trusted them. No one was giving them the benefit of the doubt.

"I grew up in Colorado," Laura said. "And the only thing I've heard about Colorado in the last week is that these terrorists have screwed things up so much that food can't get in and out of the city. The interstates are shut down. There are millions of people there. What are they going to do without food?"

"I'm nineteen," she continued. "I don't know where we go once they take us out of here, but I'm volunteering. Someone needs to fight these terrorists."

Jack found himself nodding, though that surprised him. Laura's speech made a kind of ideological sense, but nothing that he'd seen seemed to back it up. The prison was terrible. The conditions were inhumane. They were treated like criminals, not like people who were being protected and cared for.

On the other hand, the prison had security cameras. Maybe it had microphones listening in on them, too. If so,

Laura had just made a friend of the army.

Jack pointed to her water. "That stuff screws up your brain. They say you won't be able to do stuff while you're on it."

She unscrewed the cap and smelled it. "Did it change you?"

"I can't do anything," he said. "Never could. I don't know why I'm here."

Laura took a swig of the water, and Jack heard someone swear.

TWENTY-FOUR

AUBREY LAY IN HER BUNK, watching the door. Breakfast had come and gone, and Aubrey had eaten as much as she could. The food wasn't anything special—some generic brand of Froot Loops with reconstituted powdered milk, and canned peaches—but she filled up on it. She had big plans for the day, and she'd need calories. She was going to try to find Jack.

She'd spent hours talking to Alec yesterday. He'd only been in Mount Pleasant for two years, but once she reminded him of what the school was like he'd been able to remember a lot of it—and after talking to him she could recall a lot of the things they used to do together. In the fourth grade she'd played his wife in the very abridged version of *Macbeth* that the class put on—he was Macduff and she Lady Macduff.

She'd been to a birthday party at his house, and they both were in the highest-level reading group both years.

The whole thing bothered Kara, but it shouldn't have. It was nice to have Alec there, like a security blanket, but Aubrey wasn't interested in him. Kara would have known that if Aubrey dared to tell anyone what she was planning for that day.

After breakfast, Aubrey had gone to the supply shelves and asked for a bottle of water, but the soldier told her she had to get water from the main spigot—they didn't have bottles they could give out. Fortunately, she'd been able to talk him out of a few granola bars, which she hoped would help her stay on her feet. She was going to be invisible for a long time.

At nearly nine in the morning, the sergeant arrived for morning roll call. Aubrey climbed down from the bunk and dug through her small pile of clothes for her towel.

The sergeant read through the teens' names, and as they were called out, the teens went forward to have their bracelets checked against their picture. There were twenty people in Tent 209 now—every bunk was full—but the process didn't take too long. Aubrey threw her towel over her shoulder and waited.

Finally, the soldier read "Aubrey Parsons" and she hurried up to the door. They checked her bracelet twice, matching her with a picture in a notebook, and then marked her off the list.

"I want to run to the showers," Aubrey said. "Can I go now?"

The bored sergeant nodded, and Aubrey slipped past him outside. One of the tents near the fence was entirely dedicated to girls' showers, but she still had to wait in a short line for a stall to open up. No one she talked to had a good estimate of how many people were in the camp, but even Aubrey's crude calculations put the number enormously high. She'd seen tents with numbers up in the three hundreds, and her tent was smaller than some—she guessed many of the others were twice as big, if not more. So, assuming there were at least three hundred bunkers with maybe thirty in each—and she figured that was a low estimate—that still put at least nine thousand people in the camp.

And that meant there had to be other camps elsewhere. Aubrey had no idea how many teens were in the state, but there had to be way more than this. There were probably quarantine camps all over Utah—all over the country. For all she knew, this wasn't even the only camp at Dugway.

After a few minutes a girl left a stall and Aubrey hurried into it. They were only allowed one shower every other day, and the showers were timed so she needed to hurry. With only a few minutes left she poured out the entire bottle of shampoo—it was a military-grade kind that she hated—and then rinsed the empty bottle as best she could. In the remaining seconds before the water shut off, she filled the bottle and closed the cap.

When she emerged from the shower tent a few minutes later she felt refreshed and clean, and she had a water bottle hidden under her towel.

Aubrey headed south toward the fence.

It was going to be risky. Granted, it had been days since she'd disappeared and she felt fairly well rested and healthy, but what she was doing today was daunting. It would take longer than she wanted, and so much was unknown.

Upon reaching the fence, Aubrey turned right and began walking to the decontamination tents.

The first one that she reached appeared to be in use; a bus was stopped on the far side, and two freshly washed girls were sitting outside the door, waiting for their ride. They looked almost identical, except one was a little older than the other. They had to be sisters.

Wouldn't that be nice? Aubrey was enjoying the company of her new roommates—Kara and Betsy were friendly—but she longed for the company of people she really knew. Even Nicole, with her many faults, would have been comforting. In all of Aubrey's searching, she hadn't found Nicole's tent.

But Nicole wasn't Jack. He had been a better friend to Aubrey than Nicole or anyone had ever been. Jack had been more like family than her dad.

She'd promised to get Jack out. She'd turned her back on him once, abandoning him for popularity and clothes and parties, but she wouldn't do it again.

The soldiers at the fence eyed Aubrey cautiously as she passed. She smiled at them and continued on to the next tent, and then turned around the corner. Checking her pockets for the extra food, Aubrey took a deep breath and then vanished.

No one noticed her as she returned to the fence, or as she walked back toward the decontamination tent. There was a third girl on the bench now. All three looked scared and exhausted, and the sisters were holding hands.

Even now she wasn't exactly sure what the soldiers would notice, but she'd spied so much in the last six months that she guessed opening the wooden door to the tent wouldn't cause much of a stir. Aubrey still wasn't sure what they would see while she was invisible. Would they just ignore it? Would they think it was the wind? Would they not even see it open? All she knew for certain was that she'd opened doors before and it had never been a problem.

Inside were a female soldier and two more girls dressing. Aubrey hurried past them, moving quickly through the shower room and into the waiting area. Two more girls and three boys were still waiting for decontamination. Aubrey checked their faces—she tried to do that now with everyone she saw in the camp—but didn't recognize any of them. Finally, she ducked through the last door and stepped back out into the morning air.

She was outside the fence. Well, outside one of a tangle of dozens of fences.

A boxy-looking armored vehicle sat beside the tent door, and two soldiers were half-visible in the turret. One was talking on what looked like an enormous telephone. Three other soldiers were on the ground, talking and joking with each other.

Aubrey hurried past them. She wanted to run—she felt so free, away from the tents—but knew that she had to conserve her energy. It was at least a mile to the other buildings and maybe more.

Traveling down the hill was easy enough, and she actually found herself enjoying it, recalling the countless hours she'd spent hiking alone in the hills and mountains behind Mount Pleasant. But as she approached the buildings it felt less like home and more like a war zone.

Tanks and armored vehicles surrounded the complex, a few of them motionless but most moving. Soldiers waited behind sandbag gun emplacements, and two massive camouflaged trucks seemed to carry large missiles. Somehow, that actually made Aubrey feel better. Missiles couldn't be used against the people in the buildings, could they? So at least part of the army's story was true—they were protecting something. Maybe.

There was a wide flat space in front of the soldiers, and Aubrey jogged across it. Even knowing that they couldn't see her, it was uncomfortable. They were watching for someone just like her, and ready to shoot any intruder.

There was a sudden roar, and she spun to see a low-flying helicopter zoom up over a ridge and hover almost overheard. She froze.

No, it couldn't be here for her. She was invisible.

It swept side to side, rotating in midair only a few hundred feet above the ground. Finally, it turned and moved over another small hill.

Aubrey let out a long breath, trying not to panic. It was nothing. It was another vehicle moving. All the military vehicles were moving, all the time. Patrolling, she guessed.

Her chest hurt. It felt like her heart was going to pound through her rib cage. She tried to focus again.

She couldn't see any side doors to get into the complex—like her camp, it was surrounded by a double fence. Instead, she headed for the large gate guarding the main road in and out. On either side of the gate were watchtowers, and below the towers were squat, sandbag-covered fortifications. She could see the helmeted heads of soldiers peering out through narrow openings, watching for attackers.

The helicopter swooped in again, and she ducked instinctively. It moved away faster this time.

The gate was locked and closed, and she didn't dare to try to move it. Opening a door was one thing. But this gate was something entirely different: twenty feet tall and thirty feet wide. She'd have to wait for someone else to open it, and then slip inside.

Aubrey slumped down in front of the fortifications and leaned back against the sandbags. She was already feeling tired, but the weariness was still mostly in her joints and limbs, not in her head. Once she started to get dizzy she'd be in trouble, but for now it was mainly an inconvenience.

The water in her bottle had a little chemical aftertaste, but she knew she needed to stay hydrated and so drank it anyway.

A Humvee looked like it was approaching, and Aubrey stood, ready to sneak inside as it drove through the gate, but it turned and headed to the east instead.

She looked up at the sun, trying to guess the time. It couldn't have been more than forty-five minutes since she'd snuck out of camp, but the fatigue in her legs made it feel like hours.

A soldier left the other sandbag emplacement and crossed the road toward hers.

"You get the news?" he called out, ducking under the low roof and entering the fortification. Aubrey followed, standing at the door and looking in. There were two men already inside, one sitting on the ground, looking half-asleep, and the other looking out the small window.

"What's up?" the sleepy man said.

"Golden Gate Bridge," the first answered. "They knocked it into the bay."

The man at the window swore. "And we're here babysitting a bunch of kids."

Aubrey took a step back from the door. She'd never been to the bridge, only seen it in pictures, but the thought of it gone made her sick. "That's the other thing," the first man said. "There was a breakout at Relocation Seven."

"Which one's that?"

The first soldier leaned against the wall. "Amarillo. We're supposed to get briefed on it tonight, but Cummings works in the comm station and he said that the whole training facility got blown to hell. They don't know if it came from the outside or the inside, but everybody took off. I heard that they had some freak down there—took out a Black Hawk. Just jumped up and grabbed the thing and yanked it out of the air."

The other soldier shook his head and muttered something under his breath as he turned back to the window. "Hang on," he said, and pulled his radio mouthpiece down in front of his face. "We've got two inbound. Over."

Aubrey glanced back out toward the road and saw two olive-green tractor trailers approaching. Stepping away from the fortification, Aubrey stumbled on her weak legs. She moved out of the road and to the side of the gate.

It seemed to take forever for the two trucks to get approved to enter the complex, and Aubrey squatted down beside the gate, trying to save her energy. It felt like she had weights strapped to her wrists and ankles, and even pulling her hand up to wipe sweat from her forehead seemed like a chore. While she waited, she took another drink from the bottle.

The helicopter was back, holding steady over the trucks, like it was escorting them. One side of the helicopter was open, and a soldier leaned out, looking down. She tried to ignore him.

Finally, the gate was opened and Aubrey slipᵖ d inside, pushing herself to walk alongside the slow-moving trucks. There were fences in every direction, and she didn't know if she'd have to use the trucks to get back out through the gate again. She was breathing heavily as she walked, and her legs had begun to burn. This wasn't like her—she'd been hiking in the mountains for years and had always been in great health. She'd even planned on running for the cross-country team this year, before Nicole had steered her toward cheerleading instead.

The truck approached a second set of gates but as Aubrey prepared to follow it, a sign caught her eye: "Intake Station Two." She jogged to the fence to get a better view, and saw all the places she remembered—the intake station, the small annex where they'd had their cheeks swabbed, the warehouse where they'd waited, and the long walkway that led to judgment.

From the cage where their statuses had been announced, Jack would have gone to the right. She could see a short cinder-block building with no windows. There was no way for her to get inside; there only appeared to be two doors and they were both accessed through the chain-link-enclosed walkways.

So, Aubrey reasoned, *if the walkway from the judgment cage is the entrance to the building, then the other walkway has to be the exit.* Her eyes followed that walkway toward a second cinder-block building—a much larger one. The steel door was stenciled with the words "Assessment Facility."

Aubrey hurried toward that building, barely able to keep her balance over the uneven ground. She needed to find someplace where she could reappear and rest.

The helicopter was back, lower now. Sand blew in her eyes and mouth, and she shielded her face with one arm while she ran forward on shaky feet.

The steel door was just thirty feet away when a Humvee came tearing up across the dirt field behind her.

She ignored it. There was too much going on, and she didn't know how much longer she could stay on her feet. Stumbling toward the door, she saw there was an electronic keypad next to the doorknob, and her heart sank—all of this effort was a waste. But just as she almost gave in to the urge to cry, she saw someone had put a fist-sized rock in the door, holding it open.

Stale warm air greeted her as she stepped into a long, plain hallway. To her left she could see nothing but blank walls, and to her right were a few doors. A soldier in uniform was coming toward her pushing a filing cabinet on a dolly. Aubrey moved out of the way, leaning back against the hard concrete wall to avoid getting run over, and watched as the man left the building, removing the rock he'd apparently left in the door.

Aubrey was dizzy now and nauseated. She had to find a place to reappear.

As quickly as her feet would carry her, she staggered down the hallway, reading the labels on each door. The first she came to was a supply closet—perfect!—but it was locked. The rest seemed to be offices and she could hear voices inside.

There were voices behind her now, too. Whoever had been in the jeep seemed to be following her in.

No, not following me. They can't see me. She felt like she couldn't even think straight.

A door opened right in front of her and Aubrey had to jump to avoid running into the exiting soldier. Her movements were sluggish and unsteady, and she slammed into the wall, and then collapsed to the floor.

I'm going to be trapped in here, she thought, and forced herself to stand again. Her shoulder ached, and she had to keep a hand on the wall for balance as she struggled to get farther down the hall.

Pain erupted in her head as an alarm sounded and brilliant white strobes began flashing on the ceiling. This couldn't be because of her, could it? No one could see her.

She reached an open door and peeked inside. It was some kind of records room; floor-to-ceiling shelves were stacked with color-coded folders. Aubrey didn't see anyone, and took a few lurching steps in.

There was a desk, but it was stacked high with boxes and obviously hadn't been used recently. In fact, other than the door being open, there was no sign that anyone ever used the room. She read the tags on the files, and what she saw dated back ten or fifteen years.

The alarm was screaming, and Aubrey was losing her vision quickly. Boxes turned into brown blobs; filing cabinets blended into the walls.

Now needing both arms to keep her on her feet, she moved down the aisles of shelves to the back of the room. Dusty wooden cabinets lined the wall, and she fell to her knees, opening the lower doors.

Hallelujah.

There were a few small boxes stacked in the cabinet, but no shelves, and Aubrey climbed awkwardly inside.

It was a tight fit. Her knees were bent almost to her chest and she had to lean her head and shoulders forward. But, after pulling the cupboard doors closed and reappearing, Aubrey couldn't help but feel euphoric. Her lungs filled with air and her breathing almost immediately returned to normal. The returning strength in her arms and legs felt warm and invigorating. And, even though she knew she needed to fight it, knew what would happen if she was late to camp that night, she fell asleep.

TWENTY-FIVE

ALEC APPROACHED A BLONDE GIRL sitting alone in the dirt. A group of kids had cleared a semirectangular space deep in the center of the sprawling tent complex and were playing soccer. The girl seemed to be rooting for someone on one of the teams.

"Mind if I join you?" he asked.

She looked up, her eyes darting over his bruised and bandaged body. No one ever said no to him like this. He loved it.

"Sure."

It took him a minute to sit, struggling to ease himself down to the sandy earth with the help of only one arm.

"You okay?" she asked.

"As good as any of us in here," he said. "My problems are just more visible."

The girl smiled at that, and turned her eyes back to the game. A foot of dust hung in the air above the playing field as players fought for the ball.

"Why aren't you playing?" Alec asked.

"I don't know," she said. "I just don't feel like it."

"You look athletic."

She rolled her eyes. "It's not that. I just don't feel like playing right now. You know how it is—worrying about family and stuff. My roommates are playing. It just—it just doesn't feel right to play."

He nodded and leaned back on his good arm.

Alec was feeding her images now, memories of a thin, pale-faced boy from her elementary school.

"Where are you from?" he asked.

She brought her knees up to her chest and hugged them. "Brigham City."

"You're kidding," Alec said with a fake surprise that he'd now practiced a dozen times in the quarantine zone. "How old are you?"

The girl looked at him from the side of her eyes. "Eighteen. Why?"

"Alec Moore," he said. "Fourth grade. I lived there in the fourth grade."

For the first time her eyes seemed to soften. "Really? Alec? Lake View Elementary?"

"Yeah. I totally recognize you," he said, and then stared

at her, pretending he was trying to remember her name. "It's . . . it starts with a J, right? Jennifer? Jessica?"

She laughed—a real, warm laugh. "Emily Townsend. But I think I remember you—Alec Moore. You were a little guy, right?"

"Not the bulky hunk I am now," he said with a smile.

Emily grinned. "That's amazing. Out of all these thousands of people and the first person I know is someone I haven't seen since fourth grade."

"You weren't rounded up with friends?" he asked, trying to hide his annoyance. She'd be of more use to him if she had close contacts here.

"My parents sent me out of town to stay with my aunt down in Fillmore—you know, trying to get away from all the attacks. I didn't know anybody down there."

Worthless, Alec thought. But that's what he got for approaching a girl sitting all alone.

He pointed to the game in front of them.

"Where'd they get a soccer ball?"

"I heard a soldier found it for them. All these guys are from my tent. They guard that ball like it's made of gold."

He nodded. "I wish they'd give us more to do."

"I keep hearing that they're going to—more games and activities and stuff. If they don't, we'll go crazy."

Alec leaned forward and rubbed his arm.

"What happened to you?" she asked. "Did you try to

fight when they came for you?"

"I wish," he said. "Car accident."

He paused for a moment, and then thought of an opening. "You know what sucks? They took me straight from the accident to the hospital, and straight from there to here. I never even got a chance to talk to my family. They have no idea where I am."

Emily reached over and touched his arm. "That's awful."

"I just wish I could call them or something," he said. "To let them know I'm okay."

They watched the soccer game—too many kids on the narrow field, crowding around the ball too much to pass effectively. Alec had always liked soccer, and this was an embarrassing display. "It's been a long time," Emily finally said, her voice quieter.

"Since fourth grade?" Alec responded. "Yeah."

The players got close to them, kicking and tripping to get at the ball before someone finally passed it tumbling through the dirt toward his own goalie.

Alec reinforced more memories, all positive. Playing together at lunch time, going to birthday parties, even giving each other Christmas presents.

Childhood memories were easy, because he didn't need to focus on the specifics. He'd just insert a tiny fact, add a little emotion to it, and her brain would fill in the gaps. No one was expected to remember fourth grade in any detail, so none of these girls was bothered that they could only remember snippets of Alec Moore.

"So where have you been since elementary school?"

"All over," he said. "Mostly Colorado."

I'm going to go for it, he thought. He'd been playing other girls slowly, building trust over more time. But he was tired of waiting.

"How long have you been in here?" he asked.

"Four days," she said, rolling her eyes and then laughing. "I'm ready to go home."

He lowered his voice. "Can I ask you a question?"

"Sure." She met his eyes.

"I've seen people here with things, things we aren't supposed to have—like the soccer ball. And someone had a radio."

"Yeah."

"Do you know of anyone who has snuck in a cell phone? I just really need to call my parents."

Emily looked out at the soccer players and was silent for a minute.

She's shutting down. I pushed it too fast.

Her voice was barely a whisper. "There's a girl in our tent. I don't know how she got it past the guards, but she's been using it to keep track of the news. The battery's running low, though."

Alec grinned.

TWENTY-SIX

JACK AWOKE TO THE SOUND of screeching metal as his cell was opened. It was the first time it had opened since he'd been put inside, and he was overcome with a feeling of freedom. As he stood and stepped into the corridor he felt as if he could breathe easier.

Laura smiled at him as he left. "Good luck, Jack."

"You too," he answered.

Matt wished him well, followed by a couple of other mumbled good-byes.

As the soldiers led him down the corridor, he looked at the faces of the other prisoners. He was amazed at how terrible they all looked—their clothes were wrinkled, stained with sweat and grime, and their eyes sunken and weary. He had to assume that he looked the same.

His joints ached from sitting too long on the cement, and his clothes—which had spent days wet and unchanged—chafed his legs and arms.

At the door the guard placed him in handcuffs, and then attached a thick, heavy bracelet around Jack's right ankle. Jack didn't protest; he was exhausted.

They led him down a short hallway, which didn't look all that different from the cell block. The floors were still cement and the walls cinder block. There were a few doors, but all of them were closed and unmarked. After about fifty feet they turned right and came to another steel door. The guards opened it and sunlight poured in on him.

He raised his bound hands to shield his eyes from the bright light and stepped outside. He was in another chain-link walkway, except this one was short. Ahead of him was another cinder-block structure, and a sign on the door said "Assessment Facility."

As he crossed, Jack tried to look around and get his bearings, but couldn't see anything recognizable. The chain-link seemed to stretch on forever, as though there was fence after fence repeating for miles. He wondered where Aubrey was. She was probably home now, safe with the other Negatives. Would that be better, if there were still terrorists on the loose?

The guards were met at the door by two more men, one dressed as a medic and the other wearing a rumpled suit and a loose tie.

"Jack Cooper," his guard said. "One-one-seven-B-G-R."

The medic verified the number on both Jack's wrist and ankle bracelets and then motioned for the guards to bring Jack inside. He resisted for a moment, not because he hadn't resigned himself to whatever fate awaited him inside the Assessment Facility, but because the sun felt so good on his skin and the cool air smelled clean.

"Get in there," the guard snapped, pushing Jack forward. His foot caught on the lip of the door and he stumbled inside.

"Thanks, Jack," the man in the suit said. "Sorry about all of this. Hopefully we'll have you in and out real quick."

The guards led Jack into a small square room. The walls and floor were cement, except for one wall which bore a large mirror. In the center was a gurney. Jack felt his heart thump heavily in his chest; this was what everyone told him would happen—dissection and testing.

"What's that for?" he said, knowing that he couldn't fight back against the four men. He eyed the mirror, wondering who was watching.

"Oh, don't worry," the man in the suit said. "We're going to flush all those benzodiazepines out of your system. Nasty stuff. Sorry about it."

Jack nodded and the two guards helped him up onto the gurney. They removed his handcuffs as he lay down, and then wrapped his wrists and ankles with tight leather straps.

His head was spinning. He didn't realize just how tired

the medicine had made him until he'd had to walk, and even that short distance had winded him.

The man in the suit appeared at Jack's side with an IV pump and proceeded to insert a needle into Jack's arm. With the line set and the machine whirring, he turned to the guards and told them they could go.

"Sorry about all the trouble," the man said. "I know how awful this has to seem."

Jack raised an eyebrow. "Do you?"

The man got a metal folding chair from the side of the room and set it next to the gurney. He sat down. "My name is Dr. Benjamin Eastman. Pleased to meet you."

Jack didn't answer.

"You've got the Erebus virus," Eastman said. "Sorry about that, too."

"I don't have it," Jack said. The medicine coursing through his body seemed to take the edge off of his exhaustion, but he still felt weak. Even if the restraints had been taken off his arms he doubted he'd have been able to stand up straight.

"You have it," Eastman replied, holding up a sheet of paper with a list of abbreviations and numbers. "The tests are accurate."

"I'm not like the other people in there," Jack said. "They can do strange things. I can't."

"Just because you haven't manifested any symptoms yet doesn't mean that you don't have it." He set the papers down and then pulled out a stethoscope. He listened to Jack's chest for a few moments. "Tell me: Have you recently had any traumatic medical problem?"

"What do you mean?"

"It could be anything," Eastman said, tucking the stethoscope back into his jacket pocket. "Severe headaches, chest pain, memory loss. Sound familiar?"

Jack shook his head.

"High fever? Deafness? Stroke? High blood pressure?"

"No."

"No accidents in the recent past? Car? Bike? Fall on your head? Break your arm?"

"Nothing. I'm pretty healthy."

"Hold on," Eastman said, holding up a finger as he left the room. The medic was still there, standing at attention in the corner.

Images of testing moved through Jack's head—needles, electrodes, scalpels. He wished he could get out, wished he could run. The doctor insisted that he had the virus, and at that moment Jack wished that he did. If only he could vanish like Aubrey. Or if he had strength like Laura's he could break the leather restraints.

Eastman returned with a short wheeled cart. He opened a lower drawer and pulled out a scope for looking in Jack's eyes.

"Do you know why it's called the Erebus virus?" Eastman

said casually as he peered down at Jack's eye.

"Why?"

"It's Greek," Eastman answered. "Erebus was the son of Chaos. You probably know about Chaos. Darkness. 'The earth was without form and void' and all of that kind of thing." He set down the scope and made a note on his paper.

"What about sicknesses?" Eastman continued. "The flu? Chicken pox? Bronchitis?"

"Nothing," Jack said. He wanted to be brave, to stare confidently into the face of danger, but he knew that he must look terrified.

Dr. Eastman clipped something on Jack's fingertip, and then inserted a thermometer into his ear. "Anyway, Erebus was the son of Chaos, and most people think of him as the god of shadow. But, the reason that his name was chosen for the virus is because Erebus represents the place between earth and Hades."

Jack forced himself to smile. "That's supposed to be comforting?"

"Not comforting, really," Dr. Eastman said, taking the clip off Jack's finger. "It's just interesting. People with the Erebus virus are really on the border of humanity—they have strange side effects that make them almost inhuman."

Jack stared at the ceiling. The army doctors thought of the prisoners as inhuman. That explained a lot.

"Of course, it's not all flashy," Dr. Eastman said. He was

looking at his papers again. "I'll bet you a dollar that when your symptoms manifest they're not going to be anything ostentatious. Everyone talks about the big ones—the boy who can run incredibly fast or the girl who can yell at a very high decibel range. But ninety-five percent of people can only do useless things. We had a boy in here just the other day that had hot breath. Imagine that. We measured it and he got up to four hundred degrees Celsius."

Jack nodded. He wanted to ask a question, but his throat suddenly felt very dry and his chest was tight with anxiety.

"On the other hand, we had one of the most amazing young ladies come through this week, too. Simply marvelous. And she'd manifested years ago."

Dr. Eastman was quiet for a moment, fiddling with his paperwork.

"What are the bad symptoms?" Jack finally said. "How serious is this?"

"That's another strange thing," Eastman said. "The negative symptoms are as varied as the so-called good ones. And sometimes the combination is just terrible. I read the case of a boy who had amazing strength—they estimated he could lift ten to twelve times his weight—but he also had brittle bones. Ever since he manifested he'd been in a wheelchair. Imagine that—being able to do something amazing, but knowing that doing it could kill you."

"Is this going to kill me?"

"I'm not going to lie," Eastman said, looking down at Jack. "We don't know. The nation's top scientists are working on it right now. But we have very little data, and certainly not enough to determine a life expectancy."

He bent down to one of the drawers and came back up with a handful of brightly colored wires.

"Now," he said. "We're going to see if we can't get you to manifest."

"Will it hurt?" Jack tugged against the restraints, but his arms felt heavy and sluggish.

"Oh," Eastman said, attaching the first wire to Jack's forehead. "It'll hurt terribly. That's why I asked about recent injuries. Erebus manifests during periods of intense trauma."

Jack fought against the leather straps, kicking his legs and rattling the gurney.

"It's no use," Eastman said. He tapped the IV bag, which was now three-quarters empty. "You've been given a mild sedative so you won't hurt yourself. Or us."

He attached a second and third wire to Jack's temples, and a fourth to the side of his neck.

Another two medics came in from the hallway. One began removing Jack's shoes and the other used a pair of shears to cut away Jack's shirt.

"Don't I have to consent to this?" Jack said, panicked. "You can't just do this to me."

Eastman looked down into Jack's eyes. "In the event that

you actually have already manifested a symptom, but have been hiding it from me, now would be the time to say it."

"I swear I haven't," Jack said. The medics were applying the wires all over Jack's body now. "But there has to be some other way. This is crazy."

Dr. Eastman tapped himself on the head. "I almost forgot something." He gestured around at the room and then pointed at the ceiling. "This room is specially designed for this kind of testing, by which I mean that the room is designed to kill you if you should decide to attack someone. Above the acoustical tiles are high pressure valves that will drown you in seconds, and at any time we can use any one of these wires to deliver a strong enough shock to stop your heart." He smiled. "So, let's not have any trouble, okay?"

User: SusieMusie

Mood: Mellow

Holy hell, get ready for a landmark piece of information: Sara doesn't think I'm pretty. She even repeated it about a hundred times today. Erica seems to agree (duh). I often wonder why I even hang out with them. I often wonder about a lot of the stupid things I do.

TWENTY-SEVEN

THERE WERE MEN IN THE storage room. They were trying to be quiet, but Aubrey could hear the rattle of gear, the light squeak of a boot on linoleum.

She couldn't see anything besides a sliver of light. Every muscle in her body felt heavy, like she was wearing one of those lead blankets at the dentist's office. She tried to disappear and was immediately overcome with a panic attack—she felt like she couldn't breathe, like her chest was sinking in on itself.

What was she thinking coming here? How was she supposed to save Jack? She couldn't smuggle him out with her—she could barely hide herself.

She heard a box being pushed away, scraping against the floor. She heard a cupboard open, then another.

She concentrated on staying invisible. It took all her effort.

Her cupboard flew open and she was staring down the muzzle of a rifle. She let out a yelp and closed her eyes to stop herself from crying. This was so stupid.

But the soldier didn't see her. He closed her cupboard and moved on.

She reappeared, and a small wave of relaxation moved over her.

Tears came, but she didn't let herself make a sound.

She would go back—sneak into her tent the way that she'd come. With any luck, she hadn't slept through evening roll call. She had no idea how long she'd been in the cupboard, but with the pain in her back it felt like days.

"All clear in room 118," a voice said. "Over."

A radio sparked back with the command, "Leave a man there and move to the next room. She has to be nearby."

Aubrey's stomach dropped.

She'd been invisible from the moment she'd left the tents to the moment she'd climbed into the cupboard. No one could have seen her. It was impossible.

Unless—was she slipping? Could she not control it when she'd been so exhausted outside?

This was so stupid. She thought she could just do whatever she wanted, go wherever she wanted. And she couldn't. Someone had seen her. The alarm had been for her.

Had the helicopter been searching for her?

She swallowed the remaining water from the shampoo bottle, and quickly ate the last two granola bars, trying to cram as much energy into her body as possible. Then she disappeared.

Aubrey didn't worry about being quiet now. She was only concerned with speed. She pushed the cupboard door open and immediately saw the two soldiers. One was standing by a shelf, absently looking at some of the documents. The other was in the doorway, looking out. She'd have to squeeze past him.

She took a deep, painful breath, and stood. She wanted to run, but knew she was too unsteady on her feet. She moved past the first man easily, and then had to press her back against the wall to slide past the second man and out of the room.

The radio crackled to life. "Private Hickman, she's in the hallway. Over."

Aubrey froze. Someone could see her.

The soldier in the doorway yanked his radio to his mouth. "Where? I don't see anyone. Over."

"She's right in front of you, Private."

Aubrey ran, and the radio squawked behind her, shouting orders.

"Turn left. She's running toward Corridor Two. Over."

The sound of boots on the hard linoleum clattered behind her.

How was this happening? She sucked at the air, trying to

get a full breath but her body was fighting her.

She couldn't remember how she'd gotten here, or how she was supposed to get out. The two soldiers were barreling toward her from one direction, but the other way looked to be a blank hall, with no doors on either side.

The alarm turned on, buzzing and shaking her brain. Her vision instantly went blurry again.

She stopped, her back against the wall, as the soldiers approached. They were running, charging after an unseen enemy, and it was easy for her to reach out one foot and trip the first man. He tumbled to the floor, and the second soldier collided with him, falling in a jumble.

"That was her!" the radio screamed. "She's right there."

Aubrey turned and ran back the other direction. Her feet were unsteady beneath her, and she wasn't running nearly as fast as she could normally.

A door opened ahead of her, and three men stepped out. They were plainly army, but weren't dressed in the full combat gear of the other soldiers. They looked administrative. Aubrey ran past them without giving them a second look.

She turned another corner. This hall was long, lined with doors on each side. At the far end was a large round disc, but also an "exit" sign.

Aubrey didn't wait, didn't think. She was going to get outside where she could find a place to hide. She needed to be back with the thousands of teenagers in the tents and to blend in where she'd be just another face in the crowd.

And then she remembered where she'd seen the giant black disc. They'd been in the guard towers when she'd been designated a Negative. Four towers, four discs, all pointed at the small steel cage.

And now this one was pointed at her.

Aubrey was knocked to her knees by a sudden blast of sound. It hit her like a massive weight—louder than dancing in front of the speakers at the homecoming dance, louder than when she and Nicole had gone to that concert in Salt Lake. This noise seemed to shake her bones, to rattle and bruise every organ in her body, and to sap the energy out of her.

She clapped her hands over her ears, but it didn't help. She couldn't move. She couldn't do anything but try to shield her head with her arms.

Her vision was going, fading into darkness, and a splitting headache made her want to puke.

She reappeared. It was the only thing she could do to relieve her pain. It didn't help. She was flattened to the floor by a beam of sound.

When it finally stopped, she was huddled on the linoleum, completely blind.

The sound of running boots echoed in the hallway.

TWENTY-EIGHT

DR. EASTMAN'S VOICE CAME OVER a speaker. "We will begin the procedure in thirty seconds."

Jack wanted to scream for help, but the medics had put a rubber mouth guard between Jack's teeth and he could hardly make a sound.

"Ten seconds," Eastman said. His voice was calm, even pleasant.

Jack kicked against his restraints, shook his head in the brace, but nothing was going to work.

"Five, four, three, two—"

Electricity shot through Jack's body, pulsing with a pain that was both an acute burning and a dull ache, sharply stinging but throbbing slowly and heavily. The pain rested in his joints, and he felt overwhelming nausea, not in his stomach but in his limbs—like if he moved anything he'd throw up. He jammed his eyes shut, clenched his teeth on the mouth guard.

He couldn't feel his legs or his hands, and his chest heaved as though his lungs were being ripped upward. His ribs were on fire—it felt like they would burn through his flesh.

And suddenly his legs were back with an overpowering prickling, itching sensation as though he were covered in biting ants. He struggled madly against the leather straps, desperate to brush the insects from his legs. He writhed on the table, his back arching against the gurney and his muscles so tense he knew they'd tear.

The electricity now moved to his face and head, needles of pain digging under his teeth and scraping down his ear canal. The ants were on the back of his neck, their sharp teeth burrowing into his skull and spine. Jack tried to scream but the mouth guard felt enormous and oppressive, and he knew it was cutting off his air, pushing down into his throat.

Then the electricity stopped. Pain still crushed in his head and limbs, but the ants were gone and the sharpness faded into a blunt, slow throbbing.

The room was filled with light, bright enough that Jack didn't dare open his eyes. The door must have opened—he could hear the voices of several men and women. They were all talking too loudly and his brain felt too muddled; he couldn't figure out what they were talking about.

"All done," Dr. Eastman said, the loudspeaker thundering

as though the volume itself could knock down the cinder-block walls.

As if on cue, there was a tremendous shaking. Jack winced, expecting the ceiling to come crashing down. But the vibration stopped, replaced by an intense combination of body odor, cologne, and shampoo. Jack could just barely stop himself from throwing up.

"So," Dr. Eastman shouted, no longer on the loudspeaker but in the room. "How do you feel?" His footsteps thumped on the ground like an elephant's as he moved to the gurney and removed Jack's mouth guard.

"Can you turn down the lights?" Jack said.

There was more thumping, and then the brilliant flood lights were dimmed. Jack opened his eyes a tiny crack.

"That better?"

Jack nodded as much as the head brace would let him. The lights overhead were completely off, but the room still seemed to glow. He could see through the mirror now: at least ten people sat at computers, and as he watched them he noticed that it was them he could hear talking. "Tell me how you feel," Eastman said, once again pulling up the folding chair and sitting beside the gurney. There was still so much noise in the room that Eastman was bellowing to be heard above it.

"How do you think?" Jack said. His own words echoed in his head.

"Just tell me," Eastman said. "The sooner we're done here

the sooner you can go get cleaned up."

Jack tried to pinpoint any symptoms, but he still felt completely overwhelmed with pain, with noise, with the irritation of the leather restraints, with the rubber taste in his mouth. He couldn't concentrate.

"I feel like crap," Jack said.

"Be more specific."

"My head is killing me."

"Where does it hurt?" Eastman said. He removed the brace around Jack's neck.

"All over," Jack said. "My head and face mostly. And I think I'm going to be sick."

"That's fine," Eastman said with a smile. "We have a mop."

"I don't have the virus," Jack said, closing his eyes again. "I'm hurting because you almost electrocuted me. But I don't feel like I can do anything else."

"Oh, you've got it," Eastman said. "They're tracking it in the other room. You're manifesting all right."

"Can you turn off the microphone?" Jack said. "And stop shouting? Seriously, my head is killing me."

"What do you mean?"

"What do you think I mean?" Jack snapped. "You just fried my brain and now you're yelling at me. Can't we just have it a little quieter?"

Eastman frowned and then stepped out the door. Jack

didn't see him go into the room behind the mirror, and no one turned off the loudspeaker. Jack could hear the people inside talking about him—something about his brain activity.

Dr. Eastman returned to Jack's gurney with a book. He opened it, seemingly at random, and held it up.

"Can you read this?" Eastman said. "Army Field Manual. Just start at the top."

Jack looked at the page for a moment and then began reading. His mouth felt dry and swollen. "An emphasis on asymmetric means to offset United States military capability has emerged as a significant trend among potential threats and become an integral part of—"

Eastman stopped him and then moved across the room, his back against the wall. He turned to a new page. "Now read."

Jack squinted. "Stability operations in an urban environment require offensive, defensive, and support operations, combined with other tasks unique to each stability operation. Army forces conduct—"

"Extraordinary," Eastman said, closing the book. "Hold on."

Jack rolled his eyes. "Where else am I going to go?"

A moment later the chatter in the other room stopped and Jack peered over to see Dr. Eastman standing on the other side of the mirror.

"You can see me?" Eastman said.

"Yes."

"Repeat what I say." He held up the book and read from the table of contents. "Urban Outlook. Urban Environment. Urban Threat. Contemplating Urban Operations."

Jack closed his eyes. It was all he could do now to not vomit. "Urban Outlook. Urban Environment. Urban Threat. Contemplating Urban Operations."

"Jack?"

Jack cracked one eye open and looked at the doctor, who was grinning broadly.

"You think you don't have the virus?" Eastman said. "The room you're in is dark. I can barely see your silhouette. And you're hearing me through soundproof glass. I'm not using a microphone."

"What?"

"Your brain," he said. "These readings—they're off the charts. It's incredible."

TWENTY-NINE

"I'M GOING TO ASK YOU some questions," the soldier said to Laura. He had a large yellow legal pad on the table in front of him, and was scribbling in handwriting she couldn't read.

"Sure," Laura said, keeping her voice calm. She didn't want to appear overeager. The medicine helped with that—it mellowed her out, but it also dulled her senses. She needed to be on her A-game.

He set down his pen and then looked into her eyes. There was a coldness to him, and it made her want to behave even more warmly. But she held back. *Stay calm. Don't act so quick to please.*

"We haven't been able to contact your parents," he said.

Of course not, she thought. Her parents had their own jobs to do.

She paused, trying to think of how to respond. They weren't even her parents. They were more like her caretakers. Her trainers. Her teachers. She'd grown to respect them, but it was never a loving relationship.

"I'm sure they're okay," she finally said, doing her best impression of a stiff upper lip.

"Aren't you concerned?" he asked.

"Sure, I'm concerned," Laura answered, now going for indignant. "They're my parents. But my dad is good at hunting, and my mom is from Montana. They probably went north."

"Without you?"

"I got out of Denver to escape the attacks," she said. "When I left—well, when I left we sort of knew it might be a long time before we saw one another again."

She wasn't sounding sympathetic enough. She was too uncaring. Too detached.

"They would just send their daughter off with her friends?"

"I—" she started, and then stopped, trying to bring tears to her eyes. They didn't come. "I wasn't the best daughter."

He picked up his pen, but didn't write anything—just twirled it slowly in his fingers. "So you left against their permission?"

"It wasn't like that," she said, and attempted a weak smile. "I didn't run away. We . . . Well, we had gotten to the point where they knew that I was going to do what I was going to do."

This interview wasn't going how it was supposed to. She was coming across as too hard. Too rebellious. That wasn't going to help her, and she needed to fix it. She wished she could cry.

He opened his mouth to speak, but she interrupted him.

"What's happened to Denver? Is it safe?"

"You have friends there you're worried about?"

"Of course I do."

"Are you enrolled in school?"

"UC–Denver," Laura said. "First semester. I was only there a week before the attacks started and the campus shut down."

He tapped the pen on the pad now, but still didn't write anything. She couldn't read him. Was this an interrogation? Did they suspect her? Or were they interviewing all the Lambdas?

"Is there any way you can find out if my friends are okay?" she pressed, trying to look hopeful—even desperate. She'd been part of the team that had taken down Mile High Stadium, and she hoped the city was burning. But that couldn't show on her face. She wasn't as good as Alec, but she knew how to lie.

"I'll try to have someone find out for you," he replied.

"Thank you."

"Now, on to another subject," he said, and leaned back in his chair. "How long have you been aware of your strength?"

She felt a sense of relief. She was ready for this question.

"Not long. I first noticed it around graduation."

"And did you go to a doctor?"

She shook her head. "I never felt sick—I felt great. Plus, it didn't come on all at once. It grew a little every day. At first I just thought I was in good shape—that it was finally summer and my body was all excited to be outdoors again. By the time that I realized it was more than that, I didn't want to waste time going to the doctor. I was having too much fun. I'd go to Rocky Mountain National Park and run the hikes to the peaks—I mean, flat-out sprint. I've always been active—I did gymnastics and track in high school—so this was perfect. I loved it."

Some of that was true. She had practiced running the peaks, and she had loved the freedom, but her abilities had come on two years before, and she wasn't just running for pleasure. She was running with her "dad" at the bottom of the trail, timing her, over and over again. She'd free-climbed the Keyhole Route of Longs Peak, going early in the season to avoid onlookers. Cold and ice had blistered her skin, but she pushed through.

She wasn't going to let this temporary quarantine camp stop her only three weeks into the attacks. She'd trained too long and too hard.

The soldier across from her leaned forward and put both arms on the table. "And at no time did you ever think 'this is abnormal—I should go see a doctor'?"

Laura laughed, and she knew she nailed it—warm and pleasant, the all-American girl. "If you could suddenly do anything you wanted to—be any Olympic athlete you wanted to be—would you stress about what was wrong with you? Or would you enjoy it?"

He smiled at that. She'd finally made him smile.

"One last question for now," he said. "You were living the dream, and then you got picked up by some local police and put in our flimsy warehouse. Why didn't you ever try to escape?"

"I never wanted to escape," she said, her face fading from gleeful to somber. "I saw what happened to Denver. I've watched the news. You're the good guys, right? Why would I fight you?"

THIRTY

AUBREY WOKE UP IN A large room. She was lying in something like a hospital bed, with metal handholds on the sides, but the rest of the place looked oddly . . . homey. The sixteen beds all had clean, brand-new quilts, and each was next to a dresser with a lamp. She was the only teenager in there. At her feet, dropping a syringe into a red plastic box, was a man dressed in a lab coat.

"Aubrey Parsons?" he asked.

She ached all over, and her sight wasn't quite right. Something heavy was wrapped around her ankle.

"Aubrey?" he asked again.

She wanted to disappear, but for some reason her head felt cloudy, like she couldn't remember how to do it.

"Who are you?" she finally asked.

"Dr. Eastman. I have to say, you put on quite a show."

"Where am I?"

For the first time, she noticed that her wrists were bound to the sides of the hospital bed with heavy Velcro straps. Even if she could disappear, she'd be stuck here. An IV was in her left arm, connected to a bag of yellowish liquid. Electrodes dotted her fingers, arms, chest, and head.

The door was metal, and thick, with a small, square window indented and bolted into the steel.

"You're not far from where you were apprehended. I'd ask how you managed to get past the testing center, but I think that's fairly obvious."

Her eyes began to focus on the far wall. Despite the soft lighting and comfortable furniture, the walls were bare white cinder block. And there were cameras—as she craned her neck to look around the room she saw at least six.

"Yes," he said. "You're being watched. Does that bother you?"

She'd failed. She was captured, being interrogated, and she hadn't been able to do anything to help Jack. Dr. Eastman glanced down at his clipboard.

"Why did you run?"

"I didn't know what was going to happen to me," she said, her voice hoarse.

He nodded. "You realize that it doesn't look good for you."

"What doesn't look good?"

"You ran from the army when they entered your town—"

"They shot my homecoming date," she snapped.

He ignored her. "And when you were detained, you faked your test results. Then once you were in the quarantine area—spreading the virus in a clean zone, mind you—you escaped and tried to infiltrate an army facility."

She stared at the ceiling. This wasn't how any of this was supposed to happen. She was supposed to sneak in and sneak out. She was supposed to find Jack.

She was supposed to be back in Mount Pleasant enjoying high school, in a world that wasn't collapsing around her.

She was supposed to be with Jack.

"Did you do tests on me?" she asked, fighting to hold back tears.

"Yes," he answered. "Extensively."

She let out a long slow breath. She didn't like Dr. Eastman.

"Do I have a brain tumor?"

He laughed—he actually laughed. She wanted to slap him.

"No," he said. "You don't have a brain tumor. You have the Erebus virus. Interestingly, there's quite a pocket of infected people in your area. Well, that's not interesting—there're infected people everywhere—but your town seems to have produced some of the more potent presentations of the virus."

"What does that mean?"

"It means you can do incredible things," he said, with

genuine wonder in his voice. "It means that you just escaped a quarantine zone that was designed specifically to look for people like you, and then you snuck into a highly confidential military research facility. You evaded capture for hours. You made highly trained soldiers look like fools."

She snorted. "Someone propped open the door with a rock."

"I'm told," he said, "that corporal is now a private."

Aubrey didn't care about that. She'd done all the things that he'd said, and yet she'd been caught. She hadn't found Jack, let alone freed him.

"What was Nate Butler?" she asked.

"Excuse me?"

"Nate Butler. What was he?"

He flipped through the papers on his clipboard while she continued to stare at the cement ceiling.

"Nate Butler was killed trying to escape."

"He was my date."

"Were you aware—"

"No," she snapped. "I wasn't aware of any of this. I wasn't aware of a virus or that there were any others or that the army was allowed to tie teenage girls down just because they're sick. Have I been arrested?"

Dr. Eastman sighed, but she refused to look at him.

"Aubrey," he said. "You don't get it. You're a medical miracle."

She tried to disappear again, but something seemed to be stopping her. Not that it would do any good. "I'm a medical miracle that you don't trust. I'm a medical miracle that you're going to lock up."

"Not necessarily."

"What was Nate?"

"We don't know," he said. "It's next to impossible to identify a patient's symptoms postmortem. He was killed at the scene, and all we have are witness reports."

"Then how do you know he was so 'potent'?" She finally glanced over at him, convinced that her anger would elicit some response. But he was completely calm.

"Aside from the fact that he killed three soldiers and injured a fourth?"

She opened her mouth, but nothing came out. She'd seen Nate do it, of course—she'd seen him tackle those men—but it had never sunk in what he'd really done.

"I wasn't referring specifically to Nate, though," Dr. Eastman continued. "I believe you are friends with a boy named Jack Cooper?"

"He's Negative," she said quickly.

"Wrong again. He thought he was Negative, but he was carrying the virus. While his symptoms are perhaps not as showy as yours, he's really quite amazing."

"Where is he?" she asked, her voice softer.

"He's in a room that looks identical to this one. He's just fine."

"What are his . . . symptoms?"

"You can ask him yourself, soon enough, if all goes well."

"What does that mean?"

Dr. Eastman changed the subject. "Tell me about your relationship with Nicole Samuelson."

"What do you mean? We were friends."

"I understand you had an arrangement with her?"

Aubrey's stomach sank. Nicole had ratted her out. If Aubrey hadn't been caught down here, they would have come to get her at the tent.

"I was her spy," Aubrey said.

"Just around the school?"

"Why are you interrogating me?"

"It's for your own good."

"Yes, it was just around the school. Parties, too. Just normal stuff."

"And what did you get in return?"

This was so stupid. "Nicole was popular," Aubrey said. "She invited me to things. She helped me get friends."

Dr. Eastman leaned forward. "Let me tell you something. And I can tell you this because either you'll one day end up with a confidential clearance or you won't leave this building until none of this matters. Yes, Nicole helped you get friends, and she did an amazing job of it."

"I know she did."

"Nicole has the virus," he said. "It gives her kidney problems."

"What?" That couldn't be true. "She must not have known."

"Oh, she knew," the doctor said. "In fact, according to her statements, she's known she's had the virus longer than any patient we've examined. Nicole has the unique ability to control the pheromones of the people around her. When Nicole made you popular, what she was doing was, very literally, making people attracted to you. When she shunned a student, when she kicked them out of the popular clique, she literally—chemically—made people feel disgusted by them."

It couldn't be true. Nicole wasn't a freak, not like Aubrey. Nicole was so . . . perfect. Even with her sickness.

But it had to be true. Boys were paying attention to Aubrey back at school. They were fighting over her. That had never happened before this year. Aubrey had once joked to Nicole that it was like a switch had been flipped and—bam—she was suddenly pretty and popular and desirable.

And that's exactly what had happened. A switch had been flipped. Nicole had flipped it.

Which meant that it was all a lie. Aubrey *wasn't* pretty or popular or desirable. She was just regular old Aubrey. Plain, trailer-trash Aubrey.

Dr. Eastman was watching her, studying her.

"Tell me about what you can do," he finally said.

There was no point in hiding it now. Nicole had obviously explained part of it, and Aubrey had no chance of escaping anyway. So she laid it all out.

Dr. Eastman listened carefully. He took the occasional note, but mostly he just watched her.

"Can I ask you a question?" Aubrey said after she'd explained everything she knew.

"Sure," he said. "I don't know if I can answer it."

"How did you find me? The soldiers in the hall couldn't see me—only the person on the radio."

He smiled, and leaned back in his chair. "You were right about one thing when you described your invisibility. It's not a physical power: you don't bend light or turn transparent. Your brain tells my brain that you're not here. In a way, it's a form of mind control."

"That's what I assumed. But I still don't see how you found me."

"Because your brain only projects that message to people nearby. We'll need to do tests to see how far it projects, and what kind of barriers it can go through, but suffice it to say: the team watching security monitors was too far away, and to them it looked like you were right there. Same thing with the helicopters outside—they kept thinking they saw you, but as soon as they'd get close your brain would erase you from them."

It took a minute to sink in. That wasn't something she and Nicole had ever tested.

"You're a lucky girl," Dr. Eastman said. "We were getting

a sniper into position to take you down before you entered the building. You got out of his line of sight before he could take the shot."

"I could have been dead."

"Many times over," he said, his voice lighter than the subject should require. "But think of it this way: you should have been shot a hundred times during the last fifteen hours. Any normal person would have been. They wouldn't have even escaped the quarantine zone, let alone gotten all the way down in this building and then evaded capture for hours."

He smiled a cold, curious grin. "Aubrey Parsons, you are remarkable."

She didn't know what to say. If she was remarkable she would have achieved something. "So," he said, "the big question—the final question—is this: Why did you do it?"

Aubrey paused, not because she thought lying would do her any good, but because she didn't want to get anyone else involved in her problems.

"This is very important," Dr. Eastman urged.

"I promised Jack I'd get him out," she finally said. "I didn't know he was Positive."

"Why was it important to get him out?"

"I thought that was the last question."

"One more."

She sighed. "Because we all thought you'd be dissecting the Positives in here. That's why I faked my test result.

You know—military testing, dissection, like in the movies. I thought he was a Negative, and I wanted to save him."

Dr. Eastman nodded, and stood up.

"So?" she asked.

"Good answers," he said. "We'll be in touch."

THIRTY-ONE

JACK FINISHED THE TEST, FILLING in the last bubble on the scan sheet.

The room was filled with the chalky, rough sound of graphite on paper, of the repetitive and heightened heartbeats of the kids around him, of the deep, jagged breaths Matt kept taking, the tap of Nicole's fingernails on her desk as she thought.

He closed his eyes, and he could see them all. Every scratching pencil was like a GPS marker. He knew the exact direction of each one, the exact distance. It was like he was looking down on the room like a sheet of graph paper, and he could plot every student on it.

At least he wasn't throwing up anymore. For a while that was all he could do. Eating so much as a piece of bread was a nauseating assault. He tasted everything, every tiny bit of improperly mixed flour, all the mold spores that were lurking inside, not even visible yet. Even water was a disgusting slime of minerals and oils.

He could hear everything. He could taste everything. He could see everything.

He could control it better all the time; he could focus his concentration on something—staring at the cinder-block wall and counting the dimples in its texture, or looking at his fingerprints as if they were under a microscope—and that helped to block out the unwanted senses. At least now he could sit in a room with other people and not get a headache from the noise. He could have the lights on without feeling blinded.

They'd moved him to a nice dorm room, with a real bed and a dresser and a lamp. It reminded him of going to the department store: rows of bedroom sets of all different styles. This entire facility seemed to have been constructed in the last few weeks; he wondered if the army had raided an Ikea to build the dorms.

"Pencils down," the man in the suit said. He didn't appear to be military. Was he FBI? A doctor? They'd gone through three tests already today: one that checked basic school stuff, math and science and reading, one that was more about problem solving, and now this third one was an endless true-or-false personality test: "At times I feel like swearing," "I think I would like the work of a librarian," "I am sure I get a raw deal from life." Five hundred sixty-seven statements like that. When Jack finished and laid his pencil on the desk, his brain felt like mud.

As the man walked up and down the rows of desks, he seemed nervous, like he hated being so close to the kids. Jack wanted to jump, just to make him flinch. But really, Jack was one of the people in the room who couldn't hurt anyone. He could just watch and listen and smell and taste.

And touch—ugh. No blankets were soft enough for him. Everything felt like sandpaper.

With the sheaf of questionnaires in his arms, the man turned back to the group.

"You'll be meeting with me in the next few days to discuss the results of these tests." Then he turned and left.

"Can't wait," said Josi, just as the door closed.

"What a wuss," another boy said. "He acted like we were going to light him on fire. Can anyone in here do that?"

Several people laughed. Everyone knew what their abilities were now, and they were slowly getting used to them.

"Jack," Matt called out from across the room, as Jack climbed back onto his bed. "Did you notice anything? Any Sherlock Holmes action to explain what that was all about?"

Matt asked Jack that after almost every person came in the room, but Jack never knew what he was supposed to be looking for.

"Deodorant, cologne," Jack answered. "He had dandruff and looked like he bit his fingernails. Maybe if I was smarter I could put all of that together into a brilliant psychological profile."

"I saw something," Josi said.

Josi had one of the few powers in the group that Jack envied. A sort of photographic memory, combined with instant comprehension. It sounded like the kind of thing that would come in handy during a math class back home.

Everyone perked up. Josi had become a sort of de facto leader.

"We've all been classified," she said. "I saw it on his paperwork as he was going through our names."

"What do you mean, *classified*?" someone asked.

"The army—or the government, or whoever—has categorized us all according to our usefulness," Josi said.

"Usefulness for what?" Matt asked, sitting on top of his desk. He didn't sound pleased.

"Military use. They have a rating system to show how beneficial we'd be if we were in the army."

"What the hell?" a girl said. "I'm fifteen years old."

Josi shrugged. "I'm just saying what I saw."

Jack called out, "So what is it? What are we?"

"We all have something called a Lambda rating. I don't know what Lambda means—that wasn't on the chart. Jack, you're a Lambda 4T, which means you'd be best suited for tactical intelligence, which I think means reconnaissance. I'm a Lambda 4O—that's operational intelligence. I'm not sure what that means."

"What about me?" Matt asked.

"You had an asterisk," she said. "That means 'currently uncategorized.'"

"Figures," he said, annoyed. "Not much call for basketball in the army." Matt had been diagnosed with a very mild form of telekinesis: without realizing it, he'd been guiding all his throws by gently nudging the path of the ball.

Jack laughed. "Think of how well you could throw a grenade."

"And that's probably it," Matt said.

"Laura," Josi said, "you were the only five—a Lambda 5D, which means Direct Weapon Use."

"Nice," one of the guys said. "Kickin' ass and taking names."

Laura only smiled.

Josi went through the rest of the list. There were a lot of twos—designated as "Civilian Use" —and a couple of ones— "No practical use." Eddie, with the hot breath, got that one, and he was pissed. So did a girl who could change something's color by touching it. She laughed it off and said she was glad—she saw a life ahead of her as an interior designer.

The threes were all logistics—a kid who could fix anything mechanical, another who was some kind of human calculator, and a handful more.

The fours were all intelligence. Nicole got lumped in there, same as Jack: Lambda 4T. Little Cesar Carbajal, the kid who could instantly count anything he could see, was also put in intelligence, which seemed to make Eddie even angrier.

The fives were the weapons. Josi said this was broken down into several categories, but the only one in the room was Laura.

It was a 3L, a sort of healer, who asked the question on everyone's minds. "Does this mean we're all going to be drafted?"

"We're too young to be drafted," Jack said. "Well, most of us are. Who here is eighteen or older?"

Laura and Josi were the only ones who raised their hands.

"See?" Jack said. "And girls don't have to sign up for selective service. We're not going to get drafted."

"Maybe it's in case we want to join up?" Laura said.

Eddie shook his head. "Who would want to join up after this?"

"I don't blame them," Laura said. "They said that the terrorists have this same virus, and they're using it against our country—against America. I'm not just going to go back to school and the mall and pretend we're not at war."

"After what they did to you?" Eddie pressed.

"Don't you think they were right to be nervous?" she

said. "They didn't know if we were terrorists. I wouldn't trust me, if I were in their shoes. Why do you think they put these GPS trackers on our legs?" Laura pulled her leg up under her and tapped the ankle bracelet.

There was a pause, and then the 3L boy with the strange mechanical affinity pointed to his own bracelet. "They're not GPS trackers."

Everyone in the room looked at him. He was maybe sixteen, and extremely skinny and pale. "I've been messing with it. They're not GPS. They're bombs."

There was a moment of silence, and then the room erupted in noise. Jack had to force himself to lower his hearing, block out the painful sound.

It was Laura who shouted everyone down. "Get a grip, people! Shut up and let the kid talk!"

He looked at her shyly but gratefully. "It's a small explosive charge. Probably not enough to kill you, but it'd take off your foot. If you try to cut through the plastic, it will explode. And it can be detonated remotely."

Eddie glared at Laura. "These are the people who you're giving the benefit of the doubt?"

She stared back. "Yes. If you had a room of people who were potentially terrorists—who were human weapons that you couldn't disarm—wouldn't you take some kind of action to control them?"

Jack didn't want to think about it. Instead he sat back and

tried to block them out. He focused his attention elsewhere. Deodorant and cologne. He could still smell it, fainter, but present. He walked to the door and closed his eyes. The smell seemed to paint a picture in his mind, to leave a trail that filled spaces and marked objects.

The man had left their room and had gone left, his scent leaving a lingering picture of a narrow space—a hallway— before turning . . . was it to the right? Yes. To the right, down another hallway. There was a stronger scent there— a handprint on the wall, then another on a doorknob, and the man entered a large room where his scent spread to fill a much bigger space. Air vents were running through this room, but just churned his smell around, mixing it with the sage and dust of the outside air.

Jack could see it all—or smell it. It was like all his senses were blending together. He knew the shape of the halls by the way the remnants of cologne filled them. Jack knew, without a doubt, that he could walk directly to the man— with his eyes closed.

The man was still there. Jack listened. Water ran through pipes, electrical outlets hummed, as Jack retraced the path from him to the man. He could hear the air ducts in the man's room—small, whirring, and metal, probably vents in the ceiling.

The man was flicking through the papers. He was mark- ing them, the scratch of his pencil—no, a smoother sound; a pen—making notes every few seconds.

There was a sudden buzz and whir, which died down quickly, and soon the man began to type. Jack could hear each keystroke.

A hand touched Jack's shoulder and he started. He spun to see the rest of the kids staring at him.

"What are you doing?" Josi asked.

"Listening," Jack said. "He's grading our tests."

THIRTY-TWO

AUBREY WAS IN THE ROOM for three days, and it slowly filled with people. On the first day she was handcuffed to a desk while she took a full day's worth of handwritten exams. She wasn't sure what the tests indicated, but on the second day a soldier unchained her and let her roam freely around the room.

She didn't know anyone there, but they were all like her. They all took the same tests, they all were looked on with the same level of suspicion. Some tried to be studious and alert. There was a boy at the end of the row who acted like he was in the army—saluting and standing at attention and calling everyone "sir." A girl told Aubrey that he could superheat his body, whatever that meant. She never saw him do it. On the other hand, there was a girl who lay in bed all day and cried.

She never got up for announcements or for meals or for anything, and on the third day an army medic came in and gave her an IV. Aubrey didn't know what that girl's power was.

It was nearly evening; there were no windows in this room, but there was a big clock on the far wall. The door opened, but instead of dinner, it was an officer in a full dress uniform. He was young, maybe only a few years older than Aubrey, and he held a clipboard.

"May I have your attention," he said, his voice shaking the tiniest bit.

Everyone in the room quieted down. Aubrey sat up on the edge of her bed.

"The following people are requested to attend a meeting with Colonel Jensen. If your name is on this list we ask that you please exit this room in an orderly manner. There is no need to bring anything with you."

There were a few murmurs but he ignored them and began to read the names.

"Joel Read, Lambda 5M," the man said, and the boy at the end of the row shouted out a "Sir, yes sir!"

"That's not necessary," the man said, and gestured toward the door. The boy pulled on his shoes quickly and hurried out.

"Michelle Wolf, Lambda 3L?"

A tall girl on the far side of the room stood timidly, hugged a friend, and then left.

"Gary Henson, Lambda 5D?"

"Where are we going?" asked a boy who didn't stand.

"You're Gary?"

"Where are you taking us?"

The man looked back down at his clipboard. "You'll see. Next on the list, Aubrey Parsons, Lambda 4T."

Aubrey's chest tightened, but she tried to ignore it. "Here." She hurried to the door.

There were a lot more teens in the hall than the ones who had just left her room—at least thirty—and they were all heading to the right down a long white corridor.

She was overwhelmed with a strong, terrified desire to disappear. She was in a crowd, surrounded by other kids. She could get away so easily.

Until she ran into another camera. She couldn't go anywhere.

She was breathing rapidly now, wondering what new fate awaited her, and terrified it would be more of the same: more drugs, more danger, more deception.

A hand grabbed her arm, and she spun.

Jack. He looked like he'd lost weight, and the skin around his eyes was dark and sallow. She grabbed him in a bear hug.

"You're okay," she said.

"What are you doing here?"

"I came to get you," she said, pulling away from him enough to look into his eyes. "They caught me."

A voice from the back of the line shouted to keep moving, and Jack let go of her. He took her hand in his, though.

They both tried to speak, talking over each other. Finally, he told her to go ahead.

"They said you really are a Positive—a Lambda, I guess."

"Yep," he said. "I had no idea. It's nothing flashy—not like you—but I have, like, supersenses, or something. I can hear everything, and see for miles, like I'm looking through a telescope. Other stuff, too. It's nuts. How did you get caught?"

Ahead of them, the crowd was leaving the hallway and entering a room through thick steel double doors.

"I'll tell you later," she said, squeezing his hand.

They took seats in the second row, on metal folding chairs that faced a podium and a large TV. Four military personnel stood near the front, and three more who looked like civilians. Or, more likely, FBI or CIA. Or doctors. They were all very serious.

Nicole came in, surrounded by half a dozen boys. Aubrey's stomach immediately turned. She couldn't believe that they'd been so close, and Nicole had never told her. She'd made Aubrey think she was alone, the only freak.

But Nicole could never be a freak. She could be different. She could be infected—a Lambda—but she'd never be a freak. She'd never have people look at her like she wasn't good enough.

Nicole broke through the ring of boys that surrounded her and hurried over to Aubrey.

"Aubs!" she said, excited. "You're here! And with Jack, too."

"Hey, Nicole," Aubrey said. "Looks like you have friends wherever you go."

THIRTY-THREE

THE OFFICER AT THE FRONT cleared his throat loudly and Laura sat up a little straighter in her chair.

"Please settle down," the man said as he waited for the stragglers to find their seats. He didn't look like the type of person who was used to having to ask twice.

"My name is Colonel Jensen. You undoubtedly have questions. In time, they will all be answered. For now, I just want you to know that you've made a very short list. Here in this temporary facility, we're housing more than twenty-six thousand persons between the ages of thirteen and twenty. This is just one of many facilities around Utah, and there are facilities like this all across the nation now. And this virus, which you're all very familiar with, is not limited to just the United States. Countries all across the world are dealing with similar testing regimens. This operation is trying the world's manpower more than any crisis in recent human history.

"This is to say nothing of the war that we're waging here on our own soil against a threat the likes of which the world has never known."

It was all Laura could do not to smile, and she began biting the fingernail on her pinkie to keep her mouth occupied. *The likes of which the world has never known.* She'd been part of it. She'd been in the middle. It was her, and they were all completely oblivious.

If only Alec could see me now.

The officer stepped back from the podium and fiddled for a moment with the TV remote.

"You've been shielded from the news for the past several days. I don't have time to list all of the battles we've been engaged in, but let me illustrate briefly what we're dealing with."

He clicked a button and an image of a bridge, twisted and collapsed, appeared on the screen.

"The Hernando de Soto Bridge," he said. "Where Interstate 40 crosses the Mississippi. The steel beams were melted right off their piers on Tuesday. I'm told that takes 2,600 degrees."

Laura marveled at the thought. None of the teams ever met each other, but she wished she'd been able to see that one in action. Did they create fire? Some kind of energy beam?

He clicked the button again and a picture of a flooding stairwell appeared. "A coordinated attack took place on the pump stations in the New York City subway system. The cause of the damage here is less well understood, but the pumps themselves seem to have deformed in some way."

She bit down harder on her finger. *Deformed.* Deformed was good.

He clicked another. An enormous industrial pier was burning, next to a partially sinking ship. "We don't know what the hell happened here, but it was four days ago, and the fires are still burning."

He turned off the TV and stepped back to the podium. "There are dozens of other photos to show you, but I think you get the idea. This country is under attack. It's coordinated and planned. This week it was the destruction of key transportation hubs. Last week, it was power facilities. Before that it was the commercial sector—shopping malls and restaurants and theme parks."

Someone in the back row raised his hand, and the colonel pointed to him.

"Why would their attacks be coordinated, but so different from week to week?"

Laura stopped chewing on her finger and clenched her jaw.

The colonel nodded for several seconds, as if mulling over the question. "This is just conjecture," he said, "but I think part of it is because it spreads our forces. They attack dams, so we guard dams; then they attack ports, so we defend ports. We're spreading ourselves thin. Second—this is terrorism. Their goal is to hit targets that create terror and cripple the country."

Laura wondered if that really was all they knew, or if it was all he wanted to tell a group of kids. Surely they had to know how the teams operated, how they got their orders. Had things gone to chaos when Alec was killed in the avalanche?

A tall girl raised her hand. "What does this have to do with us?"

Someone else—a woman in a civilian business suit—stepped forward. "The terrorists who are carrying out these attacks are people your age—usually in their late teens, and—"

A guy stood. "Are you accusing us?"

"No," the woman said emphatically, motioning him to sit. "We're not accusing you. I'm with the FBI, and have been working closely with the Centers for Disease Control. Here's their latest information: The terrorists are usually ages seventeen to twenty-one. And they all—everyone we can identify—have the Erebus virus. This virus, unfortunately for you, can attack anyone but will only infect a host during certain stages of brain development. I could spend the day in this room with you, and touch you and share your dishes, and

I'll never become infected—the brain is fully developed during the late teen years and early adulthood, so the virus won't affect me. But at some point in your recent past, the virus infected all of you, and altered the growth of your brains."

She held up her hands, as though to stop an inevitable question.

"You might hate me for saying this, but you're the lucky ones. Everyone in this room has symptoms that can be beneficial and lack symptoms that are too detrimental to function. There are people out there who are so debilitated by this virus that they are only surviving in a hospital."

Jack—the boy who had sat in the cell across from Laura's—raised his hand. "I don't get it. You're saying we're not to blame, we're the healthiest ones—so why do you have us here?"

Another man stepped forward. Judging by the sheer number of pins on his chest, he looked to be the highest-ranking person in the room. He strode to the podium and took it with both hands.

"Because it's time to fight fire with fire. What's your name, son?"

"Jack Cooper."

"Oh, yes. Jack, you've been designated as having hypersensitivity. I'm told that you can see in the dark, can hear through soundproof glass, can read a book from a hundred feet away, and can hear a heartbeat from fifty yards, through a brick wall. Is that correct?"

"More or less," Jack said.

Laura was impressed. That was something that would have been useful on their team.

"Well, imagine the other team has someone like you. Don't you think we'd want to even the odds?"

Jack sat down and the girl next to him leaned into him a little bit.

Laura felt an unexpected pang of loneliness. She'd had friends. Well, Dan had been a friend. Alec had been an arrogant boss. Still, it'd be nice to have someone to talk to.

"Here's the deal," the man said. "You all have a bracelet attached to your legs. That's because, despite our best efforts, we can't confirm one hundred percent that you're not terrorists—or that you won't become terrorists. You are living weapons and our intel suggests the real terrorists are all American citizens—kids, just like you. On the other hand, you can be extremely helpful to our cause.

"So, if you want in, we'll take you. We train you the best we can, but our priority will be getting you out on the battlefield as quickly as possible. This is not because we don't care what happens to you. It's because every day that goes by we are losing this war. We need to get things back under control.

"We can't guarantee your safety, nor can we guarantee you'll even make it out of training and into combat. If you sign up, you'll be treated as a soldier—a special soldier, but a soldier nonetheless. You may or may not have weapons, depending on how much time we have to train you and what role you're assigned. You'll be a part of a team, and not just any team. You'll be a part of the army special forces—the Green Berets.

"Anyone who chooses to be part of this, stand up now. This isn't a draft. If you don't want in, you'll be returned to the rooms you just came from and you'll be under guard until this war is over and we can figure out how best to treat this virus."

There was a long pause, and Laura realized that he was waiting.

A boy near the front stood up, and then the guy next to him. In a moment, five more followed.

She joined them, and even let her smile show through a tiny bit. It was exactly what she'd wanted. She was on the inside.

A few more got to their feet. Others talked.

After a moment, Jack stood, and then the girl beside him did as well.

THIRTY-FOUR

JACK KNELT ON A DARK hillside, watching the broad field in front of him. He was getting better every day, and his eyes almost felt like machines now—like he could tweak the settings, zoom, focus, adjust for lighting, filter through smoke. He was no longer Jack the high school janitor; he was Jack the human telescope, the human microphone, the human sensor.

They were all stupid powers, really. They'd make a terrible comic book. But it was so incredible, so different. So not him.

Beside him on the hillside was a spotter with a headset and a scope, and behind him was an officer. Somewhere in the field a sniper was approaching. The sniper was a Green Beret, among the highest-trained soldiers in the United States

Army, yet Jack knew exactly where he was, had been tracking him for the better part of three hours.

It had taken a while to find him. There was a light breeze that made all the brush sway in the desert wind, and Jack had to struggle to pick the camouflaged man out of the background. Still, he'd done it without binoculars and without night-vision goggles.

Jack was supposed to report the sniper as soon as he saw him, but he was holding out now, just for fun. It was nearing the end of his training.

"Anything?" the spotter beside him finally said. "Time's almost up."

"Are we done?" Jack asked.

"Only if you've found him," the spotter said. "Wait. Are your eyes closed?"

Jack smiled, and cracked open one eye to see the spotter. "Yep. But not to show off."

Jack opened both eyes and clambered to his feet. He was sore from crouching. He was sore from a week of training that he had been completely unprepared for.

"*This* is to show off, though. Sorry." Jack pointed across the desert. "He started somewhere near that small hill. He scooted, facedown, for a good two hundred yards in a south, southeast direction. When he reached that taller brush, he crawled on his hands and knees. He paused for several minutes—I almost thought I'd lost him; you guys are good at controlling your breathing—and then took a lateral course over to that dry creek bed. He ate something there, or maybe just started chewing gum. He also drank, probably a fourth of his canteen. Then he headed up the creek bed on his stomach for a long time, at least an hour. Then he came out, and he's trying to get into position now to take the shot."

The spotter looked stunned. "You did that with your eyes closed?"

"There was too much movement out there in the wind. Every bush and little tree looked like a strobe light each time a gust of wind shook their leaves. So, I closed my eyes and listened and smelled. Our sniper has a pretty strong deodorant, and I think he's got moleskin on some blisters—some kind of foot ointment."

The officer, who had been quiet up to this point, stepped forward. "You're not supposed to be playing games. You were supposed to identify him as soon as you saw—smelled—him."

"I told you when I first found him. Besides, I'm not going to get any better if you keep giving me easy tasks like 'find the guy in the bushes.'"

"Well, Lambda, your training is almost over. You've been an exemplary recruit but I'm concerned about your abilities to follow orders."

"It was just a—"

"You're impressive, Lambda," the officer said, "but there's a hell of a lot more to soldiering than finding enemy snipers.

I'd advise you to get your head together. Start calling your commanders 'sir' and learn a little bit of decorum. Otherwise, you're going to get yourself or someone else killed. Do I make myself clear?"

"Yes, sir," Jack said.

"Good. We have one final test for you. No showing off this time. It's important."

THIRTY-FIVE

ALEC STOOD IN A LONG line of people. At the front it was organized and single file, but the farther back it went the more it became a mob. The desert sand bit at his face, but he ignored it. After three hours of standing and shoving he was finally nearing the fence, and the steel-and-barbed-wire passage that left the quarantine zone.

He was worried that someone would recognize him here: he'd gone through twenty-three girls in the camp, looking for cell phones and then cell phone chargers and maps and any other contraband he could talk them out of. Only four of them had anything to scrounge, and most of it was useless. Of the three phones he'd found, two worked, and just one managed to get a weak signal all the way out here.

He'd spent the rest of his time moving from tent to tent,

trying to remember the name of each girl in case he ran into her again. To make it easier on himself he'd used the same fourth-grade story each time, but there were a hundred little lies—"Oh, you went to Hawthorne Elementary?" "Yeah, I totally remember that Christmas party with the Hawaiian theme," "Mrs. Staheli was the worst!" Alec could be caught in any of those lies, or even caught stumbling over the names: Emily, Heather, Jenny, Kara, Aubrey . . . so many of them. He was an expert at creating fictional memories, not retaining real ones.

The line moved slowly forward, but he still couldn't see what was going on ahead of him.

He'd have to rejoin a group—a new group, since Laura and Dan were as good as dead. They were dead to him, anyway. Traitors. They'd abandoned him.

He wondered, for the first time in a long time, what had happened to the Glen Canyon Dam. It had to have been a total loss. Probably not the loss of life he'd hoped for, but definitely destructive to the power supply. He wondered how Hoover Dam had fared, downstream.

He also wondered, not for the first time, how many of his teams were still in action. In a way, Alec's release from the quarantine today made him nervous. Did that mean the tide had turned? Had the teams been captured? Had the attacks slowed? The little news he'd been able to read on the smartphone seemed to indicate that everything was still moving according to plan. The attacks weren't as focused as he'd prefer, but that's because he was here and not giving orders. In that event, all teams knew they should look for targets of opportunity. Even if they were only burning down an apartment building, or knocking over power lines, they still could do major damage.

The line moved slowly forward, and after another fifteen minutes of dry desert wind, he got to the table by the door. A soldier was seated, flanked by two more. Two guard towers looked on, thirty yards to each side.

"Put your hand on the rectangle," the man said, his voice monotone and dull.

Alec placed his left hand—the one that wasn't broken—on the mark, and the man at the table inspected Alec's wristband.

He consulted his paperwork, and compared his photo to Alec's face. Then he rattled off a memorized speech without bothering to make eye contact.

"Your test results show no manifestations of the Erebus virus. The US Army, your government, and the people of the United States thank you for your patience with this quarantine process. While we know you were severely inconvenienced, we hope you understand it was for your safety and the safety of your fellow Americans."

He snipped the bracelet off Alec's wrist with a pair of shears, and then replaced it with another—nearly identical, but with a barcode and the word "HEALTHY" printed in capital letters.

"You must wear this bracelet at all times," he continued, cinching it tightly onto Alec's arm. "If it is ever removed, you will be returned to a quarantine center and retested for the virus. Are we clear?"

"Yes," Alec said with a nod.

"I see you're heading to Denver?"

"Yes."

"The bus outside will take you to the Salt Lake transfer station."

And with that, one of the soldiers opened the steel-framed door and let Alec outside the fence. He was on his way to Salt Lake, and from there he'd find a team. It was time to start things moving again.

THIRTY-SIX

THIS IS IT, JACK THOUGHT. The final test. To prove if Jack could properly track someone in the real world.

The real world. Real bad guys. Real weapons.

Jack listened as the captain on the far side of the hangar ruffled through papers with the warrant officer.

A door opened, and, to Jack's surprise, Aubrey entered. A soldier pointed her to the folding chairs where Jack was sitting.

What did she have to do with Jack's test?

"She's going to be trouble," the captain said, his voice hushed, apparently forgetting how well Jack could hear.

"We knew that going in," the warrant officer said. "We caught her trying to break into a military facility, for crying out loud."

"Her psych exam showed that she could be loyal."

"She's a loose cannon. The best we can do is keep her pointed in the right direction."

The captain sighed and leaned on the table. "You think it's worth it, having these Lambdas?"

"Not my call."

"I asked what you think."

"I think they might save a few of our guys. And we just might get a couple of cheerleaders and the president of the chess club killed in the process. I don't like it."

"Neither do I."

Nothing else was said. The men flipped through papers. The warrant officer unfolded a map.

"Hey, Jack," Aubrey said as she reached him. She grinned at the sight of him. Even in olive drab she looked good.

"Hey. What are you here for?"

"My 'final test.' How about you?"

"Same."

She nodded. "They said it'd be real-world training this time. Whatever that means."

Aubrey looked out at the open hangar door and at the helicopters just outside. Jack wished that he could hear her thoughts. The best he could do was listen to her breathing and the calm, steady sound of her heart.

Jack knew his heartbeat wasn't nearly so slow.

He wondered where they were going. The captain had

said they were going into enemy territory, and it frightened Jack to think what that meant. Had an entire city been over-run? Was there a rebellion? They'd talked about that many times in training—that if they didn't get the terrorist attacks under control they'd be facing an uprising from the people. Citizens can only live so long in fear before they stop trusting their protectors.

Five Green Berets entered the room, and the captain pointed them toward Jack and Aubrey. He gathered his papers and followed.

"I'm Captain Dane Rowley," he said, looking at Jack, then Aubrey. "My men have already been briefed, and they have their maps and timetables. But for your benefit, here's the overview. A week ago, West High School in Salt Lake City was hit in a terrorist attack. Fortunately, it was at night, and there were no casualties—"

He seemed to say that just for Jack and Aubrey's bene-fit. Jack had heard of plenty of other schools being attacked; learning there weren't casualties here didn't do anything to calm his nerves.

"Salt Lake hasn't been hit as hard as some cities, but no resources have been allocated to clean up yet. This school has turned into kind of a haven for the homeless, and there are rumors of a monster living in the basement."

"A monster?" Jack said, with a small laugh that, he hoped, hid his nerves.

"Well, 'demon' is the term that keeps getting thrown around. The West High Demon. Obviously, this is a Lambda."

"A terrorist?" Aubrey asked.

"Probably not," he said. "If it was a member of one of these terrorist cells, it would be leaving to make attacks. According to our reports, it hasn't moved for five days.

"Parsons," he continued, pointing to Aubrey. "Your mission is to go dark, enter the school, and find this demon."

He reached in his pocket and pulled out a bottle of perfume, which he tossed to Aubrey. "Flowerbomb." He grinned. "I thought the name was appropriate."

"What am I supposed to do with this?"

"Spray yourself," he said simply. "Jack here can track you by your scent."

Jack exchanged a look with Aubrey. "Aren't you going to be watching her, too?" He was a guy with a really good nose, not a Green Beret. He didn't know what "demon" Aubrey was about to face, but he didn't want the responsibility solely on his shoulders. There was so much that he couldn't do.

"The school is just outside the downtown area, and our team will be stationed around the building, watching from all sides. But you're only a kid, and you don't look suspicious. You are going to be outside"—he pointed to a map and tapped on a wide lawn between the gym building and the school—"in the open where we can keep a close eye on you. You'll have a mic so you can contact us and keep us on target. Aubrey—you can probably talk to Jack after you've gone dark. He should be far enough away to hear you."

Aubrey was looking at the light pink perfume. "What am I supposed to do when I find this thing?"

"Assess and report. Give as much information to Jack as you can, and he'll relay it to us."

"Why don't I just wear a mic?" she asked.

"Two reasons. First, we don't know what this thing can detect. For all we know, it can sense electronics—we've run into that before. Second, we're going to have some of our team close to you—maybe even inside the school, depending on how things look. And we're not sure how the mic will work so close to you."

One of the soldiers spoke up. The patch on his chest read "Jolley," but his attitude didn't seem to match the name. "We're supposed to go into battle with an untested weapons system?"

"I'm not a weapons system," Aubrey snapped.

Captain Rowley held up a hand. "This isn't a battle, it's a recon mission. In the event that we see a vulnerable target, we'll move in. And yes, we haven't had the time to test all of the Lambdas to the extent that we'd like. But this 'demon' has thwarted both the Salt Lake SWAT Team and a team from the National Guard. That's why they called us."

"Is it that important?" another Green Beret—his chest patch read "Eschler"—asked. "One Lambda hiding in a school?"

"We have initial reports of a more major action taking place tomorrow or the next day. Tonight we're just testing out a possible strategy. We think Parsons and Cooper here can be a significant asset. But we've got to work together if we're going to make this happen."

Eschler sneered, as though to make it clear that he had no interest in making any of this work. Jack didn't blame him. Even though everything about her training and powers pointed that way, he'd somehow managed to miss the fact that Aubrey would be taking the lead—and that she'd be all alone. He felt an enormous weight on his chest; he was the only person who would be in contact with her. He was the one who would decide when she needed help, when it was time to call in the reinforcements and get her out of there.

Worse, he knew that no one could contact her. They couldn't order her out. She was relying entirely on Jack to make sure that the Green Berets would come when she needed them.

The captain dug into the large plastic shopping bag, from which he pulled a stack of civilian clothes. He handed them out to Jack and Aubrey. "Go change, and then get to work on these maps. I want you to know the floor plan of this high school backward and forward before we take off." He looked at his watch. "That gives us about an hour."

λ

Unmarked cars were waiting for the team when the helicopter landed in a large parking lot in the middle of downtown, and no one wasted any time in transferring their gear to the new vehicles. Aubrey and Jack were dropped off a half mile from the school, in a dingy part of the city.

It wasn't too late—maybe close to eleven—but the lights were out all over Salt Lake. The tall buildings were big black holes that blocked the view of the stars, and the only flickers appeared to come from the occasional candle or flashlight. Had the terrorists knocked out the power grid?

Aubrey followed Jack in silence as they hiked west toward the school. West High was made up of three buildings, but it was the main one—a large, three-story place that had probably been built eighty years before—that had suffered the damage. It had come tumbling down, collapsing on the north end. It looked now like the school was a sinking ship, slanted into torn-up earth. They skirted the building, as they'd been told to do, staying a block south and a block east before creeping up on it and making their way onto the lawn.

"Well," Aubrey said, spraying her neck and wrists with the perfume and then holding them out for Jack to smell. "Are you ready, Bloodhound?"

The perfume was overpowering so close, and he had to focus on something else to not gag.

"The packaging says it has freesia in it," she said with a smile. "Do you think I smell like freesia?"

"I have no idea what freesia even is," Jack answered, and then was hit by a sudden pang of worry. She was going in alone. "I'd hug you, but I don't want to smell like you. You'll be harder to track."

"I'll be okay."

Jack nodded. "If you need something—anything—just say the word and I'll get you out of there."

The microphone sounded in Jack's ear. "Cooper, this is Rowley. Everything is set on our end. We have eyes on you. Over."

"They're ready," Jack relayed for Aubrey.

She nodded, taking a deep breath, and then headed across the dark lawn.

THIRTY-SEVEN

AUBREY LIKED THE SMELL OF the perfume. It was one thing she'd never had—one thing she'd never stolen. She and Nicole had raided a Victoria's Secret once for lotions and body wash, but that was the closest Aubrey had ever come.

She focused on the smell as she walked, not wanting to think about what lay within the school. She was invisible now—she'd "gone dark" as the captain kept referring to it—but that didn't give her a lot of comfort. She'd been found before when she was invisible. The broken school almost certainly didn't have any cameras, but she was wearing perfume with the express purpose of being recognizable. She was fairly sure that if she walked through a room of people, no one would notice her, or the smell, but what about when she was gone? Would the scent linger? Was she leaving a trail for others to follow—or, at the very least, a trail that would make people suspicious?

As she reached the school, she could hear voices inside, and smell the pungent smoke of a campfire. She wondered what else had happened in Salt Lake. These people were homeless, but had they been homeless a month before? Were they just normal people trying to survive?

She climbed a pile of rubble and then ducked through a smashed window that seemed to serve as a main entrance.

"Hey, Jack," she whispered. "I'm going in. You can probably still see me."

It was weird talking to him, knowing that he couldn't communicate back. Still, it felt good—like she wasn't alone.

"I'm in some kind of classroom," she said. "English, by the looks of it. Lots of books on the floor. Ugh. *Great Expectations*. I hated that one. I can smell smoke. I should tell them they can burn these."

She moved through the room, its ceiling slanted at a sharp angle, and out into the hall.

"Man," she breathed. "What happened to this place? This building is majorly destroyed. I don't know how anyone would dare to live in here." She crept down the hall, past a man sitting on a desk. He looked like some kind of guard. A camp lantern sat next to him, illuminating his face and casting long dark shadows down the corridor.

"There's someone watching the hallway. He must be

guarding the entrance—I haven't seen anything that looks like it could go down into the basement yet. I don't think he's a Lambda—too old. Maybe in his thirties? The gun's a .38 revolver, like that one that Matt's dad used to have. The way this guy's holding it makes me wonder if he's ever used one before. Probably just defending the family."

A chill went up her back as she said those final words. This was likely a guy who lost his house. Maybe he was guarding against more terrorists, or maybe he was guarding against robbers who wanted to steal their supplies.

No, that sounded too apocalyptic, and the world wasn't like that. She hadn't heard much news in the last few weeks, but civilization wasn't completely falling apart, was it?

"I wish I had your eyes," Aubrey said to Jack, walking farther down the hall. The lantern lit up most of what surrounded her, but it wasn't enough light to really see what was in the damaged classrooms to her sides. "I don't know how many people are here. I can hear snoring. There's a baby crying."

She kept moving down the corridor, remembering the layout the soldiers had shown her. The basement was smaller than the main floor, a few classrooms and the cafeteria.

At the end of the hall she began to make out another shape in the darkness. A man, watching the other direction—she was behind him.

"There's another guy with a gun," she said. "He's

barricaded—lots of debris surrounding him, like a bunker. He's afraid of something."

Aubrey was getting tired, and the darkness strained her already-poor eyesight.

"Shotgun," she said, getting a little closer. "Pump-action. If it was brighter I could probably tell you the model. This guy is more alert, and he's holding the gun like he means business."

"Okay, I'm passing the barricade now. He has a flashlight pointing at a smashed portion of the floor."

She paused for a long time. This was what everyone was scared of. This was the demon, and the floor plan that the Green Berets had wasn't correct—it didn't include this hole in the floor.

And her eyesight was going.

"Jack," she said. "The maps are wrong. There's this hole in the floor. I'm not sure where it leads. They've covered it mostly with a piece of plywood, and the wood is weighted with bricks. There's a hole big enough for me to go in, but I don't really want to yet. I'm going to follow the map and see if I can see more of what's here."

She walked carefully around the hole in the floor, peering into the darkness below. All the images of demons she'd ever seen appeared in her mind. Leathery wings, horns, fangs, long tails. The balrog in *The Lord of the Rings*. Chernobog in *Fantasia*.

"Jack?" she asked, even though she knew he couldn't answer back. "It's a little scary down here."

She took a deep breath. "I'm okay, though. Don't send in the cavalry yet. I'll find this thing."

As brave as she was trying to sound, part of her wanted to walk out that door—to the other side of the building, where there wasn't Jack, or anyone else who could find her. She wanted to be done. She could find a place to live like this—she could disappear into the night and not be putting her life on the line.

She could not climb down into the basement with a demon.

"I'm moving past the hole," she whispered, the waver in her voice unstoppable at this point. "I'm heading farther down the hall toward the stairs."

Something ran across the rubble, and she froze. It was a rat, or a mouse, or a squirrel. Did they even have squirrels in the city? She didn't really know anything outside of her hometown.

"Jack? When we get out of here, our next mission should be to Hawaii or something. And no demons."

She reached the stairwell and found it blocked by debris— through her tired eyes it seemed a blurry mass.

"It's collapsed, Jack," she said, as she took a couple of tentative steps onto the fallen bricks and beams. She moved away, and glanced at the wall. "There's been some gunfire here. The wall over the hole got hit by a shotgun blast. Two of them, it seems like. Birdshot. Nothing that went through the brick." She forced a terrified laugh. "I don't know about you, but if I were hunting a demon, I'd use slugs."

She started back toward the hole in the floor. It looked to be the only way down.

"Then again," she said. "I guess I'm hunting a demon and I'm not armed with *anything*. How did we get into this?"

She stopped at the mouth of the hole, and looked back at the man with the shotgun. He was staring right at her, though he had no idea she was there. All she could see of him was the bright flare of the flashlight, but she knew that he was eager to fire.

"I should take his gun," she said. "But then he'd freak out, and this whole school would clear out. It would probably wake the demon." She took a long slow breath and rubbed her eyes. "I can barely see anymore, Jack. I'm going down the hole now."

THIRTY-EIGHT

"DAMMIT," JACK YELLED INTO THE mic. "She fell. She's in water."

"Is she okay?" Rowley answered.

"She says she is, but the water is gross—there's oil in it, and mud. I think it's from broken pipes, and runoff from the street. She's covered. I can't smell the perfume."

"I'm moving the team up to get ready to follow her in," the captain said. "Keep me posted."

Aubrey wheezed. "Jack, I don't know how much more of this I can do. I'm getting really weak. I almost lost it there—I almost reappeared."

Jack relayed the information to the captain.

"And Jack," Aubrey said, her voice straining to be flippant. "I was really liking these jeans. They're ruined."

There was another noise in the basement—another set of

breaths that were slower and calmer than Aubrey's. It didn't sound like a demon. Or maybe it did.

It was down there, with Aubrey, the two of them all alone.

"This is Cooper," Jack said into his radio. "There's another person down there. I can hear it breathing."

"How big?"

"No idea. The breaths are small—smaller than Aubrey's. I mean, smaller than Parsons's."

"Any idea where it is?"

"No," Jack said, annoyed. "And I still can't find her. She's down there somewhere, and I think I can hear dripping from her clothes, but the whole place seems to be dripping."

Aubrey spoke again, quieter this time. "There's a bed here—just some dirty blankets. No one is in it. And—it's warm." Aubrey's voice faltered. "I don't know how to get out of here. I'm all turned around, and I can't see."

"Captain," Jack said. "You've got to go in. It has to know Aubrey is there."

"Has it seen her?"

Jack was panicked now, ready to run into the school himself.

"I don't know. All I can hear is that low breathing. Aubrey's trapped. She can't see."

"We'll be there in less than one."

Jack wished that he could relay the information to Aubrey, but there was nothing he could do. All he could hope for was that she could stay hidden.

"I know you're here." That wasn't Aubrey's voice. It was a girl's. Young, quiet. But there was darkness in the voice—a kind of wicked playfulness.

"Jack," Aubrey whispered. "I can't see anything."

THIRTY-NINE

THE BASEMENT WAS PITCH-BLACK, AND the few bits of light—the flashlight beams coming through from the hole above—were blurred and unfocused.

Aubrey was dripping wet, soaked head to toe in filthy water. She could taste mud on her lips, and she knew she didn't smell anything like Flowerbomb anymore. Her only consolation was that she was still invisible.

She couldn't even get back out—she could barely see the hole, and it was in the ceiling twelve feet above her. She was trapped until the Green Berets showed up.

"Jack," she said. "Send them in. I can't do any more."

She'd failed. She was supposed to give them important intelligence information, but all she could do was confirm that someone was in the basement. She'd failed her test.

She'd probably get sent back to quarantine to live in one of those awful dorms.

She sat on the floor, next to the pile of blankets that was someone's bed. Loose bricks were everywhere, and Aubrey couldn't even get comfortable to rest.

"Come out and play," the voice sounded, an odd mix of little girl and menacing monster.

"Jack," she said, her hands balled into tight fists, her eyes closed. "You've got to help me."

"You're not the first, you know," the little girl's voice said. "Other people have come here, and they've done a whole lot better than you. But you can't have me. I sent the SWAT team running like scared puppies with tails between their legs."

Aubrey picked up a brick.

"And you think I'm not ready?" the girl asked. Her voice became muffled. "I'm ready. Ready and waiting."

"Jack," Aubrey said, her voice only a hoarse whisper. "If I don't get out of here . . . just . . . I'm sorry. I tried."

There was a sudden crash, and the room exploded with light and sound. The water burst upward and all around, like throwing dynamite in a pond, and all Aubrey could tell was that she was wet. She couldn't see; she couldn't hear.

In a daze, she rubbed at her ears, mashed her palms into her eyes. Things were happening all around her, but she couldn't make out what.

Screams.

There were screams—that was the first thing to break through the mud in her head. But they weren't the screams of the little girl; they were men, adult men.

She hadn't heard sounds like this before. These screams were visceral, like the cries of men whose lives were ending. Like men who were being tortured. Men who had found out their wives and children were dead.

No one was shooting. Not one person was shooting at the demon. What had happened?

She cracked an eye and the room was still a blur of brilliant white light burned into her eyes. Flashlight beams danced all around the room as the men reeled and tried to regain their composure before reeling again.

And in the middle of everything was a tiny girl, certainly no older than thirteen. She wore a gas mask on her face, and every time a soldier made an effort to stand, she would lean toward him, shouting things too muffled by the mask to understand.

Aubrey's eyes darted all around the room, looking for some other source of fear—some demon behind the little girl that she was using to mock the terrified Green Berets.

But there was nothing. Just a girl, just a gas mask, and six horrified grown men.

Aubrey struggled to stand, watching the girl to make

sure that she hadn't spotted Aubrey. But no, she was still hidden.

Aubrey stepped forward, staring mystified at the scene in front of her.

And then she smacked the girl in the head with the brick.

FORTY

IT WAS LATE—OR, EARLY. THEY'D been up most of the night, with only a couple of hours back at Dugway to sleep and recover. But the entire dorm had been awakened for a mandatory meeting in another building. Some people said it would be *the* meeting. Where they found out what would happen to them.

Jack stood outside in the cold October morning, looking up at the stars. Training was over, but it was all too clear that he had a long way to go. He could barely do the lowest levels of the fitness test, and he'd only been given the very basics of how a special forces team worked.

They hadn't gone through weapons training either, but at least that was one skill he felt he already had. He'd hunted deer every season—and then lived off the venison for the rest of the year. He'd owned his first .22 at eight years old and had a deer rifle by age twelve.

Still, he wasn't ready for war. He wasn't ready to be helping the Green Berets, for crying out loud. He wasn't even a private. He was a Lambda, outranked by every grunt in any of the armed services. And he was still surrounded by barbed-wire fences in all directions. He still had a bomb strapped to his foot.

"You're going to be late," a voice said. Jack turned to see Aubrey.

"I was waiting for you."

She slipped her hand into his. She'd been doing that lately. So had he. He wasn't sure what it meant, if it meant anything at all.

"I wonder what my parents think," Jack said. "I wonder what they've been told."

"The quarantine camps have started sending people home," she said. "I heard that a few of the camps on the West Coast are totally cleared out."

"Are you sure you want to do this?" Jack asked.

Without hesitation, she nodded. "It feels right."

Jack wished that he felt so confident, but there were too many things holding him back. He still had a family who loved him, a town that he missed.

And then there was Aubrey.

She could do amazing things. He'd followed her every

motion in the school, tracked her every step, and he'd been amazed at how much she'd changed. She acted like a soldier now, after just one week.

But she'd almost been caught. And she'd had to fight. And Jack wanted nothing more than to protect her.

He pointed up at the sky. "I wish you could see this," he said. "I've never seen so many stars."

Not just stars. He could discern the shadows on the rims of moon craters, the vague clouds of nebulae, the circular disk of Andromeda, the moons of Jupiter. The night sky seemed to be lit up with Christmas lights, and it filled everything around him with light.

He wondered how bright it really was—whether he should be able to see each of Aubrey's eyelashes, the splashes of color in her irises. He used to think her eyes were gray, but they weren't; they were blue and green and yellow and brown. They were like little impressionist paintings, filled with a hundred colors that created the illusion of gray.

"Hey," she said.

"What?"

Aubrey grinned. "You're staring at me."

He felt his face flush. "Sorry. I was just . . . My eyes are so much better now."

She laughed, and then put her hands to her face. "My pores must be enormous."

"No! No, that's not it at all." He didn't know what to say

without sounding stupid. He used to be so comfortable with Aubrey, but that was because she was just one of the guys. The one time he had tried to change things, she'd said no. That had been months ago.

He took both her hands in his. Aubrey's were cold and rough, from too many obstacle courses and push-ups in the dirt. But he didn't care. They could be coarse as dried leather and he wouldn't care.

He opened his mouth to talk, but she spoke first.

"Promise me something," she said.

"Anything."

"They're going to assign us together," she said.

"What? How do you know?"

She smiled wryly. "Because I spy on people."

"You need to be careful."

"I'm okay," she said, turning his wrist and looking at his watch. "Just promise me something. They were worried about one thing—that I'd be in danger and that you'd come charging in, being stupid."

"I'm not going to let you get hurt."

"The Green Berets have our backs," she said. "You give them info, and they'll take care of me."

"But—"

"Don't worry," she said with a grin. "If some thirty-year-old meathead comes rushing in to shoot the bad guys, I'm not going to fall for him."

She let the words hang in the air for a minute, and he didn't know what to say. *Don't worry—I'm not going to fall for someone else. Was that* really *what she meant? Did that mean she'd already fallen for him?*

There was a blare from the PA system, and it stung his ears.

"All Lambda recruits report to conference room A. All Lambda recruits report to conference room A."

"Well," he said, with a quick exhaled laugh. "That's bad timing."

Aubrey grinned, staring at him with those complex eyes. He could look at them forever.

She put a hand behind his neck and pulled him down to her, and before he could realize what was happening, their lips touched.

It was his first kiss, and he didn't know what to do, but his brain let go and emotions took over. He wrapped his arms around her and hugged her close, concentrating on the texture of her smooth, wet lips, and the smell of her skin, sweet with the lingering smells of the day—soap and toothpaste and fabric softener.

"All Lambda recruits please report to conference room A. All Lambda recruits please report to conference room A."

She pulled back and grinned. "Time for a meeting, soldier."

FORTY-ONE

LAURA SAT IN THE THIRD row of folding chairs—close enough to look engaged but not so close as to be particularly noticeable. She planned nearly everything she did now, trying to anticipate the officers' interpretations of her actions. It was exhausting, but she needed to fit in. This was a golden opportunity.

On the other hand, sometimes she wondered why she tried so hard. Looking around the room, she saw nothing but a bunch of kids. They'd all been drilled about military decorum, but they weren't soldiers yet, not by a long shot. This meeting was obviously important—there were half a dozen observers—so most everyone sat up straight and did their best to look like they belonged in the army, but Laura wondered how the commanding officers had any faith in this group.

The grizzled sergeant major stood at the front of the room and looked out over the class. "It looks like not everyone made it through training. We started with thirty-four, and we're down to twenty-six. I'd guess that if we put you through more rigorous training, that number would be cut in half, or even more. But as we don't have time for more rigorous training, we'll have to do with what we've got.

"You've all proven yourselves to be competent, and an asset to the special forces. We've been closely watching every aspect of your training, and a team of experts—psychologists, tacticians, doctors, veterans—has been evaluating how best to handle you."

He paused, watching the faces as though he expected a reaction, but Laura didn't give him one. She merely stared straight ahead as she'd been taught to, listening carefully, taking mental notes, not wanting to miss a word.

"As we mentioned last week, we're fighting fire with fire. Some of you will be formed into the exact same kinds of teams that work so well for our terrorist friends. All of you, when you leave here today, will be given a bracelet that indicates you've been tested and found healthy. You haven't been in the outside world for a couple of weeks, but these bracelets are more important than any driver's license or passport. These bracelets tell the world that you're clean—that you're just regular old teenagers."

There was a hand in the back of the room, and the sergeant

major cleared his throat before calling on the boy—Gary, a kid Laura had gotten to know. She knew most of the Lambdas by now. She wished she could recruit a few of them, but that was too much to ask for.

"Aren't we contagious? Should we really be back in the general population?"

The man turned to the FBI woman, who looked the same as she had a week ago, only with dark circles under her eyes.

"You'll be under strict adult supervision the entire time, and you will have no contact with other children—other teenagers—who you could infect."

"What if it mutates again?" Michelle asked.

"We have no idea what the long-term consequences of the virus are," the woman answered. "All I can say is that we are looking at it from every possible angle. You've been out of communication with the outside world but—"

The sergeant major looked tired of being interrupted. "But that's all a secondary concern at the moment. Right now, we have a job to do. I'm going to make this very clear, so that no one has a false impression. First of all, I've witnessed the training of each of you, and I can very clearly state that no one here is Superman. You may be able to do something very impressive, but you're not invincible. Also, the Green Berets are known as one of the finest fighting organizations on God's green earth—I'd go so far as to say they're *the* finest—but we're going to take you into combat, and in combat people die. We will not take unnecessary risks with you, but we won't coddle you, either. If you have any reservations about that, speak now. There's no dishonor in withdrawal."

An aide handed him a clipboard, and the sergeant major looked down at the sheet. "I'm going to call out your assignments and point you in the right direction. Wolf, Henson, and Read—come over here and meet with Captain Garrett." The three of them stood timidly, and then hurried to the waiting Green Beret. They were a team.

"Sola, over here." Josi stood and walked to a woman at the side of the room. By now Laura could read insignias better, and the woman was from army intelligence. It seemed like a perfect fit for an ability like Josi's.

"Samuelson," the sergeant major called.

Laura turned to look at the tall blonde and wished for the hundredth time that she had Nicole's power. It would make Laura's plans so much easier. She missed having Alec's mind-control abilities to cover up her schemes.

"Lambda Samuelson," he said, "you're in a different situation, but one I think you're ideally suited for. Please come up here and meet with Mr. Morgan from the State Department."

That seemed to make sense. Nicole's powers wouldn't be of any use on the battlefield, but she could be perfect in a diplomatic role. Or as a spy.

"Cooper, Parsons, and Hansen."

Laura sighed inwardly but stood up and smiled. Aubrey Parsons and Jack Cooper had an intriguing pair of skills and Laura had just heard a few whispers about their midnight mission together in Salt Lake, fighting a Lambda who could terrify people with her mind. They seemed like a good team. But they were a pair—a couple, it seemed like—and that would only make it harder for Laura to work with them. She'd always be the third wheel, and that wasn't good if Laura ever needed to manipulate one of them.

"The three of you come over and meet with Captain Rowley." Aubrey and Jack moved toward the captain and Laura followed behind.

He led them into a small room with a table and four chairs. After closing the door, he turned to look at them.

"Welcome to the ODA," the captain said, with a grim smile. Laura knew the designation by now—Operational Detachment Alpha. It was a Greet Beret unit.

Rowley spoke. "I'll tell you right up front that we've got a challenge ahead of us. We've got Jack Cooper, the human telescope—"

"Among other things," Jack said.

The captain stopped, as if he was about to say something, but then continued. "Then we have Aubrey Parsons, the Invisible Girl. And finally we have Laura Hansen, Supergirl, the only one of the three of you who can pass the army physical fitness test—and get a perfect score doing it."

He sat on the edge of the table and looked at Laura. She tried not to grin too much at his assessment of her.

"Hansen, it's a pity that women can't serve in the special forces, because I have no doubt that you could show our best men a thing or two. I've watched your training. Parsons, after your demonstration last night you strike me as an asset that could be very valuable to our organization, so long as we utilize you effectively. If we had six months to train you, you could be one of the top tactical soldiers this army has ever seen. But we don't have six months to train you. In fact, we have no time at all, and we're going to have to rely on your current skill set."

He looked at Jack.

"As for why we have you, it's because you and Parsons seem to be ideally suited to work together—complementary powers. I don't know how your brain works, but you're better than any sensor package."

As he spoke, Rowley gestured broadly with his hands. "Our team will be focused on special reconnaissance and Parsons, you're going to be our primary asset. Cooper, you're tasked with keeping track of anything and everything that she does. And Hansen, for now you're the bodyguard. That may change, because you have a lot of potential."

Laura nodded. It was fine, for now.

"What does special reconnaissance mean?" Aubrey asked.

"It means that we're not a combat team, at least not

primarily. It means that we—you—sneak in wherever we're going and find what we're looking for. It'll be a lot like the mission at the school—you gather information and relay that to us so we can make decisions about what action to take."

Laura finally spoke up, unable to control her curiosity any longer. "So, where are we going?"

The captain clapped his hands together. "We're getting on a plane. And we're doing it this morning."

FORTY-TWO

THE TWENTY-SIX LAMBDAS WERE LOADED onto a green camouflage bus, along with a handful of soldiers. Behind and in
front of them were at least two Humvees that Jack could see,
but he could identify a total of seven engines, so there had to
be something else in the convoy.

Captain Rowley had told them that commercial flights
had been halted weeks ago, and every major airport was
acting as a makeshift military airfield. Dugway was fifty
miles from Salt Lake International, across a mostly empty
strip of road. Even the towns on the highway were dark as
they passed, and rumor spread around the bus that whole
cities were being evacuated. Jack didn't know how much
of that was true, but it was eerie to pass the shadows of
McDonald's and gas stations—places that never closed but

were now empty and dark.

Aubrey was holding his hand but talking to Laura. It turned out that she wasn't from Utah at all, but from Colorado, and had been camping down in southern Utah when the dam had been destroyed. She was trying to run, to get far away from more terrorist activity, but ended up right in the middle of it.

"I was hitchhiking," she said. "I don't remember much. My friends wanted to go east, back to Denver, but I wanted to go farther into Utah—to someplace no terrorist would ever care about."

Jack raised his eyebrows. She was a tiny, gorgeous girl. Hitchhiking was asking to be murdered.

"Don't forget," she said with a smile. "I can handle myself in a fight. Anyway, we drove west—the trucker who picked me up said he was going to some place called Huntington. We didn't make it a hundred miles—we fell into a stupid canyon. Terrorists knocked out a bridge. I survived—" She looked a little embarrassed, maybe guilty. "I can survive a hundred-foot fall, I guess. But he didn't. Rescue teams found me at the bottom of the canyon."

Aubrey nodded and placed her free hand over Laura's. "That's actually not that far from where we're from. Huntington's kind of right over the mountain."

"I guess that's how we all ended up in the same place."

Aubrey and Laura started chatting about their abilities,

and Jack leaned his head on the window and stared outside.

Somewhere, very high up, was a bird. At first he thought it was a plane, but he couldn't get a good look at it. It disappeared high over the top of the bus before he could focus in on it.

There was a glare from low morning sun, and Jack tried to unlock the window to get an unblocked view.

"They're locked," someone across the aisle said. "I already tried mine."

Jack glanced over to see who it was—a kid who could somehow control electricity—and when Jack looked back out the window there was no sign of whatever it was.

"Keep it closed anyway," someone else said. "It's too cold out there."

He craned his neck, trying to find the bird. Something about it didn't seem right.

Jack sat back in his seat, and started listening to the conversations in the bus. He wasn't sure if that was dishonest or not. Everyone knew what he could do. He didn't even feel sneaky. He was getting better with his powers all the time, and he could focus on one conversation at a time and ignore the others.

"We shouldn't be doing this," a girl was saying several rows ahead of him. "I'm fifteen years old. I shouldn't be in the army."

"You're a freaking monster," a guy responded. "You can

take care of yourself."

She didn't seem to be offended at being called a "monster," and Jack immediately knew who he was listening to. A girl named Krezi—a powerful Lambda 5D, like Laura—who could shoot some kind of laser or fire or something from her hands.

"I know I can take care of myself," Krezi said. "But that's not the point. Should every person who can fight be forced into the army?"

"They gave you the option," the guy answered. "You didn't have to come." From the tone of his voice, they'd had this conversation before.

"Yeah, some option. We could come and fight or we could stay locked up in Dugway indefinitely. In case you haven't noticed, even though we're all helping the army now, they haven't taken these bombs off our ankles. They don't trust us. They're just using us because they don't have a lot of options."

"But isn't that the whole point? Do you think that they'd risk a fifteen-year-old girl if they had any better ideas? We're at war."

"I can shoot energy from my hands," she said. "Is that really superior to a Green Beret shooting bullets from his gun? Do they need me so bad?"

"But you don't look like a Green Beret. That's the whole point. You're—"

Jack stopped listening. He'd heard all the arguments before. He'd had them himself.

He looked out the window again. The Great Salt Lake spread out in the distance like a giant blue blanket. The lake was dead, like the Dead Sea. He'd heard it was so salty that nothing could live in it—no fish, just algae and brine shrimp that made the lake stink.

There was that bird again, flying toward them.

It wasn't a bird.

It was a—something—and it was carrying a person.

"Hey," Jack shouted, nearly tripping over Aubrey as he pushed his way out into the aisle and toward the soldiers at the front of the bus. "There's something out there. There's something—someone—flying."

Everyone jumped to the windows, blocking his view for a moment.

"It's coming right at us," he said.

There was a sudden chatter from a machine gun, behind them, and then the radio squawked. The soldier on the other end was frantic. "Unidentified bogey coming in from the south."

A second gun started, right in front of the bus—it was the .50 cal machine gun on the roof of the Humvee ahead of them.

They were the terrorists. They had to be.

And then suddenly the bus slammed to the side, rising up for a moment on two wheels, and then crashing back to the pavement. The driver tried to regain control and swerved sharply.

There was a huge dent in the ceiling, and a hand—a claw?—was tearing through the roof of the bus.

The soldiers barked at everyone to get to the floor, and then Jack was nearly knocked down by the shattering pops of their M4s.

He clamped his hands over his ears, but it didn't do any good. It was so loud he felt like he could barely move.

Someone in the bus—the girl he'd heard before—began firing blasts of white-hot light up through the roof.

The bus slowed and turned sharply, and then Jack picked out the *whump-whump-whump* of flat tires.

Jack tried to get up enough to see Aubrey, but she was out of sight—she must have been hiding down between the seats. Good.

The ceiling was perforated with holes, and he didn't see any sign of the thing that had been on the roof.

And then, as if pulled by some unseen force, the three soldiers at the front of the bus slammed into the windshield. It shattered into a million pieces, and they tumbled out onto the road. The driver tried to stop the bus, but it rolled right over the men.

The radio was filled with shouts—frantic, desperate calls for help and barked orders.

The driver was yanked from his chair, his seat belt shearing, and he flew to the pavement. Jack jumped forward, mashing his foot on the brakes and trying to get control of the wheel.

Ahead of him, the two Humvees were stopped, dealing with their own attacks. Someone—a small person dressed all in black—was climbing on the roof of one, trying to open the gun hatch. Another was crouched in the street, throwing something—or shooting something?—at the other Humvee.

There was a sudden *whoosh* and rush of air, and someone swooped into the bus through the missing windshield. He was dressed in black, like the others, and Jack could see his face—he couldn't have been any older than Jack. He raised his hands, but was immediately thrown back onto the pavement by Krezi's bolts of energy and a blast of lightning from the kid.

With a screech, the clawed thing on the roof began tearing through the sheet metal again. It only took a quick swipe for the already-damaged roof to give way, and the Lambda collapsed into the bus.

He looked like Nate, back at the dance. His skin wasn't skin—it was something else, some kind of metal or stone. His hands were three-fingered hooks.

And he was where Aubrey had been only moments before.

Jack searched for a gun, but there was nothing—they'd all been thrown out with the soldiers.

Laura tackled the beast, smashing him down to the floor with an enormous crash. The guy tried to speak, but his voice was an inhuman rumble. People were shouting for Laura to get out of the way so they could shoot him, but Laura didn't listen. She threw a punch into his face, connecting with a sickening crunch. Before she could throw another, the thing launched her into the ceiling. Her body tangled against the jagged hole.

The monster stood, and was instantly hit by Krezi's energy blasts. He stumbled backward, but the attacks only seemed to push him, not hurt him.

He took a step forward, and fell flat on his face.

Aubrey. It must have been her—she'd tripped him.

A soldier shouted at Jack, and he turned to see a whole team of Green Berets in front of the bus.

"Open the door," one called. Jack searched for a moment before seeing the bent lever. By the time he got it open, the soldiers were spreading out around the bus. Someone stepped inside and started grabbing kids, pulling them from their seats and ordering them onto the street.

The monster was getting up again, but the blasts were targeted on his head now, and he was trying to shield himself with his arms.

Someone grabbed Jack, and pulled him from the driver's seat.

On the street, it was harder to see what was going on inside the bus. He hoped Aubrey was keeping hidden. The whole convoy was devastated, every vehicle either damaged or burning, and the street was filled with soldiers who were trying to tend to the injured, or beat back the remaining enemies.

The bus shuddered, rocking back and forth, and then a hole erupted from the back. The monster fell out onto the pavement and began running in slow bounds off the road and into the brush.

The soldiers gathered the Lambdas from the bus and formed a defensive perimeter. Within minutes aircraft appeared, flying low over the demolished collection of vehicles. Jack could hear them overhead for quite a while, but they'd missed all the action. There was nothing for them to attack.

Cesar Carbajal was dead. He was the only Lambda to die. And though the soldiers didn't make an announcement, Jack could hear every word they whispered to one another. Cesar hadn't been killed by the terrorists—he'd taken a bullet. Sure, it was the terrorists' fault that the battle started in the first place, but it still felt like a punch in the gut. This war—this thing they'd agreed to do—was deadly. Cesar had no way to defend himself; his power was all mental. He wasn't even trained for combat.

Aubrey sat across from Jack on the pavement, her knees tucked up to her chest, her arms wrapped around her legs.

"This isn't like what they talked about," she said. "It isn't like the girl at the school."

"I know," Jack answered.

"So many," she said, gesturing weakly to a row of bodies lined up a few car lengths outside the perimeter.

Jack glanced over at the dead bodies. Eight teenagers. Just

like him, except driven by—what? He'd never heard any demands from the terrorists. Did they just want to watch the world burn?

Aubrey spoke, her voice barely above a whisper. "In training they said the terrorists worked in groups of three or four. They didn't talk about big attacks like this. They didn't talk about battles. The terrorists never come out and fight the army."

"They must have known who we are—what we're going to do. They wanted to stop us."

Jack crossed over to sit next to Aubrey and put his arm around her waist.

"I didn't think it would be like this," she said. "I mean, so many . . ."

Jack couldn't see where the other bodies were being collected, but he heard the radios talking about more of them—the soldiers killed in the attack. There were three, and several more wounded.

This didn't seem like any terrorist act he'd heard of. Granted, not a lot of details were ever given, but they never seemed like suicide attacks. Had they just underestimated the army? Were they unprepared?

Aubrey laid her head on his shoulder.

From the distant skies, Jack could hear the thumping of helicopter blades.

FORTY-THREE

THE HELICOPTERS EVACUATED THE LAMBDAS to the airport, where a variety of aircraft was waiting. Aubrey stared into the dim morning light around them, wondering what other dangers were lurking in the shadows, what monsters she was getting ready to fight.

They'd all started like she had. She'd been a normal girl until she got the virus. It hadn't taken long before she shoplifted her first thing—a box of medicine that she couldn't afford. It hadn't seemed evil. It was for her dad, not her, and she knew the pharmacy could take the loss—it was owned by one of the wealthiest families in town. Still, she'd cried that night, all night, afraid that she'd be found out.

It got easier after that. She needed supplies for school—notebooks and pens and a new backpack—and then she needed school clothes. Nicole was helping by that point, telling Aubrey what to choose—which outfits were in style and which colors complemented Aubrey's skin and hair. It had been so easy to steal—a sweater from here, a pair of jeans from there. They were big companies with plenty of money; Aubrey knew that a pair of jeans didn't cost one hundred and fifty dollars to make—it was just a greedy corporation that could get away with huge prices. If they missed one or two pairs, then what difference did it make?

Aubrey couldn't make a direct connection between shoplifting and terrorism—that was crazy—but there had to be some path, some series of bad choices. Like when Nicole had dared Aubrey to steal the principal's car, and Aubrey had faked an ankle sprain to get out of it. What if she hadn't? Stealing jeans was one thing, but stealing a car? And what about the parties she'd been to, the party where Jeff Savage brought ecstasy and Aubrey could have stolen all of it. Selling that would have paid their rent for months.

She wasn't a terrorist, but what was she? A criminal? A thief who just wasn't stealing anything at the moment?

She'd be better, she promised herself, though it felt hollow. How could she truly be better when she didn't have any reason not to be? There was nothing here to steal, nothing to gain.

When the helicopter touched down at the Salt Lake airport after a short flight, Captain Rowley directed them to a waiting truck. Another of the Lambda teams was in tow, an officer leading them. The other groups—including Nicole—were being sent elsewhere. Everyone had a different flight to catch.

Aubrey's team and the second group loaded into the truck, which took them to a small commuter plane guarded by four soldiers in full combat gear. The plane was only sparsely filled—ten soldiers were relaxing, their packs and weapons in the seats next to them. When they saw Captain Rowley, they stood as much as they could in the cramped plane and saluted.

"Men," the captain said. "These are our Lambdas. They'll be joining us for the next couple of missions."

The men nodded as though they knew what was going on. Aubrey recognized a few of them from the mission at the school. None of them seemed thrilled at the prospect of working with kids, and one of them openly grimaced at Aubrey and Laura—two small high school girls.

The Lambdas made their way to the back of the plane, to where seats were still open.

In a moment the captain and the other team leader were in the small first-class cabin, looking over some paperwork. The aircraft began to taxi without any announcement from the cockpit. Aubrey had only ever flown twice—on a school choir trip that she'd gotten a scholarship for—and this all felt new and weird. She missed having a flight attendant to explain what was going on.

"So you're supposed to save the country?" one of the soldiers asked, turning in his seat.

None of the teens answered.

"I asked you a question, Lambda," he said, smiling but grim. "Don't forget that we outrank you."

"That air force puke up front outranks you," another one said. "The guy who refueled the plane outranks you."

"I'm nineteen," Laura said defensively. "I could join—"

The first man, a broad-shouldered guy with a square face and a scar along his chin, cut her off. "You could join, but you didn't. You haven't even made it through basic boot camp. You probably can't do a push-up."

"She can do a push-up," Aubrey said. "She can do more push-ups than all of you combined."

"Is that your superpower?" the second man said. "You're Push-Up Girl?"

Aubrey wanted to say that Laura could break any of them in half, but she held her tongue.

"How about you, kid?" the square-faced soldier asked Jack.

"Just trying to help out."

"Are you the one who is about as useful as my binoculars?"

Jack opened his mouth to answer, but the soldier laughed and smacked another man with the back of his hand. "They tell us we're getting help and they send us a kid who can do everything that our equipment already does."

"What about you, honey?" the other man asked Aubrey.

"She rolled her eyes!" the first laughed. "It's going to be *great* working with kids."

A voice from farther forward called back, "Shut up, guys."

"I just was asking the nice young lady what amazing miracle she can perform."

But before he could finish his sentence, Aubrey disappeared, and stood from her seat. His laugh faded a little into confusion as she climbed forward in the accelerating plane and took the man's Beretta M9 from his gear. She removed the magazine, and then pulled the slide from the frame, just as she'd done a hundred times when target shooting in the hills of Mount Pleasant.

She reappeared in front of him, and dropped the three pieces of the gun in his lap.

"What the hell?" he shouted, grabbing at the gun. "What's wrong with you, freak?"

"Don't call me 'honey.'"

"Hey," someone called back, pointing angrily at Aubrey. "You do not touch weapons. That's part of the deal."

The exchange got the attention of Captain Rowley up front, who was hurrying awkwardly down the aisle as the plane bounced through the air.

"What's going on?"

The square-faced man jabbed a finger at Aubrey. "She stripped McKinney's sidearm. She was just suddenly here, with the thing taken apart."

Aubrey was fully expecting the captain to tell his men to

shut up and knock off their attitudes, but instead he barked at her.

"Is that true?"

"Well—"

"Yes or no, soldier."

She was getting mad. "You told me I'm not a soldier."

"You're a Lambda," he scolded, nearly shouting. "When you raised your hand a week ago and agreed to join the war effort, that put you in the army, and it put you under my command. You will respect these men and the orders they give you."

Jack touched her arm and she shook him off.

The captain turned to face the other Lambdas. "You're not here to put on a show, and we're not here to baby you. If that's what you expected, then you should have stayed in Dugway. There's a war on, and if you can't handle a little ribbing from your fellow soldiers then we can't use you in this unit."

He finally turned to the soldiers. "As for you, keep your mouths shut and your minds on our mission. We're flying into hostile territory, and you can use that time to review our planning session. Do I make myself clear?"

"Yes, sir," was the chanted reply.

He turned back to the Lambdas. "Do I make myself clear?"

"Yes, sir."

FORTY-FOUR

AUBREY SLEPT THROUGH THE FLIGHT. It was only when the plane touched ground with a sudden uneven bump that she was jarred awake.

Jack was sitting quietly, looking out the window, one hand balled in a fist and pressed to his lips.

"Welcome to Seattle," Rowley said, seeming to be in a better mood. "It's one of the hardest-hit cities so far, and if you've ever been here before I think you'll be surprised at what you find. I'm told the city center is a ghost town, and many of the suburbs are emptying out. Everyone's heading inland."

More military vehicles met them at the airport and drove them into the center of the city. They spent the day and night at a Marriott commandeered by the military. It was strange to see a Marriott surrounded by army vehicles. And not just Humvees, but some kind of big armored trucks. There were roadblocks on every street nearby, and some military personnel on the roof with enormous floodlights.

Aubrey and Laura were put in a room together, and the relative luxury felt like the opposite of everything they'd experienced for weeks. It had only been this morning when they'd woken up in the Dugway dorms, only this morning when Aubrey and Jack had kissed in the starlight.

That seemed like years ago. It had been before she'd really been inducted into the military, before all those deaths on the road. It was a different world now.

She wondered if her kiss with Jack was from a different life. Had she changed too much? She felt like a different person.

Laura let Aubrey have the first shower. By the time she dried her hair and went to bed, Aubrey was already mostly asleep anyway. It didn't take much longer to drift away.

Breakfast came without them having to ask—it was room service, though it couldn't have been the kind of room service the Marriott usually delivered—everything was in packages: boxes of cereal, cups of yogurt, and plastic bottles of milk. Still, it felt fresher than the MREs that they'd been eating for the last few weeks, and Aubrey was glad to get it.

Laura sat down in a big plush chair across from Aubrey's

bed. "So, I have a question. I wanted to bring it up last night, but you were kind of out of it."

Aubrey nodded wearily. "Yesterday was . . . long. What's up?"

Laura peeled back the lid of her yogurt and licked it. "The attack on the bus? I don't think it was terrorists."

"What do you mean? Who else would it be?"

Laura lowered her voice even though it was only the two of them in the room. "I heard about something similar before I got caught. And I heard about it again at Dugway. There's a rebellion."

"A rebellion?" Aubrey said. "Against what?"

"Against locking up all the Lambdas. Apparently there are Lambdas who have gathered together to fight against the army."

Aubrey took a bite of cereal. "But we're at war."

"Did you want to get caught?" Laura asked. "Did any of us want to get caught?"

"The country needs us."

Laura smiled and took a big spoonful of yogurt. "Tell me that you felt that same way when you broke in to the assessment facility to try to rescue Jack."

"That's different," she said, though she wasn't quite sure if it was.

"I think those Lambdas yesterday were part of the rebellion and they were trying to free more Lambdas to join their cause. Think about it: Would terrorists attack a full military convoy?"

Aubrey shrugged. "I don't know."

"I don't either," Laura said. "But it doesn't seem to fit anything we've heard about them. They don't do suicide attacks, and they act in small groups."

"But if it's a rebellion, so what?"

Laura shook her head. "I don't know. I just think it's interesting."

"I don't think I'd want to be part of a rebellion that was killing American soldiers."

"Even if the American soldiers are locking up American kids? Forcing them to kill?"

"Maybe I'll think about it differently when they force me to kill," Aubrey said, laughing a little and trying to pass it off as a joke.

"It's not funny," Laura said, suddenly more serious. "What do you think my job is? You're the spy, but I'm the bodyguard. You spent the last week training how to sneak around and pick locks; I spent it learning how to fight."

"Are you saying you're going to join the rebellion?" Aubrey asked. She didn't know what to make of Laura. She made Aubrey uneasy.

"No," Laura said, with a wave of her spoon. "I just don't know what to think about this."

"Neither do I."

They met upstairs in a suite that had been turned into a command room. Jack was already there, dressed in casual civilian clothes. It made Aubrey think about something she'd heard in history class, about combatants needing to be in uniforms or else they'd be called spies. That probably only mattered when you were fighting in another country, not against terrorists.

"Good morning," Rowley said a little sharply. Aubrey thought they'd come on time, but he didn't seem happy with them.

"Sergeant Eschler has our briefing this morning." The captain gestured to the other man.

"Thanks," Eschler said, and rolled out a map on the table. Everyone moved in a few steps.

"We have received intel that a terrorist cell in the area is planning on hitting the Space Needle today."

"The Space Needle?" Jack asked. "Isn't that just a restaurant?"

"It's a landmark," Eschler said. "A few landmarks were hit yesterday: the St. Louis Arch, Old Faithful, a couple others. It seems like they hit similar targets all at the same time, or within a couple days of each other."

"It's more than just a landmark," Captain Rowley added crossly. "It's six hundred feet of concrete and steel that could collapse in the center of Seattle."

Eschler nodded. "We don't know where the attack is going to come from. There is a terrorist cell working in Seattle that has some kind of superheated power that can be used to melt steel. Or there's another group that has a kind of jackhammer effect. We're not sure how that one works. It could be them, or it could be something else entirely. Or it could be all of them working together.

"The plan that we've worked up is simple, but it ought to be effective. We'll have snipers in place in three areas—on the Children's Museum, the Pacific Science Center, and this business complex on Broad Street. The remaining three of us will be an assault and command team located in the music museum. Our Lambdas will be filling similar roles to what they trained for. Parsons, you'll go dark up by the Needle and watch for anything and everything. Cooper, we'll have you near the music museum with us. We'll have eyes on target, but I want you listening in on every conversation and every creak that thing makes when it sways in the wind."

"What about me?" Laura said.

"You'll be bodyguard," Rowley answered. "And you're backup to pass information to and from the primaries."

"Now," Captain Rowley said, staring at the Lambdas. "You have your genuine I-Don't-Have-the-Virus bracelets so that no one will question you out there. But if you think those are your tickets to run away or betray us, remember that I have this." He pulled the ankle-bomb detonator from his pocket and held it up. "I'm sure I won't need it. But you can never be too careful."

FORTY-FIVE

"I'M SURE I WON'T NEED it," Aubrey said, mimicking the captain's voice. "But you can never be too careful."

She sat on a bench, eating her lunch—a Subway sandwich she'd bought at the only open shop in sight.

"You can probably hear me chewing," she said to Jack. "That's got to be disgusting. Sorry."

She was bored out of her mind. She'd been sitting in the park for hours, patrolling while invisible and sitting visible while resting, and she hadn't seen a thing. Maybe the Green Berets had spooked the terrorists. Maybe they'd seen the snipers. Maybe they wondered why one teenage girl was wandering around the Seattle Center in the middle of a war, when everyone should have been too paranoid to be outside.

She took a bite of her sandwich. She felt ravenous—eating always seemed to renew her energy after being invisible—but she was trying to make it last. At least chewing on a sandwich made it look like she was doing something.

Aubrey glanced up toward the Children's Museum, but didn't see any sign of the Green Beret snipers. They were good at what they did, even if they treated her like crap.

Well, she'd saved their butts at the school. They were good at what they did, but she was good at what she did, too.

"Hey Jack," she said, clearing her mouth with a sip of soda. "About yesterday. Well, a lot happened yesterday, but I'm talking about the beginning—about the morning. I'm talking about the kiss—I'm talking about our kiss."

She paused. She suddenly didn't know why she'd brought it up. This was stupid. He had better things to be doing right now.

She took another bite of sandwich and wiped a glob of mayo from the corner of her mouth. She tried to think how long it had been since she'd seen someone—anyone—out by the Space Needle.

"Wait," she said quickly. "Jack. I just realized I'm totally leaving you hanging. I don't want you to think that anything I have to say about the . . . about the kiss is bad. I'm glad we kissed. I'm not saying, 'It was a moment of foolishness and we need to pretend it never happened.' That's not what I'm saying at all. I'm definitely pro-kiss."

She wondered if anyone was watching her. If the terrorists had someone on a roof nearby, they'd see her. Then again, if someone was up on a roof, then they'd see the snipers before they'd see her.

"The thing is," Aubrey said, "I'm sorry about everything back home. I probably should be saying this to your face—and I've wanted to. You don't know how much I've wanted to. But I'm just so sorry that I ditched you for Nicole. It wasn't right, and it only led to trouble. Every time I tried to do something good I screwed things up even more. I treated you horribly, and I did horrible things. Nicole wasn't buying stuff for me all the time. I was stealing it. I was stealing just because I could and because I wanted to be pretty like Nicole. Maybe you already guessed that, but I wanted you to hear it from me. Assuming you're even listening, which I don't know if you are."

She walked to the Space Needle for the tenth time and looked up at the structure. No one was there, doing whatever a terrorist would do.

"You were always there for me," she continued. "And I turned my back on you. I betrayed a lifetime of friendship for—"

There was a pop, and then three more pops. She knew the sound the instant she heard it. Gunshots. She spun in place, trying to look for the shooter, but it was too much of a bowl—the shots echoed off every building.

"Jack?" she said. "Jack!" She started running for the music museum. Before she got far, she saw Jack running toward her, blood streaming from his head and down his shirt.

She reappeared as she ran, and Jack altered his course to meet her. He seemed to be running fine, but there was blood everywhere.

Aubrey threw out her arms to hug him, but when he reached her, he just grabbed her and kept running.

"They tried to kill us," he said, panting.

"Are you okay?"

"We have to get out of sight—away from the snipers."

She tried to look at him as they ran, but her eyes were too blurry to see his wound. He seemed to be bleeding above his right ear, but he was moving too much to be sure.

"Why?" she shouted.

"I don't know."

They ran in between two buildings, out of the view of snipers—or at least, she hoped so. It should have been out of the soldiers' view if they didn't move. Jack began to stumble, and pulled her behind a Dumpster with him.

"What's going on?" she asked, her hands on his head, trying to stave off the bleeding. His blood leaked through her fingers and down her arm, dripping from her elbow onto the pavement.

"I don't know," he panted. "Everything was fine. It was quiet. We were watching, and Rowley was getting routine checks from the snipers. And then all of a sudden he was pulling the detonator from his pocket, priming it." Jack paused and wiped blood from his eye.

Aubrey couldn't get the bleeding to stop. She pulled her sweater up over her head, ignoring the cold, wet Seattle weather in her flimsy military T-shirt. She mashed the sweater against his wound.

"The detonator?" she asked, panicked. "You mean, like, the ankle detonator?"

He nodded, and then winced at the movement. "It was all of a sudden. He didn't say anything—he just heard something on his radio and pulled it out of his pocket. I swear, he was about to push the button."

"How did you stop him?"

"Laura did," Jack said, leaning his back against the filthy Dumpster. "She hit him and took it—she's so fast—and I think she broke his arm. That's when the fighting started."

Aubrey peeked around the edge of the Dumpster toward the way they'd come, and then glanced up at the rooftops. She couldn't see anyone. But she needed Jack's eyes. She wouldn't have been able to see a sniper on a rooftop even if her head wasn't filled with adrenaline.

"What happened to you?" she asked, turning her attention back to him.

"McKinney tried to shoot me," he said. "Right as Laura tackled him. I swear, she saved my life. Twice."

"Where is she?"

She could feel him try to shake his head, but her hands

wouldn't let him. "I don't know. The captain gave the order to the snipers to take out the Lambdas."

"What? Why would he do that?" She felt herself starting to cry, and she pushed the feelings down. "Did you know why? You could hear the radio in his ear, couldn't you?"

Jack smiled weakly. "I blocked it out because I was listening to you."

"Oh great," she said, forcing a laugh. "Good job, Aubrey. We have to get out of here."

"Uncover my ear," Jack said. "We've got to find Laura."

FORTY-SIX

JACK TRIED TO PUSH EVERYTHING else out of his mind—the throbbing in his own head, his labored breathing, Aubrey's poorly hidden sobs. He closed his eyes.

The pain was unbearable, and he kept trying to turn off the sense of touch—turn off the nerves in his own head. But it was an almost overwhelming task. He felt every shred of torn skin, every scrape against his skull, every broken blood vessel. It was excruciating.

There weren't any voices, not from the music museum. He could hear one person's breathing. He didn't know if it was a soldier or Laura.

It had to be a soldier. None of the Green Berets would have left Laura alive, not after she attacked them so viciously.

But if she was dead, they'd have the detonator. Both he

and Aubrey would have lost a leg by now.

He heard the sound of someone on a roof, but he couldn't pick it out. It was near them—rubber soles on a steel roof. That had to be a sniper, unless Laura was climbing onto roofs now.

He tried to concentrate even more, but it was nearly useless. Every time he moved his head, trying to locate a sound, the rough rubbing of the bloody sweater distracted him.

Jack could hardly believe he was still alive. The bullet had come so close. He'd felt every bit of it, as if time had slowed down. He'd felt it rip through his skin, then skid around his skull. He wondered how much farther it would've needed to be to the left to have killed him instead of grazing him—a millimeter? Two? He could have been dead right there. No one would have alerted Aubrey, and she'd have been killed by a sniper.

There was a clatter on a rooftop, the sound of—of a gun? And then quiet. Breathing. Two people had just fought and one of them had beaten the other, and he had no idea who had won.

"We have to get up," Jack said, looking in Aubrey's eyes. He moved the sweater from his head—it was now just a soaked rag, and it was stopping him from finding help.

"Why?" she asked, plainly terrified.

"To find Laura. Now."

Aubrey stared back at him for a moment, and then nodded.

She stood, still hunched so she wouldn't be seen over the Dumpster. She gave him her hand, and he pulled himself to his feet. He felt dizzy and tired, and he wondered if this was the right choice.

The breathing on the rooftop moved, quickly now, faster than a Green Beret could move. It had to be her.

Why was she fighting the snipers? Why weren't they just getting out of there? Was it rage? Revenge? Did she think they were going to track them all down?

"You stay here," Aubrey said. She reached into her small bag and pulled out the light pink bottle of Flowerbomb. It was a ridiculous image—she was wearing jeans and T-shirt, both her hands were smeared in his blood, and yet she was spraying herself with perfume.

His nose was immediately filled with the aroma of roses and orchids, mixed with the pungent iron scent of blood.

She smiled at him. "You look terrible."

"You look like you just murdered me," he answered.

She kissed him quickly, and then vanished.

She shouldn't have done that. The smell was on him now, right under his nose. He scrubbed at his face with sticky, red fingers to remove the perfume.

There was so much blood. He was going to pass out.

He leaned a shoulder against the Dumpster and tried to focus on the remnants of her perfume that were left trailing in the air behind her. She headed back down between the buildings, and it seemed, though he couldn't be sure, that she was stopping at the corner.

There was no more breathing from the roof. He tried to focus on the other roofs, where he knew the rest of the snipers were supposed to be, but it was too big of a plaza and he couldn't be sure of anything. Sounds bounced back and forth.

Someone was running, their shoes smacking hard against the pavement. It couldn't be Aubrey—she didn't run when she was invisible because it made her so unsteady.

Jack moved out from the Dumpster and down the alley. He wasn't walking in a straight line, and he knew that he wasn't going to catch up with anyone.

Everything had fallen apart. This morning they'd been part of a team of Green Berets and now they were the enemy. They were terrorists. Laura had killed soldiers—she was defending Jack and Aubrey—and now no one would ever believe them. They were outlaws. They were exactly what Captain Rowley had thought they were when he pulled out that detonator. They were killers. It didn't matter that Jack and Aubrey didn't kill—he would have certainly killed Captain Rowley to save Aubrey's life if he'd been able to do it. The fact that Laura did it instead didn't make him any less complicit.

Something was burning as Jack reached the end of the alleyway. He could smell it. And he saw Aubrey's bloody handprint on the wall where she had paused and waited.

The running feet were somewhere on the other side of Seattle Center, but they seemed to be coming toward him.

He shouldn't be there. Those running feet could be a soldier—someone chasing after them, pounding across the cement to get revenge—and Jack was standing around like an idiot. He didn't have a gun or even a rock. He was half-conscious.

And then the source of the footfalls appeared—Laura, running at full speed down toward the Children's Museum. He wanted to shout, to get her attention, but he didn't want any more attention for himself.

Where was Aubrey? There was too much for him to keep track of. Aubrey's perfume wafted in the breezeless, humid air as she made her way toward the center of the—

What was that burning?

Bang!

Jack watched as Laura, running at full speed, stumbled a few more steps, and then plummeted forward, tumbling head over heels across the pavement. There, at the entrance of the Children's Museum, was Sergeant Eschler with his pistol.

Jack ran. He didn't know why. It made no sense, but the only thing going through his mind was the throb of blood and the terror of seeing his bodyguard get murdered right in front of him.

Eschler saw him coming, and raised his pistol.

But the sergeant flew into the glass doors of the building,

as though pushed by an enormous gust of wind.

It wasn't wind, Jack knew immediately. It was Aubrey. She wasn't strong, and she'd only caught him off guard. The pistol was still in his hand, though Jack could tell that she was fighting him for it.

It only took a minute for the man to throw her off him, invisible or not. He swung the gun at empty space and fired.

"No," Jack breathed. All he could tell was that she was there, somewhere. Her perfume was all over Eschler and the ground.

Eschler fired a second time and then a third.

Jack was racing wildly, knowing that he'd be just as ineffectual as Aubrey had been—worse, because he was visible.

Eschler turned, leveling the gun.

And then, as though launching from a cannon, Laura erupted from the ground and shot forward, tackling Eschler and smashing him into the cement wall of the front of the Children's Museum.

The red-painted concrete crumbled around the impact, leaving a man-sized gash in the facade of the building. Laura stumbled backward, bleeding from her stomach.

Aubrey appeared, grabbing Laura as she fell.

That was three times Laura had saved him today.

Jack took the soldier's bag and dumped the contents onto the pavement. With shaking, wet fingers, he picked through the first-aid gear and found a roll of gauze and an Ace bandage.

"What's that smell?" Aubrey asked.

Lying on her back, with glazed eyes, Laura pointed upward. Black smoke was roiling from the Space Needle, about a third of the way up. And at the center of the smoke was a blinding white spot.

"Oh my . . ." Aubrey didn't even finish—she just stared.

They'd failed. Everything had failed. They'd fought the very people that they'd come here to help—or, rather, those people had fought them—and the terrorists got to the target anyway.

There was no way to stop them, Jack thought as he stared at the brilliant glowing center of the smoke. Laura was the only one who could do anything like that, who could possibly climb to where the damage was being done, and she was lying on the concrete bleeding from her stomach.

"We have to get out of here," Jack said, his eyes locking on Aubrey's. Without another word, she began lifting Laura to her feet, and Jack scrambled to gather as much of the soldier's gear as he could, throwing the first-aid kit, the flashlight, and the Beretta all into Aubrey's bag. He pulled one of Laura's arms over his shoulder, and Aubrey did the same on the other side. They hobbled as quickly as they could toward the alleyway, trying to put as much distance between them and the Space Needle as possible.

There was a metallic screech, and Jack hurried his steps. Laura was moving surprisingly well, but she'd always been tough. He hoped that she'd live long enough so they could thank her.

They moved down the side alley, which spread into a wider road, and a block later they reached a street. Jack didn't care who was watching. He used the flashlight to smash in the window of a car, and then knelt on the ground to hot-wire it—a skill he'd used a dozen times to start the run-down tractors he worked with in Mount Pleasant. He took the driver's seat, despite the blood that was still flowing from his head, and Aubrey helped Laura into the back and then sat with her, already applying first aid before Jack put the car into gear.

He pulled out into the empty street, and watched in his rearview mirror as the Space Needle fell.

FORTY-SEVEN

ALEC COULDN'T BELIEVE HIS LUCK, nor could he stop the grin from covering his face.

Laura, he thought. *The stupid little bitch.*

She'd put up quite a fight, but he'd seen the final bullet, seen it hit her in the chest. Laura was tough, but she couldn't take a bullet so close. He was sure of it.

His team hadn't had trouble with the Green Berets. They were so predictable, so ridiculous.

As soon as Alec had heard that the army was trying to create superpowered military strike forces—teams like his—he'd known they'd be simple to defeat. If anything, adding untrained superpowered teenagers to an army team made it weaker, not stronger.

It was fear. No one trusted a kid with that kind of power.

Even Alec's own trainers—his "parents"—had trouble trusting him, and that was after years of working together, years of testing and training and teaching. They were afraid of him, because he had a weapon they could never take away. And he was young. Adults instinctively distrusted the young.

So it was easy to implant a memory to make the Green Berets detonate the bombs.

Alec hadn't even had to approach the captain. One of Alec's new team members had lifted him into position near one of the snipers, and minutes later that sniper was sending panicked radio calls that one of the Lambdas was planting bombs near the Space Needle.

Alec didn't know what happened after that. The army team was in complete disarray, Laura managing to escape with another Lambda, only to be shot in the chest.

And while all of that was happening below, the other two members of Alec's team launched up to the center of the Space Needle. Lee—a Lambda like Alec had never imagined—superheated his body into a white-hot ball of flame and melted through the steel supports.

It was all perfect. Better than perfect. They'd taken the thing down in front of a team of Green Berets, a team of Lambdas, and Laura had been shot.

He had more important targets to focus on now, but he'd never forget this success.

FORTY-EIGHT

"WHAT HAPPENED?" AUBREY SHOUTED, LOOKING out the back window.

Laura didn't care—her side was screaming with pain as she lay awkwardly in the backseat. Blood was soaking the makeshift bandages.

Jack was driving the car, bleeding from his head, and Aubrey was trying to treat the bullet wound to Laura's torso.

Laura took a gasping breath and then gritted her teeth.

It had come down. Whatever team had been attacking, they'd succeeded, and Laura couldn't help but be pleased. And she'd even killed a few Green Berets while she was at it.

But her side—her rib, her whole body—felt like it was on fire.

Aubrey had saved Laura's life, and if she could have

breathed better she might have found it funny. Aubrey, a loyal soldier, saving the life of her enemy. If Aubrey hadn't slammed into Sergeant Eschler and knocked him back Laura would have been dead. And if Laura was dead, Jack would have been dead. The three of them were on their own, and Laura needed to keep herself together and stay in control.

Jack kept wiping blood from his face as he moved through the mostly empty Seattle streets, flying well over the speed limit. The Space Needle had come down, after all—who would care about a speeder?

"They turned on us," Laura said, and dug in her pocket, wincing in severe pain as she did so. At last she pulled out the detonator, now a crumpled mass of electronics, smashed apart in Laura's brutal hands.

"But why?" Aubrey asked, trying to inspect Laura's wound in the bouncing car. "What did we do wrong?"

"Nothing," Laura answered. "We did exactly what they wanted." It wasn't even a lie. Laura hadn't done anything to prompt the detonator, and neither had Jack—she'd been right next to him. And Laura was sure that Aubrey hadn't; she was a complainer, not a rebel.

Aubrey looked to Jack for an answer. "What do you think?"

Laura had to keep that in mind, too. Aubrey and Jack were totally devoted to each other. She couldn't play one against the other. They'd always pick each other over her.

Jack glanced back at them. His face looked awful, like something from a horror movie. Aubrey's hands shook even harder. Head wounds bleed a lot. Laura had heard it forever. Head wounds bleed—they look worse than they are.

"We didn't do anything," he finally said.

Aubrey had pulled up Laura's shirt to expose the bullet hole in her second-to-bottom rib. Blood was seeping from the wound, but not like the bright red gush from Jack's head. It was just a simple hole, not the violent tear above Jack's ear—Laura could even see the butt of the bullet. It looked like it had hit a rib and just stopped, flattened.

There weren't any tweezers in the first-aid kit, but Aubrey found some in her purse. She tore open a packet of antibiotic ointment and squirted it liberally all over the tweezers, and then positioned them on the bullet.

"This will probably hurt," she said.

Laura strained to smile. "I've already been shot. How much worse can it get?"

"Jack," Aubrey said. "Slow down for just a minute."

Jack slowed and pulled to the curb, turning to watch the surgery.

Aubrey wiped the exposed bullet with gauze to dry it. She positioned the tweezers and pulled.

It didn't come—the tweezers slipped off and Laura let out a little gasp.

It felt like a drill was boring down into her—even now,

even with the bullet motionless.

"Hang on," Aubrey said, whispering something to herself and repositioning the tweezers. They weren't made for surgery. They were for plucking eyebrows. They barely fit around the bullet.

Aubrey pulled again, the tweezers hanging on a second longer this time, but eventually sliding off.

"Dammit," Laura wheezed, and brushed Aubrey's hands away. She grabbed the bullet between her thumb and two fingers, dug deep into the skin with a guttural groan, spit curse words through gritted teeth, and yanked the bullet free. She gasped and exhaled, and threw the bullet at the window, cracking it.

Bright red blood bubbled from Laura's chest, and Aubrey immediately placed a heavy gauze pad over it, and affixed it in place with surgical tape.

The immediate pressure was gone, but the burning, searing pain remained.

Aubrey sat back in the car, plainly exhausted. She looked at Jack. "We need to find a place to get you cleaned up."

"And then we need to get out of this car," Jack said. "It looks like a murder scene."

Laura tried to sit up more in the seat, wincing as she did but not stopping. "We need to figure out where we're going to go, too."

"We have these bracelets," Aubrey said, pointing to her

wrist. Her bracelet was splattered with a little blood, and she wiped it clean. "They're supposed to be like a free pass, right? They say we're healthy."

"They're a free pass assuming our faces don't show up on any wanted posters," Laura said. "The only reason the captain would have used that detonator is if he thought we were terrorists. And nothing happened back there, so the only reason he would have thought we were terrorists is if someone radioed it to him. Someone whispered in his ear that he needed to disable all of us."

"Speaking of," Aubrey said, "we still have these things on our ankles. I assume they're tamperproof."

"I destroyed the detonator."

Jack spoke. "Do we know if that's the only one? Can they be detonated by someone else? More remotely?"

"Listen," Laura said, pointing ahead and talking through gritted teeth. "Look at that neighborhood. What do you bet that half those houses are empty? Let's go get cleaned up."

"What if they have alarms?" Aubrey asked.

"The freaking Space Needle just collapsed. I don't think police are going to care about a burglary."

User: SusieMusie

Mood: Whatever

It's time to talk about the military, I guess. I was lucky, too young to go. But now they're talking about kids my age having to go there, too. Be fearless, everybody. They say there's a virus or something.

FORTY-NINE

JACK LET AUBREY DRIVE THE rest of the way. Her eyes were much worse than his, but he felt too light-headed to stay behind the wheel.

They picked a road off a major street, and searched for houses that looked empty, unprotected. It seemed like no one had cars here. Rowley'd said that Seattle had been hit harder than many cities, but would that make everyone flee? Maybe it was just because these houses were more expensive—these people could afford to run for the mountains, or Canada, or the little islands in Puget Sound.

Aubrey checked several houses—invisibly peering in windows—before they broke into one.

There didn't seem to be an alarm—there were no keypads anywhere—and they took turns in the shower.

It was the first time that Jack had looked at himself in the mirror, and he was horrified. The grazing wound over his ear had mostly stopped bleeding, but his hair was matted and tangled in dark patches, and his entire left side was soaked, from his shirt to his shoes.

He washed quickly—the hot water was off. He wondered if that was a precaution the family took before evacuating, or if terrorists had hit the natural gas lines somewhere in the city.

He tried to scrub around the cut, but even so there was a constant stream of red dripping down his body and into the drain. And he couldn't control the raging, splintering pain in his heightened senses. He had to give up, trying to rinse and numb the wound with cold water.

When he was out of the shower, Aubrey appeared with the first-aid kit. She had him kneel in front of the sink, and she gently—excruciatingly—rubbed at the wound with a washcloth. It took three clean towels to dry his head and dab the blood from his gash before she was willing to put the antibiotic gel on the skin and wrap gauze around his skull like a headband.

"You're enjoying this just a little too much," Jack said, as she finished the painful process and taped the gauze in place.

"I'm not going to let you get infected," she said. "You have such a nice face."

Laura came down the stairs wearing clothes that looked a little too old for her, a little less trendy, but they fit well enough. Aubrey was in a similar style, though she was drowning in a two-sizes-too-big fleece jacket.

"We need to talk, guys," Laura said. She was walking a little more gingerly than before, but you could hardly tell she'd been shot in the abdomen. Not for the first time, Jack thought that he'd love to trade powers with her.

Laura tossed a bottle to him. "Painkillers," she said. "I found them upstairs."

Jack took a tablet and swallowed it.

"I assume," he said, "that you want to talk about what we do next?"

Laura nodded as she sat, and Aubrey plopped down in an easy chair, stuffing her hands in the pockets of the jacket.

"We can turn ourselves in," Jack said, not because he really believed it, but because he wanted to get it out on the table. To his surprise, it was Aubrey who spoke first.

"No," she said. "They want to kill us. And, even if they didn't want to before, they do now."

"It could have been a mistake," Jack said.

"Do we all want to risk our left foot on that?" Laura said.

"So what other options do we have?" he asked. "Hide out somewhere? Go on the run? Escape to Canada?"

"There are terrorists in Canada," Aubrey said, and the other two stared at her. No one had heard that.

"The newspaper upstairs," she said. "It's dated three days ago. It says there have been attacks all through British Columbia and Alberta."

"That doesn't make any sense," Jack said. "Since when do terrorists go after more than one country?"

"When more than one country is pissing them off," Laura said. "Al-Qaeda went after the US, but they also went after all sorts of places in Europe and Africa. They just don't make the news because we don't care as much unless it's happening right in front of us."

"So we go to Mexico," Jack said. "Any terrorists there?"

Aubrey shrugged.

"Do you guys have any place you can hide here?" Laura asked. "Any contacts?"

"We're from the same town," Jack said. "They're armed, and I bet they've formed a friggin' militia to try to get their kids back, but I don't trust the town to keep a secret long. It's too small, and everybody knows everybody else."

Aubrey nodded. "We can't go back."

No one spoke for a long time. Jack thought about Mexico. It sounded awful. He knew that Aubrey had taken a class or two of Spanish, and she almost certainly got A's, but that didn't mean it was going to be easy to flee there and live in peace.

Besides, betrayal or no betrayal, he didn't want to just run away and watch while America burned to the ground.

"I know some people," Laura said. "I haven't been totally honest with you guys. But I've been aware of my powers for a long time—like you, Aubrey—and a couple of my friends have, too. They hid out better than I did, I think. We could see the writing on the wall and we started to get ready for the government to come after us. We built bomb shelters and things—well, not bomb shelters, but you know—storage."

"What kind of storage?" Jack asked.

"Just food and stuff. We didn't get as much as we wanted, because we were only in college. We didn't have a lot of money."

"So," Aubrey said, "you're saying we should find these storage places? Would they be enough for us to lay low and hide?"

"Probably not," Laura said. "I'm saying that we should do exactly what we've been doing—infiltrating the enemy—but Aubrey, I think you should get into the military base—where we were yesterday?"

"What?" Jack said, before Aubrey got a chance. "If you haven't noticed, every single one of these 'infiltrations' have been disastrous."

"And what would I be looking for, anyway?" Aubrey said.

"If we can find these guys, then that's five of us instead of three. And for all I know, they've been working more on storage. They might have a safe place we can go. More important—we need to find out how to get these bombs off our legs."

"Is this about the rebellion you were talking about?" Aubrey asked, suddenly sounding suspicious.

"Not really," Laura said. "We weren't part of the rebellion, and I don't think they would be now. They definitely wouldn't be part of a violent rebellion like the one that attacked us. I'm just saying that I don't think this is all black-and-white: that we're either on the run as criminals or we're helping the army catch Lambdas. There has to be a different way to live."

Jack looked at Aubrey and she stared back at him. She didn't appear at all convinced. Neither was Jack, but it wasn't like he had a better solution. He definitely had no interest in a rebellion, and even though he didn't mind the prospect of spending all his time with Aubrey he wanted to be legal. He didn't want to be on the army's list of most wanted. He didn't want to have an explosive tied to his foot for the rest of his life. He didn't want to live in fear, marked as a terrorist.

"What if we do something easier?" Jack said, still looking at Aubrey. "What if we just infiltrate the army base, find out why the order was given to kill us, and see if we can make things right?"

Aubrey was clearly discouraged, though it looked like she was trying to hide it.

Jack continued. "I'm just thinking that if we know why they're after us, then maybe we can make things good? Maybe we won't be criminals if we can give them what they want?"

Aubrey spoke. "I screwed up breaking into a demolished school full of homeless people, and you think I can make it into a military base?"

"You didn't screw up," Jack said. "You got in. You assessed all of the dangers and gave an exact account of the guards.

Then you got down to where the girl was, and when the Green Berets couldn't take her down, you did. It was a huge success."

Aubrey exhaled long and slow. "It felt like a failure."

"And today wasn't your fault," Laura said. "You saved my life. He was going to take another shot at me."

Aubrey stared straight ahead.

Jack spoke. "You're good with computers—you get straight A's in everything—and they'll probably be everywhere. Just get into one of them. You probably won't need to hack a password—use a computer while someone else isn't watching."

"And it's not even a real military base," Laura said. "It's a Marriott. There will be a lot of soldiers everywhere, but there shouldn't be too much security. There'll probably only be the cameras that the hotel already has."

Finally, Aubrey sighed and looked over at Jack. "You'll have my back?"

"I'll follow every step you take. And if you get caught, I'm coming in there with you. I'm not going to let them split us up."

"But you're not going to get caught," Laura said.

"What are the names of the people you want me to find?" Aubrey asked.

"Alec Moore and Dan Allen. They're both from Denver, like me. I'll write it down for you."

FIFTY

JUST AS LAURA HAD PREDICTED, the main benefit of having a makeshift army command center set up in a hotel was that a hotel wasn't designed to be an army base. It was close to other buildings, and there were a lot of entrances to guard. In the case of the Marriott, it was on the waterfront, so that vantage was blocked, but it wasn't hard to move from building to building, climbing over barricades, slipping around vehicles, moving from bush to bush, column to column.

The place was prepared for World War III. Aubrey hadn't realized that the first time they'd arrived. In addition to the jeeps and armored vehicles there were trucks loaded with surface-to-air missiles. Aubrey had no idea what they'd be needed for—she'd only seen the one Lambda who could fly—and could a missile really track a flying person?

The entire street, Alaskan Way, was blocked off, and the

marina in front of it was emptied. It took Aubrey a long time to get all the way from the first roadblock to the hotel. She'd hoped to find some kind of large fern or patch of trees to hide in and reappear—to give her a chance to get her energy back—but the only trees in front of the hotel were planted into the sidewalk.

So instead, she waited at the front entrance for someone to open the door, and then slipped inside.

The entrance was beehive of activity, and Aubrey didn't know where to look first. But she knew she needed to keep moving—the lobby had to have security cameras.

She hurried toward the back of the hotel, following signs that directed her to the ballrooms. She didn't have a lot of experience in big hotels—the biggest place in Mount Pleasant probably had twenty rooms, and she'd never stayed there. But, she figured that the best place to not be seen was the kitchen. Their room service hadn't been cooked, which meant most of the staff was gone. There'd be no reason to set up much of a military kitchen if everyone was still eating MREs.

Her eyesight was getting worse as she entered the main ballroom, but she kept going, tripping over a cord and stumbling to stay on her feet. The ballroom appeared to be the central hub. A dozen long tables were set up, and cords were strewn everywhere to support the computers, laptops, servers, and who-knew-what-else that the army had arranged. There was a PC open and available right in front of her, but she could hardly make out the words on the screen. She headed toward the back of the room and through a door to the kitchen.

It was empty.

She breathed a sigh of relief and moved from cupboard to cupboard, trying to find one big enough to fit her inside. Finally, she came across a walk-in pantry with a heavy door. She made sure she could get out—there was a lever inside, too—and then pulled it closed. She sat in the corner, tucked between an enormous sack of potatoes and a crate of old oranges.

Aubrey smiled, smelling the old produce around her, and wondered what Jack would have thought of it. She'd noticed he was losing weight. The plainest of foods—bread or rice or even water—were so overpowering to him that he rarely ate as much as he should anymore.

She also wondered what he was thinking of her now. He knew that she was going to look for a place to hide, but the scent of Flowerbomb almost certainly couldn't make it out this heavy door, and she'd seem to have disappeared completely. If he could track her at all. He swore he could, but he and Laura hadn't been able to get very close. They were in an apartment nearly half a mile up the road.

So far, things had gone well. But all she'd done was get inside. She hadn't tried to access a computer yet, or navigate the army's systems. For now, she needed to rest. She took a drink from her water bottle and leaned back.

λ

Aubrey didn't know how much time had passed, but she felt stronger now. Her eyes were refocused—she was practicing reading the box labels across the pantry, and everything seemed to be clear. She had more energy and was ready to disappear again.

She reached in her fleece pocket and felt for the paper Laura had given her. There was also the little bottle of perfume, and she sprayed herself again before leaving. She was starting to love the smell.

She eased the pantry door open. The kitchen was still empty, the fluorescent lights only half-lit.

Aubrey hurried back to the ballroom. If possible, the room was even busier than before, with more soldiers at computer terminals and officers marching around giving angry commands.

Aubrey waited in a corner, away from the action for several minutes, watching for a computer to open up.

An officer walked nearby, talking on a cell phone and jamming a finger in his other ear so he could hear over the din of the room.

"Just get the message to him," he said.

Aubrey moved a little closer to eavesdrop.

"I don't give a damn about the Space Needle," the officer said. "It's a stupid tourist trap, and it was evacuated anyway. This is Boeing I'm talking about."

There was a pause. Aubrey thought she knew what Boeing was, but couldn't put her finger on it.

"You let him know," the officer continued, "that we're being destroyed out here. We can't guard every business. Hell—we *were* guarding Boeing and it didn't do any good. I'm not exaggerating when I say that we could be facing another Chicago up here."

Boeing. They'd flown in a Boeing airliner. Was Boeing in Seattle?

A man stood and left his computer. Aubrey was tempted to stay and listen in on the conversation, but she didn't dare.

She took his chair, sitting on the edge of it, exactly the way that he'd left it. He was still logged in.

The system wasn't what she was expecting. It was older, less intuitive. She looked through the files on the screen, but didn't see anything about the Lambdas.

She found a search bar and typed her name.

Aubrey Parsons Lambda

A picture of her appeared—a photo taken all the way back when they'd first been tested.

Aubrey Parsons
Lambda 4T: Limited form of invisibility (click here
for medical report)
Special Forces 19th Battalion, ODA 9117
Currently stationed: Seattle, WA

The text continued, outlining her background and her eyesight problems, but there was nothing interesting there. It was all basic information—information she already knew and obviously not updated to reflect anything that had happened today.

Toward the bottom—she almost missed it—was the line *"Ankle Band Detonation Code: 431-866795."* She deleted the number, and then searched to see if there was some kind of edit history where it could be retrieved, but the program looked old and all she could do was hope.

Next she searched for Jack.

Jack Cooper
Lambda 4T: Hypersensitivity (click here for
medical report)
Special Forces 19th Battalion, ODA 9117
Currently stationed: Seattle, WA

She deleted his detonation code and then searched for "Laura Hansen Lambda."

It was more of the same. Old information, probably not updated since they left Dugway a few days before. She deleted Laura's detonation code.

She pulled the paper from her pocket.

Alec Moore Lambda

His picture popped up.

Alec Moore
Tested in the Dugway Quarantine Facility
No symptoms of the Erebus virus or Lambda
attributes (click here for medical report)
Released to Salt Lake City transfer station
October 9th

That picture. Aubrey recognized it. She knew him from somewhere. . . . Alec Moore. Who was that? It felt like only half a memory, like she'd seen him in a dream.

It was probably nothing. He'd been at Dugway. She'd probably seen him.

Next she searched for the other name Laura had given her.

Daniel Allen
Lambda 5M: Ability to manipulate the movement
of minerals (click here for medical report)
Special Forces 19th Battalion, ODA 9128
Currently stationed: San Francisco, CA
Was found outside Price, UT, and surrendered
willingly. Claimed to be hitchhiking to his home
in Denver, CO, and his father corroborated the
story.

Aubrey jotted down notes on where Dan Allen's unit was located, and stuffed the paper back in her pocket. She deleted his detonation code as well; if they ever got to him, it needed to be deactivated.

She looked up to see where the soldier was, and found him a few tables away, talking to an officer. If anyone glanced over, they'd see the computer screen changing. She had to work faster.

She exited Dan's profile and searched for "Space Needle." The results came up empty.

Next she tried "Sergeant McKinney."

21 results found.

Too many to dig through. Aubrey tried a couple more.

Sergeant Eschler
14 results found.
Captain Dane Rowley
2 results found.

She clicked on the first and knew instantly from the picture it wasn't who she was looking for. She clicked the second.

His picture and profile were there, but above them, in bold type, were the words:

Killed in action while on a Special Reconnaissance mission watching over the Space Needle in Seattle, WA. Investigation is ongoing. It is known that he was given the order to terminate his Lambda team, and the Lambdas attacked and killed all but one member of his team. Shortly thereafter, the Space Needle was destroyed, collapsed by some unknown explosion or force. Initial reports indicate that the Lambda team assigned to CPT Rowley could not have accomplished this on their own, due to their particular skill set, and it is theorized they had additional help with the destruction.

It is also not yet known who gave the order authorizing the termination of the Lambda team, or why. The radio transmission is being reviewed.

FURTHER INFORMATION WILL BE POSTED AS IT BECOMES AVAILABLE.

Aubrey exited the personnel records and returned the computer to the original screen.

"Jack," she said. "I don't know if you can hear me, but this isn't good."

FIFTY-ONE

AUBREY DROVE THE CAR, HER vision supposedly much better after having rested for a night in the apartment. Jack sat next to her in the front seat, watching the winding road ahead for the ever-present roadblocks. Laura would have preferred that he drive, but every time he did he got twice as many questions from the police—everyone wanted to grill him about his bandaged head.

It was hard for Laura to hide her happiness that they were going to get Dan with them. She'd done what she could to subvert the Green Berets, but that was all over now, and she needed help to hit important targets—she couldn't do it on her own.

And she was looking forward to getting rid of the two lovebirds up front. Everything scared them; everything made them second-guess her. But once she was back with Dan, they'd come up with a way to get rid of Jack and Aubrey.

Laura had found keys to this sedan in the apartment they'd been hiding in. It was nice to not have a filthy car with busted windows. This one looked like three late-teens should be driving it; it was old enough to not look stolen, and it was intact, with one dent on the front fender.

"Roadblock," Jack said, sitting up a little in his seat. "A couple miles ahead."

Laura stowed her smartphone in the seat pocket. She'd stolen it from a neighboring apartment and had been messing with it all day. She'd been watching the news, tracking the other terrorist groups.

"Old Faithful is a pile of rubble," she said, sitting a little straighter for the police.

"Weird thing to blow up," Jack responded, staring ahead at the upcoming barricades.

"Not really. If the point is to scare people, then destroy the things they love. What's more American than Old Faithful? You can't even call it that anymore—they said it's just a mound of rocks that kind of bubbles like a little fountain."

"I never got to go," Aubrey said.

"Me either," said Laura. Not that she'd ever wanted to.

Aubrey turned to glance at Laura. "Did they say anything about Chicago? That was something that I heard in the hotel—that Chicago was bad."

"Oh yeah," Laura said, her voice a little quieter now. She'd been paying special attention to that. "A couple days ago— well, maybe about a week ago. It was like everyone—all the terrorists, I mean—converged on Chicago at the same time. The internet is spotty about reports, but most agree it was pretty well devastated."

She paused, thinking of the implications.

"Devastated more than Seattle?" Aubrey said. "That place was a no-man's-land."

"Yeah," Laura said. "More than that. Listen, I have friends there—I *had* friends there. I don't want to talk about it, okay?"

That should keep them quiet.

Jack glanced at Aubrey, who just nodded and said, "Okay."

The roadblock was set up like most of the others, with three police cars blocking the road in a sort of Z pattern. Road flares were burned down to ashes, unnecessary in the daylight. The police car read "California Highway Patrol."

Aubrey pulled to a stop and put the car in park, and after unrolling her window, she put her hands on the steering wheel. She'd learned from hundreds of miles of experience what the policemen liked to see.

"Where are you headin'?" he asked. He was an older man with a paunch and a gray mustache.

"San Francisco," Aubrey answered.

"License?"

She held out her wrist bracelet. "I don't have my real license—it got lost when I went through quarantine. But this is me. We all have them."

Laura leaned forward and held up her wrist and the tamper-proof ID tag that declared her to be negative for the Erebus virus. The army couldn't have given her a better present.

"What's in San Francisco?" he asked, jotting down the identification number off Aubrey's bracelet. All of the police wrote down the number, but no one had ever checked it, so far as Laura could tell.

"We have family there," Aubrey said. She sniffled and wiped her eye. For being a goody-goody, Aubrey knew how to lie. "At least we did have family. We haven't heard from them since the Golden Gate came down."

"I don't know if I'd head into the city right now," the officer said. "It's getting pretty bad in there, and I'm not talking about the terrorists. I'm talking about what happens when people don't have any law and order and they all go crazy. To tell the truth, that's where we should be, but the governor has us here watching the damned border."

"We'll be careful."

He leaned down on the car window and pointed to Jack. "You take care of these ladies."

"I will, sir."

"What the hell happened to your head?"

"We were in Seattle when the Space Needle came down," Aubrey answered for him.

"You'd never believe it," Jack added. "We were half a mile away, in an apartment, and a piece of steel as big as a tree trunk came flying through the wall."

"Oh, I believe it," the officer said, and stood up. "You ask me, this is the start of World War Three. We just haven't figured out who the damned enemy is yet."

"I think you may be right," Aubrey said.

"Well, you'd better get moving. With all these roadblocks you've probably got another six, seven hours before you hit the Bay. Good luck to you."

"Thanks."

She rolled up the window and shifted the car back into drive.

"One of these times," Jack said, "someone's going to check out our story."

The beginning of World War III. Laura covered her mouth to hide her grin.

FIFTY-TWO

THEY DROVE THROUGH THE DAY, and when it got dark Jack took over—Aubrey's eyesight just wasn't good enough at night.

Not much was open anymore, but they found a McDonald's outside of Vacaville. There was an armed security guard—not a cop, but a scary-looking mammoth of a man who had a Taser on one hip and a gun on the other. After everything she'd seen, Aubrey thought it was laughable that anyone thought this guy could stop a terrorist Lambda. But, at least the McDonald's was open—the three of them were starving.

Aubrey ordered the food while the other two—both still injured and looking terrible—sat in a booth toward the back. Aubrey had noticed that there was a spot of blood showing though Laura's shirt, but Laura refused to acknowledge it. It was like she was a machine—single-minded in whatever it was that she was trying to do. Aubrey just didn't know what that was.

Aubrey didn't have any great ideas for what they ought to be doing, but she didn't know why Laura's plan was any better than anything else. Why were they looking for Laura's friends instead of Aubrey and Jack's? They could track down Matt Ganza. He had to be somewhere. Or Nicole. She was with the State Department now, and if anyone could get them out of this mess, Nicole seemed like a good choice.

Aubrey wished that she had thought of that when she was going through the army's computer.

While Aubrey stood at the counter, she watched the fry cook. The guy was skinny and pale, and Aubrey wondered what this kid thought about everything going on around him. He was still coming in to work, which had to mean something: the kid had hope. Or desperation, maybe. At the very least, it meant that someone was still giving him a paycheck. The world hadn't completely collapsed if a McDonald's in Vacaville was open at midnight.

He was skinny and pale. . . . It reminded her of that picture—Alec Moore, Laura's friend. Something about him had been nagging at Aubrey since she'd seen it. Had he been on TV? Where had she seen him before?

The food came, and she thanked the skinny fry cook.

Alec Moore. Who was he?

She took the tray of hamburgers back to the table, arriving just as Laura was gingerly standing and heading to the bathroom. She was holding her side.

"Do you know who Alec Moore is?" Aubrey asked, as soon as Laura was out of earshot.

Jack unwrapped his burger. "Laura's friend? No."

"I've seen him before—they had a picture on the computer—and it seems like I remember meeting someone named Alec. It's weird. It's like it's been on the tip of my tongue since Laura first mentioned him, but I can't place him at all."

"Maybe you're thinking of Alec Baldwin," Jack said, with a smile. He took a bite of fries.

"I'm not thinking of Alec Bal—wait. Do you remember going to school with someone named Alec? Way back in like the third or fourth grade?"

"I don't think so."

It was coming back to Aubrey. Alec Moore. The guy she'd met in the quarantine zone, who had made a connection with her, to the other girls' dismay.

"There was a guy," Aubrey explained. "Back at Dugway. He said he lived in Mount Pleasant for a couple years when he was a kid. His name was Alec, and I'm pretty sure it was Alec Moore."

Jack continued eating, but Aubrey had stopped.

"That's a big coincidence, don't you think?"

He ate another fry. "I'm pretty sure I don't remember any-one named Alec in elementary school."

"Neither do I," she said. "But—I don't know. Maybe I do. Back there, it seemed like I knew him."

"Either way," Jack said, "I don't think it changes anything. If he grew up in Mount Pleasant, then that's good, right? Kinda makes me trust him a little more."

Aubrey shrugged. "I guess. But remember—we're not going after him right now. We're looking for this Dan guy."

"I wish we were looking for our friends, not hers."

"Exactly," Aubrey said.

She glanced over at the bathrooms. Laura was still gone. Aubrey lowered her voice. "I don't know if I totally trust what we're doing. Are we actually getting help? Or is Laura just going AWOL and wants our help to find her friends? You and I are the recon team—she couldn't contact Dan without us."

Jack chewed thoughtfully for several seconds, watching the bathroom door. He finally swallowed. "I'm open to other ideas. I just don't know what to do. This seems dumb, but we're on the run from the friggin' US Army. What's dumber than that?"

The bathroom door opened.

"I don't know," Aubrey said.

Maybe Dan could help them hide out. Maybe they really did have storage hidden somewhere—some kind of bomb-shelter hideouts where they could be safe.

Jack took another bite of hamburger and stood up. "I'm going to go check out this cut," he said as Laura came back.

"The bathrooms aren't very clean," Laura said. "Take some of the antibiotics with you."

He nodded and Aubrey dug through her purse for another packet of medicine. They were running low.

Jack took it and headed off.

"So," Aubrey said. "Any idea how we're going to find Dan once we get to the city?"

"There's a military base," Laura said, pulling out the smartphone. "I looked it up. Camp Parks. It's training for the army reserve, but I bet that's where they're running things."

"I don't know if I can do a real army base," Aubrey said. "Remember—anything with a long line of sight is dangerous. Plus, I can be invisible, but what about Dan? How will he get out of there?"

"What if we can arrange a meet-up somewhere?" Laura said. "Find out where their next mission is, and help break him out."

Laura was digging into her food like it was the first thing she'd eaten in days. Maybe superstrength gave her a high metabolism. Or it was recovery.

"I've got a question," Aubrey said, nerves sending a chill down her spine. "You said that Alec is from Denver."

"Yep."

"How long have you known him?"

"Forever, I guess," she said. "It seems like we've always been friends. Kinda like you and Jack."

Aubrey ate a french fry, slowly, wondering if she should continue. Laura made her nervous.

"I think I met him," Aubrey finally said. "In the quarantine zone. He said he remembered me from school—and I kind of remembered him. He said he grew up in Mount Pleasant."

Laura looked startled. "Well—well, maybe you're thinking about someone else."

"He looked just like the picture on the army computer."

"I don't know what to tell you." Laura took a huge bite of her Quarter Pounder, and looked down at the paper advertisement on the food tray.

"And another thing," Aubrey said, her voice soft and careful. "You said that he was a Lambda, like you and Dan. But he was in the quarantine zone, and they let him go."

Laura seemed to chew for a lot longer than was needed. Aubrey wished Jack was back. Not that he could help, but she didn't like being alone with Laura.

"You were in the quarantine zone," Laura finally said. "You wouldn't have been caught if you hadn't tried to escape."

"I wasn't—" Aubrey stopped herself. She didn't want to argue. "What is Alec's power?"

"He can talk to you with his mind," Laura said, still staring down at the paper. "What's that called? Telepathy? Even if he was tested, the army probably wouldn't have any purpose for him, I don't think. They probably would have labeled him a Lambda 1 or 2, and he'd have to sit out the war in those Dugway dorms."

Aubrey glanced at the bathrooms, wishing Jack was back.

"Laura," Aubrey said, her hand gripping the edge of the table. "Do you really think this will help? Getting Dan and Alec, I mean? Or is this just . . ."

"Just what?" Laura said, finally looking up.

"Just—I don't know. Are you . . . are you just going AWOL?"

"Excuse me?" Laura said, her eyes suddenly furious. "Didn't you see that bastard shoot me? Try to kill me?"

"Yeah, I—"

"And didn't you see me save you and your boyfriend?"

She pointed to the bathroom, where Jack was coming out of the door. He looked concerned. He'd been listening.

"I know you did," Aubrey said. "I just—I don't know if this is—"

Laura grabbed Aubrey's wrist and began to squeeze. It felt like the bones were grinding together, and Aubrey let out a yelp.

"Stop it," Jack said.

"What the hell do you people want from me?" Laura

said, still crushing Aubrey. "I'm trying to help you. Haven't I always tried to help you?"

It was hard for Aubrey to talk through the pain. "Are you trying to help us?" she wheezed. "Or are you using me because you can't get in there yourself?"

Laura's eyes widened, and she released the grip. Aubrey immediately disappeared, slipping away from the table.

"Maybe you can talk some sense into her," Laura said to Jack, glaring at the empty space where Aubrey used to be.

"Let's all calm down," he said, looking only at Laura. "Aubrey's sticking her neck out for you. I think it's only fair that she ask some questions."

"There's a difference between asking questions and making accusations," Laura snapped. She grabbed her hamburger and took another huge bite.

Aubrey sat down at the table across the aisle and reappeared. Laura glared at her.

"Listen," Jack said. "We can work together, or we can split up right here. It's your choice, Laura. But if we're going to work together—if we're going to be a team—then we all have to be on the same playing field."

"So what do you want to know?" Laura snapped. "Am I lying? After everything I did for you guys, you want to know if this is a big con?"

"For starters," Jack said, "you can swear on whatever you love most that you won't touch Aubrey again."

Laura laughed darkly. "Or what?"

"Or we're gone, and you can do this all on your own."

"Fine," Laura said. "And in exchange I'd like a little bit of trust. I think I've more than proved myself to you. I don't deserve this crap."

Jack looked at Aubrey and she stared back at him. Jack didn't look certain—didn't seem like he knew what to do.

"Fine," Aubrey said. "We'll help you, and we'll work together. But that doesn't mean I trust you—not after what you did."

Laura took the final bite of hamburger and chewed slowly as she eyed Aubrey.

"Fine."

FIFTY-THREE

THERE WAS A PROTEST OUTSIDE Camp Parks. Jack could see tents in the distance—the camp was another quarantine/ training facility, and the angry mob at the fence were parents and family.

Well, they didn't seem angry anymore. The protest was weak and tired, with families sitting in camp chairs and talking among themselves, only getting angry and yelling when a Humvee or armored vehicle went in or out of the gate. A few people held signs—"Give us back our children!" and "Rest in Peace: US Constitution"—but the wind seemed to be taken out of their sails. And, Jack guessed, anyone in those vehicles wasn't very important. There was a steady stream of helicopter traffic—those were probably all the special forces teams, all the VIPs.

Jack stood back from the fence, wearing a woolen winter cap to hide the bandage around his head. It wasn't that cold in California, but he didn't look entirely out of place or suspicious.

And he listened. He listened to the patrols, the radio chatter as they monitored the fence. There was no mention of him, which was good. He didn't know if there were wanted posters out for the three of them, but he hoped the hat would help with that, too.

Farther inside the base it was a mess of noise—talking from the quarantine zone, radio blasts from somewhere inside the buildings. Phone calls, arguments, orders given and orders received. A lot of "yes, sir" and "no, sir."

He stood outside that fence for hours, shifting his focus from one building to the next, room to room, listening for any mention of ODA 9128, Dan's team. Somewhere in the suburbs behind him, Aubrey and Laura sat in the car, not speaking to each other and waiting for him to give them news.

In a way, he was relieved. If they couldn't find Dan, then that would still keep the odds in Jack and Aubrey's favor. He still wasn't sure if that mattered, but it felt like it did. After the way Laura had acted at the McDonald's the night before, Jack was nervous around her. She wasn't who he wanted to be on the run with.

He just didn't know where else to go. At least she seemed

to have a plan, which was more than what he and Aubrey had.

Mexico was looking more enticing. They could go there and live completely off the grid—live like kings. They'd be criminals—they'd have to live on whatever Aubrey could steal until they could get on their feet, but that's no worse than what they were doing now—stealing cars and wallets and breaking into abandoned homes.

But he had his family to worry about. The US could fall into ruin and he might find safety in Mexico, but what would happen to his mom and dad? They ran the thrift store, after all; they hardly had any income as it was—they'd be hurting really bad now that people moved into a survivalist mode: no one would be giving them donations, and no one would be spending money.

Going back to them wouldn't solve anything. It would just be one more mouth to feed. If it was true that Laura, Dan, and Alec had stockpiled supplies, then he could take care of himself and Aubrey at least, and if things went well then he could help his family, too.

"—the 9128 is on their way out there right now."

Jack's focus narrowed instantly on a blocky, two-story building, an upstairs room.

"They're not going to be there in time," a woman's voice said.

"It's the best we can do. Besides, the place was evacuated

weeks ago." It was a man. He sounded tired.

"It's San Francisco City Hall. It's a national landmark!"

Jack started walking away, back to the car.

"Do you think that matters now? They're hitting landmarks because all the important targets are either hit or guarded too tightly."

"So we should just give up on it?"

"I told you," the man said, "9128 is on their way out there right now."

Jack broke into a jog.

"Isn't the 9128 the one that accidentally destroyed the Dumbarton Bridge? With Lambdas like these, who needs terrorists?"

"I don't need to remind you," he said, "at this point, our goal is not to save monuments and buildings. Our goal is to find and destroy these terrorist cells. If city hall comes down, so be it. Besides, how big of a deal can it be? I've never heard of it."

Jack broke into a run. He'd only ever seen San Francisco on maps, but he knew they were on the wrong side of the bay. Hopefully the roads were as empty as the city seemed to be.

FIFTY-FOUR

THE CAR RIDE WAS TAKING forever.

Laura sat in the backseat with the smartphone, keeping an eye on the battery. She didn't have a charger, and it was already down to half power.

Military targets. That was what she was after. Military targets she could hit with Dan. And, maybe if Jack and Aubrey were dumb enough, they'd help out. Alec had always thought Laura was the dumb one, but she'd played these two kids easily. They had a common enemy, and Laura had slipped into a position of authority—she was the oldest, the most powerful. And they were scared; they were scared of her, but they were also looking for someone to tell them what to do.

She scrolled through websites over and over again, searching for something good—something important. Some of the sites had obviously been censored in recent weeks, removing a lot of information about the military, but nothing was ever entirely erased from the internet. She just needed to find it.

Dan was in San Francisco, but there weren't many targets nearby—a couple of Coast Guard stations. Farther to the east were three air force bases, but she doubted that there was much Dan could do there—he couldn't get close enough to disrupt a runway or knock down a tower. And Laura didn't feel like taking any more bullets.

There was a naval college to the south. That was probably the least protected option, but it didn't seem like a very enticing target: any damage she did there wouldn't make an immediate impact in the war.

But the farther south they went, the more bases popped up: air force, army, navy—even marines. There had to be something good in one of them, some weakness that could be exploited.

She looked at maps of the bases, and she focused on mountains—somewhere Dan could bring down another avalanche, or cause an earthquake. But there just wasn't a lot in Southern California. Plenty of bases, but nothing next to a hill or a cliff or a mountain range.

She scrolled farther south.

Wait a minute.

She pulled up a topographical map.

It was a gamble, but if it worked . . .

She turned off the phone and leaned back in her seat, a plan already forming in her mind. Now she just needed Dan.

FIFTY-FIVE

IT TOOK THEM THREE HOURS to get to San Francisco. The Bay Bridge was bumper-to-bumper traffic with a military roadblock at each end. Still, the bracelets and cover story seemed to work just fine. The military was obviously looking for someone else—something more specific. They checked the trunk, and looked under the car with long mirrors on sticks, but eventually let them pass. Aubrey drove as quickly as she dared through the hilly streets of San Francisco until they got within a quarter mile of city hall.

There was no plume of dust and smoke, no sounds of settling steel. If the terrorists were really going to come for city hall, they were taking their time. But that was no different from the attack on the Space Needle—an anonymous tip that didn't pan out for hours.

They parked near a tall office building, and Jack got out of the car and listened. Aubrey stood next to him, holding his hand and trying to make him look as little like a terrorist as possible. With her other hand, she was downing power bars, loading up on calories. "They're there," he whispered, leaning in close so his voice was barely audible. "I can hear the radios. I'm not sure where they're stationed. I haven't heard specific mention of a sniper. There's a Lambda who seems to have some kind of night vision. That shouldn't do anything right now. The other one is really fast."

"Do you think the night-vision one can see me?" she asked.

Jack shook his head. "They're not even having her do anything. She's sitting back with the warrant officer."

"Any snipers?"

"There have to be," Jack said. "It seems like they'd set it up similarly to the Space Needle. I just don't know."

"Are there other people there?"

"City hall is empty," he said, "but some of the other buildings are still occupied. There aren't many people on the streets, but there are a few."

Aubrey turned to Laura. "Then let's do this. You two walk together down there, out in the open, and don't do anything. You're the right age for terrorists, so they'll watch you. I'll walk with you, and Jack, when you can find Dan or the warrant officer, then you let me know."

"Why do you need the warrant officer?" Laura asked.

"Because he's got the detonator," Aubrey said, annoyed

that no one else seemed to have thought of that. She had to do more than just walk away with Dan—she had to disable the bomb on his ankle. She'd made the deletions on their files, but did that really mean anything? Did that automatically deactivate the detonator? She didn't want to take the chance.

Laura nodded. "For all we know, his detonator works on our bombs, too."

Aubrey rubbed her hands over her face. "Let's get this over with. Dan had better be worth it."

There was a large open plaza a few streets up from them, with dried autumn lawns and rows of flags. No one was in sight, and the three of them strolled out into the middle. Aubrey wasn't invisible yet—there was no point. Any sniper would see her out here, but it wasn't her plan to stay in the center of the action for long.

"I can hear them," Jack said. "But . . . I just don't know where it's coming from. It should be over there." He gestured with his head toward an empty playground.

"Could they be invisible?" Laura asked.

"No," Jack said. "We already know what they can do."

Aubrey's hand slipped down into Jack's and she laced her fingers with his. "I want you to be careful," she said, her voice so quiet that she could hardly hear it.

He replied with a squeeze.

"I mean it, Jack."

"It's under us," he said out loud, and smiled. "There's a parking garage underneath us."

Aubrey looked over at the playground and saw the now obvious railing that blocked the ramp downward.

"Is Dan down there?"

"They're talking to him on a radio," Jack said. "But he hasn't responded to pinpoint him yet. They're also talking about us. They don't seem to think we're a threat, but they're wondering why we're all standing here."

"Well," Aubrey said. "You guys get out of the plaza, away from snipers. I'm going down the ramp."

She disappeared, and even though she knew he couldn't feel it, she kissed Jack on the cheek. She didn't know how long it would be before she'd see him again, or if she would.

Aubrey made her way to the playground. The ramp was more visible now, but she wondered what the best way was to enter it. Should she hop over the side to suddenly get out of the snipers' view? Or should she casually stroll down so she didn't look like a threat?

She wished she had more training—more time back at Dugway to really learn how the Green Berets react in situations like this.

She walked to the entrance of the ramp and started down.

She could barely keep her eyes open, she was cringing so much.

And then she was in the parking garage.

A Green Beret spun from the shadows, bumping into her and then suddenly looking confused that she wasn't there.

"What the hell?" he said, spinning all around looking for her.

The insignia on his shoulder indicated he was a sergeant—. not who she was looking for.

"Jack," Aubrey said. "You'd better be out of sight. They know I'm a Lambda."

The sergeant put his hand to the mic at his mouth. "She's gone. I don't know where she is. Anyone have eyes?"

As her vision adjusted to the darkness, she saw the other three: another sergeant, the warrant officer, and a girl in camouflage without any insignia. She was the Lambda. There was no sign of Dan.

All three soldiers had their guns readied, searching the dim light for her, not knowing she was just inches from them.

She ran to the warrant officer and gently patted his chest pocket. The detonator was there.

"Kubato," the officer said into his radio. "I want you to find those other two. Get eyes on them, and then radio me. Don't get shot."

"Jack, they're coming for you. Get out of there."

Aubrey very gingerly—well, as gingerly as possible— attempted to open the pocket.

Crap. It was Velcro. She wouldn't be noticed, but would ripping open a Velcro pocket be?

It would put suspicion on all the Lambdas on team 9128. They were going to get shot, because someone was stealing the detonator.

She couldn't let that happen.

But the other Lambda—the fast one—was chasing down Laura and Jack. He was going to lead the other Green Berets to them.

Aubrey had to do something.

She could tie this girl to the officer—that way if he blew up the leg, he'd hurt himself.

No, that was stupid.

She could appear—announce that she wasn't with them, and make a show of leaving the girl alone.

No. She'd get shot as soon as she appeared.

She'd have to make him forget about the detonator. That was the only way. Make it so far from his mind that he wouldn't ever consider it.

"Jack," she said. "You're going to hear gunshots. Ignore them."

Aubrey took a breath and pulled the officer's sidearm from his holster. Just as he was turning, feeling the motion, she emptied the magazine, firing wildly into the few cars that remained in the parking garage. Glass exploded and tires boomed. Gas was leaking from one, but nothing was on fire.

The soldiers were scrambling now, searching everywhere, panicked and calling for backup.

She disassembled the M9 and dropped it on the ground with a clatter, then moved to the next soldier. She yanked the pistol from his hand and did the same, though she was firing into the puddle of leaking gas now. On the third shot there was a spark and the small sedan burst into flames.

"Get out!" the warrant officer barked. One man grabbed the Lambda girl by the collar and pulled her toward the exit ramp. The warrant officer followed and Aubrey tripped him. He splayed out on the concrete, and as he tried to get up she tore open his pocket and stole the detonator.

The group dashed up the ramp, and she followed, running in weird loops and circles around the Green Berets. The snipers could see her now. They could take a shot, and she had to make it too hard for them to take her out without shooting a fellow soldier.

It was stupid. She didn't have the energy for this. She wasn't in as good of shape as they were anyway, much less so when she was invisible. She hadn't thought this through.

But then the men stopped at the top of the ramp.

"There's a terrorist here?" the officer shouted into his mic. "What do you mean you can see her?"

She grabbed the third soldier's pistol—not because she knew what to do with it, but because it might make the snipers pause. She kept moving around the soldiers, inches from them. She was shorter than all of them, which made her feel better, because any headshot on her would hit a soldier in the chest. No sniper would take it without risking their own man.

Another man was running toward them across the plaza. Dan.

She was stumbling now as she moved around the men. She yanked the microphone from the officer's ear, and cut through the cable with his knife. She jumped to the next man and did the same, but by the time she got to the third, he was holding on to his—the snipers must have been telling them what was happening.

Dan approached cautiously.

And then suddenly the ground erupted, like an earthquake, and everyone fell to their knees. She tried to hold on to a soldier, but she was an open target.

She jumped up and dove for the cover of the ramp, and the ground bounced under her feet. She couldn't tell if the cracks and pops she heard were shattering stone or rifle blasts, but she was a sitting duck.

The ramp bounced again, the cement sides starting to crumble inward, and she rolled to the center. Dan couldn't see her—he must have just been incapacitating her.

She spun, tried to run, and tumbled farther down the ramp. She was almost out of the snipers' view, almost under the cover of the smoke-filled garage.

The ground thumped again, and she was underground, bits of cement dropping all around her.

Dan was standing at the top of the ramp, the battered Green Berets all around him. Aubrey stood and reappeared, only for an instant, and waved for him to come forward. Then she disappeared again, and ducked into the darkness of the garage.

The place was thick with smoke and the scent of burning oil. She leaned against a pillar, the pistol in one hand and the detonator in the other.

Dan appeared out of the darkness.

She made herself visible, and held up her hands.

"I'm a friend," she said, and then tossed him the detonator.

His eyes went wide. "How did you find me?" There was an uncertain grin on his face.

"I have Laura Hansen with me."

"Laura? I didn't think she survived. But, of course she did." He was marveling at the little device in his hand.

Aubrey looked past him. "They're going to be here soon. I can't make you invisible. And the snipers can see me."

He looked up at her, his face full of confidence. "I can get us out. Can you run?"

"Kind of," she said. "This wears me out."

Dan looked like he could hardly control his happiness. "I'm going home."

"First we have to get out of this garage."

"Easy," he said. "We just need to get to the top of the ramp and then out to the road. Roads are easy."

She had no idea what he meant, but she nodded. "I'm going invisible. Just know that I'm with you."

He nodded. "Like old times. For my mother and yours."

She stared awkwardly for a minute and then disappeared.

"There's going to be some dust," he said, looking where she had been.

He walked to the ramp and saw the three soldiers, their M4 carbines drawn and pointed down at him. "It's okay," he said.

For just a moment they relaxed, and then the entire ramp exploded in a puff of fine white concrete powder.

"Run!"

He darted through the cloud and Aubrey followed on wobbling legs. There was another tremendous crash and when they reached the top of the ramp all three men and the Lambda girl were on their backs, clutching at their feet and ankles.

Dan jumped into the street and as she followed, a wall of asphalt and dirt jutted up out of the road, creating a barrier between them and any sniper on the surrounding buildings. With the wall in place, she reappeared to get some of her strength back, and they sprinted down a side street, the path and wall forming just in front of them as they ran.

He was amazing—far more powerful than anything she'd seen in the training area at Dugway, or even when the terrorists attacked the convoy. And as she ran, her stomach fell, wondering what kind of monster she had just unleashed.

She prayed Laura was telling the truth—that her actions the night before had just been moody, not sinister.

When they were four blocks down, she stopped and called for him to wait. The streets of San Francisco were a wasteland behind them. Aubrey bent over, crouching to catch her breath. She pulled the bottle of Flowerbomb from her jeans pocket and sprayed herself, much to Dan's confusion.

"Trust me," she said, with a gasp. "It's how they'll find us."

She looked back the way they came and let out a small laugh. Like Jack and Laura would need much of a map to track them.

And then a dot appeared, coming at them impossibly fast.

"Dan—"

Before the word had escaped her lips, the road bulged upward. The dot, which became the shape of a man, couldn't stop in time and rocketed up the bulge and over their heads. He flailed through the street, arms scrambling for hand holds in the empty air, before landing with a crunch.

Aubrey's heart sank. The man didn't move. No, he wasn't a man. He was a Lambda. He was a teenager, just like her, and now his broken body lay in the street, motionless.

She wanted to throw up. He was dead. Just like that. Killed as casually as swatting a fly.

"Where's Laura?" Dan asked.

Aubrey stood and stared for several seconds.

"They're going to come after us," Dan urged. "Where's Laura?"

Aubrey stared. Without even looking, she disassembled the M9 and dropped it to the dirt.

"Come on," Dan said.

She took a deep breath, and then pointed in the direction of the car.

"They'll follow me," Aubrey said.

FIFTY-SIX

LAURA SAID THAT DAN HAD a storage shed in Southern California that would be the closest place to hide out. Jack drove, completely silent other than a few glances at Aubrey. At one point he thought he heard her say, "I'm scared," but it was too muffled by her raspy voice to be sure.

Dan was more than Jack had expected, but he should have thought about it. Dan was a Lambda 5M—that had been in the file Aubrey had read, and a 5 was just like Laura. They were both powerful weapons.

It was getting late, and Aubrey asked Jack to pull the car into the parking lot of a gas station. There was a big spray-painted sign out front that read "No Gas," but Aubrey insisted she needed to go to the bathroom and get something to eat.

She took his hand before getting out, and pulled him

across the car toward her. He wasn't expecting it at all, but she kissed him on the lips and then on the cheek.

"Listen." One word, breathed beside his ear.

He sat behind the wheel and watched her walk away. Laura and Dan were in the back, talking about something on the smartphone. Jack wasn't focused on it—all his attention was on Aubrey. Every footstep, the tiny grains of concrete rubbing under her shoe, the wisp of her fleece sleeves as they drew back and forth, the rapid beating of her heart, the unsteady, nervous inhalation of air.

"They're not who they say they are," she said, disappearing through a creaky door into the bathroom. "You should have seen the way that Dan killed that kid—he didn't care at all. He seemed proud of it.

"And remember what Laura told you about how she got caught? She was hitchhiking, alone, and was in a car accident at a bridge collapse, down on I-70. And the military records said Dan was caught up by Price. But when I told Dan that I was with Laura, he seemed surprised she was alive. He said, 'I didn't think she survived.' How would he know that she was in an accident unless he was with her?

"They're lying, Jack," Aubrey continued. "I don't know about what, but something isn't right. I don't think we want to be with them. But I don't know how to get away. I mean, I can, but can I get you away? They'd both have to be asleep."

Jack turned to Laura and Dan. "I'm going to grab a drink.

You guys want anything?"

"I'll take anything—donuts or chips or something," Dan said. "I'm so sick of those MREs."

"Just a bottle of water for me," Laura said. "Power bars, if they have them."

Jack stepped out of the car.

"I don't know who they are, Jack," Aubrey said. "They might be terrorists. Think about it—they knew each other from before, they're both superpowerful. And that Alec guy. I don't know what the deal is with him, but when I was with him I swore I knew him. I swore we were old friends. I don't know if that's some kind of power, but it fits the whole profile, doesn't it? Three terrorist teenagers, all together and aware of their powers before the government cracked down."

Jack was in the store now, looking through the bottles of soda. The selection was small, as if they hadn't had a shipment in weeks, and the drinks cost nearly six dollars a bottle.

"Anyway," Aubrey said. "I just think we need to be careful." He could hear a smile in her voice. "Now quit listening, Jack. I'm in the restroom." She laughed.

Jack put the food on the counter and waited for the cashier to ring it up.

"You can't talk like that," Laura whispered. "He can hear you."

Dammit. He'd missed something.

The cashier began making small talk about a storm

coming in off the Pacific. Jack replied awkwardly, trying to listen to the car.

All he could hear now was the electric clicks of typing on the smartphone. They were hiding information from him.

Aubrey emerged from the bathroom just as Jack took the bag of snack foods from the counter. It had cost a whopping thirty-eight dollars, but Jack guessed it didn't matter. They were still spending money from someone else's wallet.

"I agree," Jack said, as they walked out of the convenience store. "They're writing on the smartphone so I won't hear. We have to get away from them." He paused to kiss her again before reaching the car. He looked into her eyes. "We have to wait for them both to sleep. They're too powerful for us."

Jack cracked open a packet of Tylenol and took the pills with a swig of Mountain Dew. The pure sugar was almost overwhelming, but the store was out of bottled water.

"You want me to drive?" Aubrey asked.

"How are your eyes?"

"As good as they get. I can take over for an hour or so."

They climbed back in the car.

"Where are we going?" Aubrey asked immediately, opening the paper map that had been in the glove compartment.

Dan turned to Laura. "Where's the closest stash?"

"Take I-5 into San Diego," Laura said. "I'll give you directions from there."

Jack leaned back in the passenger seat, watching the road

ahead of them in the darkness. Aubrey seemed to be doing fine with driving, so he didn't mind relaxing his head a little bit. He lowered the headrest as far as it would go and slumped in his seat.

He could hear the clicking in the backseat. It wasn't stopping.

They had to do something.

His view outside was blocked by a little glare from inside the car. He could see through it, but it was annoying.

He shifted his head to figure out what it was. The skin along his scalp throbbed as he moved.

And there it was, as plain as day.

The screen of the smartphone was reflecting off the back window and onto the front window. He didn't even have to transpose the letters—it was being written out for him as clear as if the phone were in his own hands.

What's in San Diego?

We're supposed to go after military next, right? San Diego has a HUGE naval base. Subs. Carriers. Everything.

And we can do anything about that? We're 2 people.

Hang on.

Laura took the phone from him and looked up a map. Jack could see every detail—he saw the glow of Laura's finger as she pointed out the Coronado Naval Base, the enormous bay that held a hundred ships, in the satellite photo. And then she pointed to a narrow channel. She tapped on it, and then pointed to some land to the west. It read "Point Loma."

She closed the map and resumed typing.

Dude, it'll be your biggest score ever. There's only 1 way in and out of that naval base and it's that little channel.

That "little" channel is half a mile wide. Didn't u look at the scale?

☺ **That's the best part. Point Loma is a massive rock— way tall. IDK how you do your stuff, but u get up there on that thing and knock the whole damn point into the water, houses and everything.**

Seriously?

Look at the map again. Look up Point Loma. It's gonna be AWESOME. Alec will freak.

Wow.

For your mother and mine.

Dan took the phone and switched back to the map.

They didn't type anymore, and now that they weren't holding the phone between them, Dan's head blocked the reflection.

"How much longer are we looking at?" Jack asked. "I've never been down here."

"The last sign said seventy miles," Aubrey answered.

"Where's that map?" he asked, digging around in the foot-well. It was the only reason he was asking about the distance.

He found the map of California, and a close-up of San Diego.

"I've always wanted to go to the zoo," he said, trying to sound casual. "Probably not on this trip." He turned back to look at Laura and smiled. She gave him a half smile in return.

The map was clear, and Laura had been right. The naval base was huge. Miles and miles across, with dozens of major piers—room for hundreds of boats.

Jack didn't know what enemy he had sitting in his back-seat, but they wanted to stop the military. They wanted to freeze them in their tracks.

And after seeing what Dan did to downtown San Francisco, Jack had no doubt that he could obliterate Point Loma, turning it into a massive avalanche that would tumble down into the narrow channel and block every single boat in the harbor.

FIFTY-SEVEN

THEY ARRIVED IN SAN DIEGO to find the city under a rough lockdown. Aubrey drove through roadblock after roadblock, and though everyone eventually let them pass, she was almost wishing that they wouldn't. Jack had exchanged enough worried glances with her that she knew he was onto something. Maybe turning themselves in would be the best course of action. They'd be arrested, but they wouldn't get shot. Hopefully.

Unless Laura and Dan turned on the military at the roadblocks, which they almost certainly would. They were on the run, trying to do something wrong—Aubrey didn't know what yet—but it had to be criminal. She'd completely given up on the lie that there was any secret stash of supplies somewhere. Aubrey and Jack were transporting fugitives.

Aubrey and Jack were fugitives, too. But maybe they could get some leniency. They didn't know what the others were planning.

But it would be their word against the army. During a time of war.

How much longer could they run?

Laura steered them through the city. Streets were blocked with heavy cement road barricades to prevent cars from going in a straight line, and the skies were patrolled by helicopters. Aubrey's eyes were getting tired and blurry.

"Can we pull over, guys?" she asked.

"We're not far," Laura said, "and then we can get out and relax."

Aubrey nodded, and tried to keep her eyes on the road. They were going through residential neighborhoods, climbing a hill in the darkness. She couldn't see much else besides what was right in front of her.

Jack took her hand. The sky might have been getting lighter in the west. Was it morning already? She needed sleep.

They continued on a few more blocks, and through another, even tighter roadblock. Laura had the story this time—that she had a grandma up here. Aubrey had no idea if it was true, but Laura gave the name and the soldier waved them through.

"Okay," Laura said, sounding plenty awake. "We need to make sure that the site isn't compromised. Aubrey, can you come with me?"

"Hey," Aubrey said sincerely. "I can barely see. I need to close my eyes for a little while." She pulled the car over to the side of a wooded street.

That seemed to throw Laura for a loop, but she thought for only a few moments before patting Jack on the shoulder. "You and me, 'kay?"

Aubrey and Jack kissed, and she was sure he said something to her, but she was too tired to understand the words. As nervous as she was around Dan, she leaned back and closed her eyes. She didn't dare fall asleep, but she needed her strength. If Dan tried to hurt her, she could disappear, but only if she had the energy.

"You get tired?" she asked him. "I swear, this virus . . ."

"I used to. Not so much anymore," he said. He sounded nervous. "The doctor back at the base gave me some pills."

"I wish there were pills for sleepiness." She opened her eye and looked at him. "I mean, aside from meth or something."

He laughed.

"So you can turn invisible?"

"I can," she said. "With limits."

"Pretty awesome."

"You know what I used to do with it?" She was talking now mostly to keep herself awake.

"What?"

"Shoplift. That was my big contribution to society."

"Like, steal jewelry?"

"Nope," she said, enjoying the reclined seat. "Just crap.

Clothes. I stole school supplies, if you can imagine it. Pens. Paper. Notebooks. I always really wanted to have a nice stapler, so I stole one."

He laughed. "Rebel."

"As bad as they come. Who would have thought we'd end up here?"

He paused. "Where?"

"Running from the army," she said, suddenly a little more alert. He was testing her.

"What do you think we should do next?" he said. "I mean, I know what Laura thinks. What do you think?"

"I don't know," Aubrey said, shaking her head. "Maybe go to Mexico. Maybe something else."

"Don't you have a family back home?"

"I have a dad," she said. "Who sold me and Jack out for beer money. I'm in no hurry to see him."

"What about Jack?"

"He has family. Well, parents."

"That's not what I mean," Dan said. "I mean, is Jack like family?"

She paused. She wasn't expecting that question, especially not from someone like Dan.

"I . . . I don't know. I mean, yes, I think. The closest thing I have." She turned in her seat. "What about you? Family?"

"My old man was from Denver," he said. "But he died a couple years ago." Aubrey had read something like that in

Dan's military file—that he was from Denver.

"What about your mom?"

"My mother?" he asked, with a little smile. "Old. I don't see her much—haven't seen her in years. She didn't like the way my dad was raising me."

"She in Denver, too?"

"No," he said. "Chicago."

Aubrey sat upright in her seat.

"Are you serious?"

"Yeah, why?"

"Haven't you heard?"

Dan's face went pale. "Heard what?"

"Where's the smartphone?"

"Laura took it with her."

"You need to find a computer," Aubrey said, opening the car door. It was dark, and she was incredibly shaky on her feet, but she pointed to the house in front of them. Dan was out the door and at her side, holding her up by the elbow.

"What happened to Chicago?"

"It's not good."

Dan almost carried her the remaining steps up the path. The house was completely dark, and as Dan strode forward the cement porch buckled upward, splintering the wooden door in half.

A man in his underwear ran out into the living room.

"What are you doing?"

"Where's your computer?" Dan demanded.

"We're not going to hurt you," Aubrey said. "Please tell us where it is."

"I have cash," the man said. "Just leave us alone."

"Tell us where the computer is," Dan shouted.

The man pointed down the hall.

Dan almost ran, leaving Aubrey to rely on the walls to support herself. She got to the room just as the start-up screen began to glow.

"It's not good," Aubrey said again.

"It's the third-biggest city in the country," he said, seething. "Second-biggest financial district. Second-largest labor pool."

"What are you talking about?" Aubrey sat down in a chair behind him. She heard the man in the other room calling the police.

"Kraft Foods, McDonald's, Motorola, Sears, United Airlines, Abbott Labs. Railroads. Ports. Tech companies."

He opened a browser and began typing into the search bar.

"It was supposed to be off-limits. It was supposed to be off-limits."

The pictures were worse than Aubrey had feared. The entire city was on fire. A thousand columns of smoke all merging into one.

"That bastard," Dan seethed, his teeth clenched. "It was

supposed to be off-limits." He smashed his hand into the end table, punching the wood over and over until it had broken and his hand was a mess of blood and cuts.

He went back to the search engine, his blood dripping on the keyboard. He pulled up a blog.

It was purple lettering on a pink background: "Susie's Musings."

The posts were all short, and he scrolled through them, his finger leaving a red dribble down the screen.

"There it is," he said, leaning back in the chair. "I try to save his worthless life, and this is how he repays me."

Aubrey read over Dan's shoulder.

User: SusieMusie
Mood: Pissed off
Have you ever seen that movie Chicago? Erica =
Roxie, and Sara = Velma. Both should be locked up
ASAP. They're both crazy and they deserve each
other. They are a severe, SEVERE pain in my butt.

He smacked the screen, leaving a handprint. "Seventh word is the target. Eighteenth word is the time frame. Thirty-first word is additional notes. Chicago, ASAP, severe."

"What does that mean?" Aubrey said, but Dan was up out of his chair. He pushed past the bewildered man and charged back out the front door. The man tried to grab Aubrey and she disappeared just long enough to slip from his grasp, then reappeared and ran after Dan.

"Where are they?" Dan said to Aubrey.

"I don't know."

"Spray that stuff," he said. "That perfume."

FIFTY-EIGHT

JACK SMELLED IT ALMOST IMMEDIATELY. A strong—a very strong—whiff of Flowerbomb.

"I've got to go," Jack said, turning away from the rocks that overlooked the Coronado Naval Base.

"Do you have a count yet?" Laura asked, peering into the darkness.

"Why are we doing this? I thought we were going for supplies."

"We're doing this first." She had hold of his wrist.

"I can smell the perfume," Jack said. "They need us back there. Didn't you hear that big crash a couple minutes ago?"

"What big crash?"

"We need to check on them," Jack said, pleading.

He'd listened to the whole conversation, ever since he

heard Aubrey get out of the car. He didn't want to take any chances, especially leaving Aubrey with Dan.

"How many boats?" Laura said, squeezing his arm.

"I don't know—a hundred. A hundred and fifty."

"Count them," she said.

"I can count them five minutes from now."

Laura got in his face. "You can hear everything going on over there. You tell me why we need to get back."

"Because Dan freaked out and someone called the police," Jack said.

Laura paused. "Why would he freak out?"

"Something about Chicago."

"Oh, hell."

She shoved Jack back onto the rocky outcrop and he landed with a rough thud. His head wound screamed with pain. With all the strength he could muster, he rolled onto his side and moved to his knees. He could hear Laura running, pushing through trees and smashing through a fence that they'd carefully climbed over only minutes earlier.

He followed, staggering to his feet and pressing one hand to his head as he chased after her.

"Why didn't you tell me?" Dan shouted.

Aubrey was there. She was breathing hard.

"Because it was too late."

"Too late for what?"

"Too late to save her."

414

"I'm only in this for her."

There was a massive thud, and the sound of cracking wood. Aubrey gasped.

Jack pushed through the broken fence and saw them in the front yard of a badly damaged house. A man in his underwear was standing in the street. Aubrey was standing away from the fight, and her eyes connected with his. "We have to get out of here. I'm coming to you."

She faded from view.

Laura pointed a finger at Dan. "Alec only followed through on what he'd always promised. You help us or your mother gets it."

"Gets it?" Dan said, with an incredulous laugh. The entire lawn, sidewalk, and trees all lifted a foot into the air and collapsed back in a crash. Jack fell on his face, and saw the trees surrounding the house tipping at dangerous angles.

A siren sounded in the distance. No, it was three.

Where was Aubrey?

"My mother 'gets it'?" Dan said again, walking toward where Laura had fallen. "How dare you? What did she ever—"

Laura leapt forward, smashing into Dan's chest, and Jack heard the distinct sound of bones breaking.

"You've never been committed to anything," Laura spat at his groaning body. "You know how worthless a team is when you have to blackmail your muscle? What did you think would happen when you tried to kill Alec in an avalanche?"

The ground swelled again, knocking Laura off her feet, and a tree came crashing down, missing her by inches.

She jumped to her feet.

"I didn't try to kill him," Dan wheezed. "You were supposed to save him. It was your fault."

She kicked him, and he screamed as his knee shattered.

A massive clod of dirt flew from behind her and exploded around her, but she managed to keep her feet.

"We could have taken it out," Laura said, pointing toward the bay. "And you had to cry about your mommy."

The sirens were getting closer, and were being followed by something louder—something bigger.

Jack felt himself lifting up, and he turned to see Aubrey reappearing. She had a cut on her cheek.

"Let's get out of here," she said.

"Yeah."

They backed away from the fight.

Three police cars arrived, sirens blazing, and behind them was an armored personnel carrier. It came to a stop and soldiers began pouring out.

A loudspeaker blared. "Cease and desist. We will use deadly force."

Dan was in a crumpled heap, and Laura couldn't keep her footing with the constant minor earthquakes.

She threw a punch and it was deflected by a flying paving stone.

"You want an avalanche?" Dan said.

And then the earth folded over both of them, like enormous waves, and the entire lot—house and trees and fence and all—sank away down the side of the mountain. Jack jumped back, pulling Aubrey with him, and they watched as the tornado of dirt and wood and stone tumbled to the road below.

Finally it was over, in a monstrous cloud of dust.

Aubrey took Jack by the hand, and they stumbled through the remaining yard next to the sinkhole. They reached the street, and the stunned police officers just stared at them.

"We'd like to turn ourselves in," Aubrey said.

FIFTY-NINE

ALEC SAT IN A MOTEL room across Sinclair Inlet from the Kitsap Naval Base in Washington, an hour from Seattle. From here, he could see the devastation and the navy's scrambling efforts to get ships out of the narrow inlet and off to sea.

His team was gone. A suicide mission. It was necessary—and it had been worth it.

Kitsap had the largest fuel depot of any naval base in the country, a series of fifty-three underground storage tanks spread across the facility. Alec's team couldn't hit them all, but he could wreak havoc. Now the base was on fire—huge plumes of black smoke curling up into the early morning air. He didn't know how long it would go. They'd opened valves—destroyed some—and much of the fuel would have to burn off on its own.

Alec was no use to them on this mission. He'd planned it, of course, and he'd even assigned a job to himself—a job that he didn't bother doing. It was nonessential, and it helped them feel a sense of solidarity to make this one final suicide mission. They were all in this together. They'd all taken their deep breaths, they'd all praised their purpose, and they'd all drunk a small toast in honor of this, their final battle.

They knew what they were getting into. That Alec didn't die alongside them would never be known to the rest. He was needed for other, bigger things. He didn't know what yet—he never knew what the ultimate plan was going to be—but he knew the timetable.

And so he watched Kitsap burn. He expected that soon the entire inlet would be evacuated—it amazed him that a military base of such importance could be surrounded by civilian neighborhoods. But he would wait until he was forced to leave, and he would keep a running mental tally of the ships that he saw leaving their docks. Two aircraft carriers. Four submarines. A missile cruiser. Two destroyers. A handful of other ships that he couldn't identify. Alec would memorize these ships—memorize the numbers emblazoned across their superstructure—and he would report.

He'd meet up with whoever he could contact. He still had a few numbers, even though cell service got worse every day. And he had anonymous email addresses, contacts on the deepnet. He'd tell them what he'd seen, give an accounting of what he'd done, and await orders.

It had all gone amazingly well. Sixty groups of three. One hundred and eighty teenagers. And they'd brought the world's grandest superpower to its knees in just over a month.

Alec took a drink, pouring himself a glass from the same bottle his comrades had used for their final toast.

He would be a hero.

SIXTY

"SIX DAYS, JACK," AUBREY SAID to the wall. "I hope you don't mind that I'm still talking to you. It helps me stay sane. It's nice that they don't drug the water here. At least, I don't think they do. I feel like I can still turn invisible, if there was a reason to."

She played with the food on her plate. It was chicken and rice, but didn't look appetizing.

"Do you think they just put the food from the MRE pouches on a plate? Or does no one in the army know how to cook? Or the navy, or wherever this is. I think it's the navy."

They'd been taken in the back of the armored personnel carrier, with new detonators coded for their ankle bombs. Where they'd gone from there was anyone's guess. It hadn't been a very long drive, but the vehicle had been in a warehouse when it opened to let them out. They hadn't gotten any sunlight.

That had been the last time they'd held hands.

"You know what I wish, Jack?" she said, leaning back on her bed and staring at the plain white ceiling. "I wish that I'd said yes. When you asked me to the dance last year. I wish we'd gone, and I wish you'd worn jeans and I'd worn that awful flower-print dress I always wear to church. I should have said yes. I'm sorry."

She put the cover back on her food so she wouldn't have to smell it.

"I wouldn't mind having worn some of that Flowerbomb stuff, though. It's really grown on me."

The deadbolt unlocked, and she shot upright. No one had been in the room for six days, not since she'd explained everything that happened—every detail in Seattle and San Francisco and Point Loma. No more lies. Let the chips fall where they may.

With a squeal, the heavy metal door opened, and a soldier stood looking at her.

"Aubrey Parsons?"

"Yeah?"

"Your presence has been requested in the briefing room."

She followed the soldier down a long corridor. Two others walked behind them.

The soldier turned the corner and pushed a door open for

her to go through.

Jack was in there, his head sporting a newer, smaller bandage. He smiled at her and waved from his desk.

"Hey," she said as she came up and sat next to him. "I hope you got my messages."

"I didn't want to eavesdrop," he said with a grin, "but I would totally go to prom with you."

She reached across the gap between their desks and took his hand. His skin was cold and dry and comfortable.

Aubrey didn't know what was going to happen anymore. She didn't know if they were going to be kicked out of the army, or court-martialed, or put in lockdown back at Dugway. But at least they were together for now.

The door opened again, and a bald man in full dress uniform entered. He sat on the edge of the table at the head of the room, and set down a small stack of folders.

"Let's cut to the chase," he said. "Your information has proven very useful. While we have yet to apprehend Alec Moore, we have managed to shut down the website he's been using to communicate to the various terrorist cells.

"It has also been determined you should be exonerated for the tragic events that took place in Seattle. While we do not have a solid confirmation, we actually believe that the order to terminate you came from a . . . compromised individual."

Jack raised his hand. "What does that mean? A gun to his head?"

"In a sense. Alec Moore, we've gathered, has some form of mind control. We don't know the details. He's used this many times to get past guards, to convince people he's on their side, or even that he's their superior. Ms. Parsons, I believe he convinced you that you were in school together."

She nodded, embarrassed that she'd fallen for it.

"We believe that it was either him on the radio giving the order, or it was someone he had influenced. Either way, he is conclusively linked to the terror cell that destroyed the Space Needle."

Aubrey spoke, her voice quiet. "Does that mean that we're free to go?"

The colonel sighed. "I wish I could say that the answer was yes. The terror cells are now disorganized and making mistakes, and our boys are ferreting them out—with the continued help of Lambdas like yourselves. This phase of the war is coming to a close."

Aubrey looked at Jack. He spoke first. "This phase."

"I'm afraid to report that this has all been a prelude. The terrorists stretched our forces thin, destroyed our infrastructure and our ability and will to fight. And, as of this morning, Russia has invaded Alaska."

ACKNOWLEDGMENTS

AS ALWAYS, THIS BOOK WAS written due to the long suffering and patience of my wife and best friend, Erin. She's stood by my side through every hardship and been the anchor I hold on to when things are tough. And she's believed in me and my dream of writing perhaps even more than I have—always pushing me to keep going, keep working, keep writing.

I also owe a huge debt of gratitude to my writing group: Sarah Eden, Michele Holmes, Annette Lyon, Heather Moore, J. Scott Savage, and Lu Ann Staheli. They read versions of this book when it was middle grade, when it was YA, when it was first person, when it was third person, and when it was generally terrible. I think they read at least five different Chapter Ones for this thing before I got it right.

I need to thank Gary Hansen for his book *Wet Desert*, which I used as a reference when I was blowing up the Glen Canyon Dam. I also want to thank Larry Correia and Sergeant First Class Ethan Skarstedt of BSC 1/19th SFG(A), who both gave me invaluable advice about the military aspects of the book. If there are any errors (as there likely will be), I take full responsibility. And many huge thanks to Katherine Applegarth and the people of Mount Pleasant, Utah, who helped so much in setting the groundwork for my characters.

I have a troop of amazing beta readers who gave incredible advice: Krista Jensen; Stephanie, Amy, and Shauna Black; Ally Condie; Patty Wells; Jenny Moore; Nancy Allen; and Josi Kilpack.

And I would be nowhere without the ridiculously talented people at Harper. I probably only know a tenth of the names of the fantastic professionals who made this book what it is, but major props to Christina, Tyler, Casey, Patty, and of course Erica Sussman, my editor. And a big special thanks to Erin Fitzsimmons, who designed this awesome cover. You guys rock!

And none of this would exist if it weren't for the world's greatest agent, Sara Crowe. Without her, I'd be back in my old real-world job, sitting in conference rooms and using the word "webinar" all the time.

KEEP READING FOR A SNEAK PEEK
AT THE EXPLOSIVE SEQUEL

ONE

ZASHA LITVYAK FLEW ACROSS THE northern Pacific, low enough
that she could feel the salty spray as the ocean surged. This
was the culmination of years of preparation; everything had
led to this moment, and the work that would follow.

The Russian Federation had invaded Alaska.

It sounded worse than it was. It was a tiny landing force at
the northernmost part of the state, just enough to startle the
residents and seize the oil reserves. The real invading force
was coming now.

Fyodor Sidorenko groaned as he dangled in a harness
underneath her.

"Shh," Zasha said. "It's about to start."

"We've been waiting long forever," he replied, pain apparent in his voice. "Let's get it over with."

He'd do his part soon enough. He was the real weapon. She was just the transportation.

"They're here," she said as she spotted the lights of the American task force in the distance. She saw the first carrier, 70 painted on its superstructure. "The USS *Carl Vinson*. And behind it is the *Ronald Reagan*." In addition to the carriers, Zasha could name most of the destroyers and frigates in the group. But there were a dozen support craft that she couldn't identify. They were auxiliaries that had fled the terrorist attacks at Bremerton: research vessels and hospital ships and cargo carriers. This group was a cluster of unprepared misfits, not a war-bound task force.

"I wish I could see," he said.

"You'll see the fireworks."

He laughed at that—a wet, raspy laugh in which she could hear the damage to his body. Too many drugs.

No, that wasn't right. It was the perfect amount of drugs— a formula that had been tested on him time and again until they'd gotten the results they wanted. Fyodor meant *gift from God*. It was his new name, given by their overseers at the training facility. And if this plan worked, he would be.

Zasha liked her new name, too. No longer was she Inna Fedorov, a name that meant little. Zasha meant *defender of the people*, and her surname came from Lydia Litvyak, the world's top female flying ace. At training school Zasha had put on a dour expression and pretended the title was a solemn honor, but out here—soaring over the ocean—she adored it. Soon she would be an ace, a flyer who aimed her weapon with such precision and grace that the enemy wouldn't even know how they'd been hit.

Zasha moved slower now, so she could fly closer to the rolling ocean. Two teenagers wouldn't show up on the fleet's radars; even if someone did track them, they'd give off signatures no different from birds. And should anyone catch sight of them from the deck, their black-and-white camouflage would blend in with the dark sea and breaking waves.

As Zasha neared the fleet she felt her heart leap, knowing that the plan was going better than they had hoped. The flagship was the legendary USS *Nimitz*. Two carriers was a feat. Three carriers was a miracle. Of course, the carriers were surrounded by a host of defensive ships and air cover, but that was what Zasha and Fyodor were for.

Zasha checked the GPS on her wrist. Everything hinged on being in just the right place. She glided around a tall, blocky cruiser—the USS *Princeton*, she noted, the names drilled into her by her trainer—and moved farther back into the group.

She checked the GPS again. Just about right. She made an adjustment, flying two hundred yards to her right. Fyodor had a range—a diameter—of just under twenty-six kilometers. Zasha hovered in place and pulled a syringe from her hip pouch. It was already filled, and she checked it for air.

"I'm ready," Fyodor said through a tense jaw. They both knew the pain he'd feel. Maybe she knew it better than him—her mind was clearer while it was happening.

"You're going to be a hero." She jabbed the needle into Fyodor's shoulder and depressed the plunger.

He strained, his whole body going rigid. She gazed up at the stars, waiting for the inevitable, and a moment later she saw it. First one, then two, then four fighter jets fell from the sky, careening uncontrollably. Soon all the aircraft that had been flying above the carrier group were falling, followed by their parachuting pilots.

One plane was in the distance—outside of Fyodor's range. It was foolishly moving back toward the group. A moment later it began a sharp descent into the inky black sea. No parachutes emerged from that one.

Every ship was dark. Every door light, every cabin window, every beacon. Everything. It was just like Zasha had imagined, and it thrilled her.

She checked her watch—an old wind-up one that didn't rely on batteries; Fyodor's abilities shut down anything with an electric current. She was right on schedule, which meant her backup wouldn't be far behind.

Thirty-two Backfire bombers were coming at the carrier group, flying low over the ocean, using strategies not seen since the Second World War.

It was an old admiral who had come up with the plan, or

so the story around training camp went. In World War II, torpedo planes would fly low to the water—hoping to dodge the incoming anti-aircraft fire—and then drop their torpedoes.

The problem now was Fyodor's dead zone. The Backfires needed to get their projectiles through the bubble without entering the dead zone themselves; Fyodor's abilities did not distinguish between friend and foe. The Backfires had been equipped with special torpedoes, created just for this mission. Long range, accurate, and with an impact detonator. Each plane would drop two torpedoes without having to watch out for anti-aircraft fire. The only challenge was to aim.

Zasha wondered what was happening on the American submarines caught inside the bubble. They'd be nothing more than steel pipes in the water, completely dark and powerless, drifting aimlessly. Their crews would have no idea what was happening on the surface—no sonar, nothing.

And then Zasha saw the first of the Russian Backfires, screaming up and away, its torpedoes dropped.

She checked her watch. The torpedoes had a range of eleven kilometers.

"Four minutes," she said to Fyodor, even though she knew he couldn't understand. Or maybe he could understand—maybe he just wouldn't remember any of this.

The sky was filled with Backfires now, pulling back and turning away from the dead zone. One didn't make it—it pushed too far and came to a stop in midair, then began to spin down into the ocean. The first Russian casualty of the American War.

Fyodor was writhing in his harness, the powerful drugs amplifying his abilities and wreaking havoc on his mind. Zasha had sympathy for him, but his name was accurate: he was a gift from God, and a gift to be used.

Two minutes to go. She hoped the torpedoes would get past the ring of ships at the outside of the carrier group. For that matter, she hoped that the torpedoes would be on target at all. She knew the Backfire pilots had been practicing for months, but it was a tricky maneuver, and trickier still under pressure.

Somewhere in the distance, the Backfires were reforming, opening their bomb-bay doors and getting ready to drop heavy missiles.

For just a moment—an instant—Zasha had a flicker of remorse. Or was it pity? More than thirty American ships, including three Nimitz-class carriers—three of the largest ships ever to sail the oceans—were about to be destroyed. It was easy for a Backfire pilot to fire an anonymous torpedo and watch it sail away into the dark. It was harder to be among the ships—to hear their crews' calls as the sailors scrambled for some kind of defense.

The first torpedo hit, a geyser of flame bursting upward from the side of a frigate. Zasha was thrown backward a dozen yards by the impact blast. Before she could get her bearings there was another impact, and then another. The sky was blazing with orange-white fire.

Three ships were engulfed; soon it was four, then six, then eight. Finally, the first carrier was destroyed—the *Ronald Reagan*. Then it seemed as though the entire *Carl Vinson* rolled, hit by half a dozen torpedoes in a single moment. Zasha could see sailors falling overboard as the massive steel beast shuddered and swung back to right itself.

"Look at it, Fyodor," she said in awe. "Look at the fires."

Smoke was pouring from a dozen ships now, billowing in the Pacific winds and obscuring her view. Zasha watched the raging inferno, pride swelling in her chest. The American fleet was in ruins.

She checked her watch and marked the time, then flew east, away from the burning ships. Now she would set the trap.

It had to be done by sight. She couldn't administer the drugs to Fyodor to calm him down; she wasn't done with him yet. So she couldn't use her GPS to track the thirteen kilometers she would need to fly to move the bubble off the carrier group—she'd have to do it by sight. But she'd trained for this, long and hard. She could judge thirteen kilometers on land, or on sea, in the light or the dark.

At thirteen kilometers out she stopped, hovering over the waves. She watched the undamaged ships' lights come back on.

She checked her watch again. It had been two minutes. By now any carriers that were still operational would have launched their first wave of waiting aircraft. Zasha knew the fighter jets wouldn't pursue the Backfires, not yet. Not until they had a substantial force in the air, and not until their radars saw the Russian planes returning.

Fyodor groaned and mumbled something that she couldn't hear over the rush of the ocean. She wished he could see this. He was her partner. She was the gun and he was the bullet.

"It's okay, Fyodor," she told him. "Everything is okay."

The burning ships were oddly beautiful, like a distant row of campfires billowing in the night sky. She wondered what the sailors on board were doing—what procedures they had in place to deal with this kind of unexpected attack. Fire-fighters would be out in force, and the captains and admirals would be scrambling to save their vessels. They'd be waiting for another attack, watching their radar, anticipating a return of the Backfires.

But they wouldn't be anticipating a return of Zasha. She flew back toward the fleet, watching as lights began to disappear on the nearest boats, and made her way to the center of the fleet. She arrived just in time to see one of the Nimitzes' catapults—running on steam power, not electronics—launch a powerless fighter jet over the edge and into the water. She knew that the rest of the air patrol would be falling now, and she strained to see them, but there was no sign of the planes against the darkened sky.

And again she would wait, her bubble directly over the carrier group once more, disabling all their sensors and radar. The Backfires would return, their bays open and their missiles ready for a killing blow. They'd be followed by Mainstays with radar arrays to guide them in, and Fullbacks to provide fighter support. Not that they needed it. Fyodor was stopping every American aircraft that was trying to move.

It was a longer wait this time, but Zasha didn't care. How many years had they planned this? Decades? It was ever since they learned of Fyodor's abilities, and then they'd sought out a flyer with Zasha's strength and intelligence. Not many could make the distance, or hold so steady over the water. Not many could follow the exactness of the plan.

The thought struck her: How many men would be killed in this glorious battle? Carriers had nearly five thousand each. A frigate had about two hundred, and a destroyer had as many as two fifty. And who knew how many all these extra ships had.

More than fifteen thousand. Maybe twenty?

She checked her watch one last time. The missiles would be nearing her bubble now, and it was time to get out of there. She only needed to stay long enough to keep the missiles off the radar. Zasha turned and headed east again. As she flew she withdrew another syringe from her pouch, flicked away the air pockets, and stabbed it into Fyodor's arm. He'd drift to sleep, and the electronic interference would melt away. She could return to the Varyag to debrief and celebrate. And then the preparations for landing the ships in Seattle would begin.

The invasion has begun.

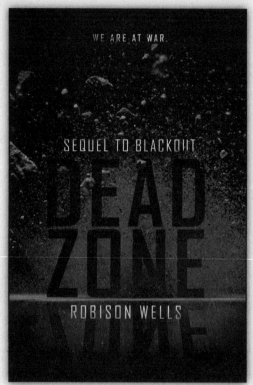

WE ARE AT WAR.

SEQUEL TO BLACKOUT

DEAD ZONE

ROBISON WELLS

The time for choices is over—and the rush to the front lines is about to begin in the sequel to *Blackout*.

Don't miss *Going Dark*, the digital original prequel to *Blackout*!

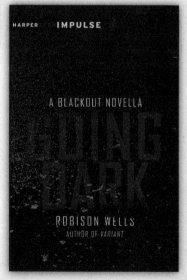

HARPER   IMPULSE

A BLACKOUT NOVELLA

GOING DARK

ROBISON WELLS
AUTHOR OF *VARIANT*

HARPER TEEN
An Imprint of HarperCollinsPublishers

www.epicreads.com

Also from Robison Wells

"**I loved it!** The twist behind it all is my favorite since ENDER'S GAME."
—James Dashner, *New York Times* bestselling author of the Maze Runner trilogy

TRUST NO ONE.

VARIANT

ROBISON WELLS

Follow the rules.
Stay off their radar.
Trust no one.

THEY ARE NOT ALONE.

FEEDBACK

Sequel to VARIANT

Don't miss a
single page of the
pulse-pounding
Variant series.

HARPER TEEN
An Imprint of HarperCollinsPublishers

www.epicreads.com

ROBISON WELLS

JOIN
THE COMMUNITY AT

Epic Reads
Your World. Your Books.

DISCUSS
what's on
your reading
wish list

FIND
the latest
books

CREATE
your own book
news and
activities to share
with friends

ACCESS
exclusive
contests and
videos

Don't miss out on any upcoming EPIC READS!

Visit the site and browse the categories to find out more.

www.epicreads.com

HARPER TEEN
An Imprint of HarperCollinsPublishers